ZAYDE'S ARCADE

Coming of Age in Coney Island

ANDY SMITH

Copyright © 2019 Andy Smith
All rights reserved.
Printed in the United States of America
Published by Author Academy Elite
P.O. Box 43, Powell, OH 43035

www.AuthorAcademyElite.com

All rights reserved. No part of this publication may be reproduced, stored in a retrieval system, or transmitted in any form or by any means---for example, electronic, photocopy, recording---without the prior written permission of the publisher. The only exception is brief quotations in printed reviews.

Paperback: 978-1-64085-418-5
Hardback: 978-1-64085-419-2
Ebook: 978-1-64085-420-8

Library of Congress Control Number: 2018955349

This book is a work of fiction. The names, characters, businesses, places, events, locales, and incidents are either the products of the author's imagination or used in a fictitious manner. Any resemblance to actual persons, living or dead, or actual events, is purely coincidental.

Cover Photo: Courtesy of Blair Collins

DEDICATION

To my wonderful, colorful family who lived, loved, dined and argued together over many years. I could not have conceived of this or written any of this without you.

To my children, Josh, Tessa, and Jared. You are my jewels.

To my partner, Liesje Wagner, without whose wholehearted encouragement, backbone and heart, this novel would never have been written and completed.

And to Brooklyn's Coney Island that I had the privilege of getting to know … and to the Coney Island I will sadly never know.

PREFACE

I have long felt the need to tell this story, to breathe life into and to adorn this rich, formative period of my life. It is the least I can do to honor the memory of my family; their feisty energy, their tenacious character, and their resolve.

To convey the spirit and the energy of these colorful characters as well as the era, I have used many Yiddish expressions and have some of the characters speak in English using old world pronunciation.

Throughout the novel, depending on the circumstance, several of the characters are referred to in different ways; using different names to address the same person. For example, depending on the context, I have referred to Jason's grandfather using several different names. While his American name was Harry, the Yiddish equivalent is Herschel as well as the various terms for grandfather, grandpa, and the Yiddish equivalent, Zayde.

*"Up like a rocket ship
Down like a roller coaster
Back like a loop-the-loop
And around like a merry-go-round."*

Palisades Park
Freddie Cannon

CHAPTER 1

*"Baby, baby
Where did our love go?
Ooh, don't you want me
Don't you want me no more?"*

Where Did Our Love Go?
The Supremes

Sunday, August 22, 1999

Jason's stomach groaned as he drove his leased car. He hated the fact that he felt like a trespasser every time he had to visit what had up until recently been his own house. But Lyla had insisted that he make it his business to remove the last of his things from the garage after the divorce. So begrudgingly, he had to drive over to the house today to retrieve the last of the remaining boxes. His only satisfaction was knowing that he hadn't first gotten the okay with her, as she had insisted.

Heck, we're not married anymore. What's she going to do? Shoot me? Besides, stopping there would at least give him a chance to see his little girl, Tess. That's the problem with divorces. They separate you not just from your spouse, but also from your kids.

Jason gazed down at the new Barbie doll he planned to give his daughter. He'd picked it out while he shopped for toiletries. His cousin Mitch had been nice enough to let him stay at his place for a while. But Jason couldn't stand that smelly soap of his.

To brighten his spirits, he reached over and turned on the radio. He felt a whole lot better when he heard the opening strains of *"I Still Believe"* by Maria Carey. However, no matter how fervently he rocked and swayed to the music, it couldn't hide the fact that he'd soon have to face the ogre.

The light turned red as Jason was approaching the intersection. The beat of a competing rap song soon took over as another car pulled up to the left of him. He turned to look, ready to stare down some smart-aleck sixteen-year-old who was showing off. Instead, he saw two lovely young women with a certain familiar look, both brunettes, smiling, chatting, and bouncing joyfully to the beat of the music. Out of embarrassment, he turned away and snuck a look at himself in the rearview mirror. *This damn divorce is making me look way older than my years.* Jason then glanced back at the girls. To his surprise, the girl in the passenger seat was staring at him. She waved gleefully.

"Hey. How are 'ya?" he yelled to her, grinning a bit too broadly. Groan.

As soon as the light turned green, the other car sped off. Halfway down the street, a hand stuck out of the passenger's window and waved goodbye. Jason's face flushed with heat as he focused on the road and patted the steering wheel in time with the music. *What am I, stupid? How are 'ya? What kind of line is that?* He shook his head. *Next time, I should say, Hey, beautiful day, isn't it? Or, Say, don't I know you?* Jason gave a resigned sigh.

But lately something odd was happening. It seemed everywhere he looked there were young women reminding him of his first love, Anna. A love he'd lost long ago when he was all of sixteen years old.

If he was being honest with himself, none of the relationships which followed ever had the same passion, that same ineffable feeling you get deep down inside. Funny, when he thought about it more, he'd never experienced that since. And he wondered aloud whether he'd ever have that sensation again.

Five minutes later, he swung his car into the all-too-familiar driveway. The living room curtains were closed. He purposely gave the car door a good slam as he got out. Jason's eyes were suddenly drawn to the far living room window. When the curtains were pulled back, Jason's daughter, Tess, stood in full view. He felt a momentary pang seeing those bright blue eyes of hers and her recent pageboy haircut.

Jason smiled and Tess waved excitedly at him. He happily returned the wave and before he knew it, she'd opened the front door, yelling, "Hi, Daddy."

"Hey, Tess."

She looked so happy rocking back and forth on her heels. Jason got out of the car and leaned back into the open passenger window to grab the new Barbie doll he'd bought, hiding it quickly behind his back.

"How's my girl?"

"Good," she replied bluntly.

"Guess what Daddy got his special girl?"

Tess's eyes lit up. "What?" she squealed as she ran to him in her socks.

"Tada!" Jason said, pulling the Barbie doll from behind his back.

Tessa grabbed the doll out of his hands and studied it with glee. While she played with the doll's hair, Jason bent down and gave his daughter a gentle hug.

"You happy, my little cutie pie?"

"Yup," Tess said, studying the Barbie doll's dress. "Not like my friend Kate."

"Oh."

"Yeah. Her dad left home. Now, she's sad."

Jason cringed at the thought that when Tess fully understood the recent turn of events that she too might be sad. "I'm sorry to hear that," Jason said, brushing his daughter's hair from her eyes.

"But not as sad as her mom," Tess reported. "She cries a lot."

"Oh?" Jason considered that for a moment. "How about your mom? Does she cry too?"

"Nope. Not at all."

Jason couldn't help but smile. At that moment, the front door swung open. His estranged wife Lyla was leaning against the doorframe, her arms crossed. *Oh, that stance of hers.* Jason could feel his stomach tighten.

"Didn't I distinctly ask you," she said, "to call before you came over?"

Jason had always felt Lyla got entirely too much satisfaction from her interrogating ways.

"Yes, you did, "Jason replied. "But I was in the neighborhood and ...."

"Yeah, but why didn't you ...?"

Jason raised his hand, cutting her off. "I distinctly remember you saying that you wanted everything out of the garage. So, I came by to pick them up."

She considered that a moment. "Well, okay," she said. Though she'd never admitted it, Jason could tell Lyla was embarrassed. *There's gotta be a stitch of warmth in there somewhere. She can't be as perfect as she thinks she is.* Lyla looked at her watch. "Come on in, Tess. Your friend will be over soon."

"Friend?" Jason asked.

"You remember Julia, don't you Dad," Tess asked.

While Jason had never met her, he'd heard a lot about her. He nodded in agreement.

"Her mom's bringing her over."

"Great," Jason said. "Well, have fun."

"*Au revoir*, poppa," Tess said.

"*Au revoir?*" Jason asked, impressed. "Where'd you pick that up?"

"Julia taught me. She lived in France."

While her mom was shutting the door, Tess gave her dad a final wave. Suddenly alone, Jason felt his shoulders sink. He lumbered over to the garage and yanked the door open. When he'd trudged up the creaky wooden stairs leading up to the attic, he spotted the last remaining boxes stacked in the corner. *There's nothing harder than divorce,* he repeated to himself. *Nothing's harder than divorce.* He and Lyla had signed their divorce agreement only two days earlier.

Jason took his time lugging each of the old boxes down the stairs and over to the car. Then, he packed as many of the boxes as he could fit into the trunk. The rest he put on the backseat. On Jason's last trip, he spotted a familiar red Miller High Life logo printed on the side of the last box as well as the words 'Coney Island' handwritten in black marker. This intrigued him.

Crammed into the box were an assortment of long-forgotten items; newspaper clippings, documents, a plaque, various papers, and a faded diploma, and if the tip of it weren't already sticking out, Jason would never have found the postcard. It looked strangely familiar.

Long ago, when he was all of sixteen, he had worked for the summer in his grandfather's penny arcade. On his first day of work, he had spotted the postcard tacked to a wall in the arcade's private bathroom. Jason leaned down and carefully removed it from the box. A faded photo of a young woman appeared on the cover.

As Jason's gaze lingered on the photo, a flood of memories swept over him for a brief moment. When they'd faded, Jason filed it back in the box and placed the box on the backseat of the car. Then, Jason hopped in. As he turned on the ignition, he took one last look back at the house. *God bless her.* Then, he shifted the car into reverse.

As he was about to drive off, a second car pulled into the driveway. Jason briefly glimpsed a young girl sitting in the passenger seat as well as the profile of a woman driving. *Now that's strange. What is it about today? Another woman who reminds me of Anna.* Jason shook his head and turned the radio on. To his delight, the strains of Martha and the Vandellas' *Dancing in the Streets* filled the car.

> "*Calling out around the world*
> *Are you ready for a brand, new beat?*
> "*Summer's here and the time is right*
> *For dancing in the street …*"

With the music quickly transporting him back in time, Jason suddenly felt the scorching heat of summer. The sand on his feet. He distinctly heard the deafening roar of a roller coaster screeching down a track, inhaled the sweet smell of cotton candy and savored the smoky crunch of a steaming Nathan's hot dog.

Beep! Beep! Jason was suddenly jolted out of his reverie by the blare of a car horn behind him. His car had been sitting at an intersection and the light had just changed. As he sped away, the intoxicating memories faded all too quickly.

Jason thought about Mitch's offer. *Nice of him to let me stay at his place.* But, while Jason appreciated Mitch's gesture, he had mixed feelings about his cousin. Sure, family came first. But Mitch was not the easiest person to be with. He was a stickler for facts and details and Jason found that a bit tiresome. No one else could come up with as many odd facts about sports and bits of trivia. And damn him, Mitch invariably backed them up with statistics. Statistic after damn statistic.

One Sunday afternoon decades before, Jason recalled, while the family was gathered around a dining room table, Mitch, who couldn't have been more than seven at the time, had blurted out, "You know who still holds the record for the most losses of any baseball team in the Major Leagues?"

Everyone turned to look at him.

"The Cleveland Spiders."

"Really?" Mitch's dad finally said with skepticism. "And when did that happen?"

"They lost 134 games way back in 1899," Mitch had said matter-of-factly.

Jason took great delight in teasing his cousin about his obsession with details. Jason loved messing with his head. As they sat around the table one evening, Jason, knowing that Mitch's family lived in the Brighton Beach neighborhood of Brooklyn, asked his cousin, "So, Mitch. How long does it take to get from Brighton Beach to Coney Island?"

"23 minutes," his cousin shot back without missing a beat.

"23 minutes?" Jason asked. "You sure about that? Not 20 or 25?"

"Nope," Mitch said. "23 minutes."

Who could argue with him? Or for that matter, who wanted to! Being a stickler for details, Mitch often bored Jason to tears as he droned on in that dry monotone of his about subjects Jason cared nothing about. Mitch was the only person Jason knew who got excited about tax policy and dental care or annuities.

The problem was, Jason's parents thought the world of Mitch. In their eyes, Jason's older cousin was a model child, that he could do no wrong. They raved about him. How smart he was, how hard he worked. From time to time when Jason's parents claimed, "You know, your cousin's going places," all that came to Jason's mind was, "Yeah ... and I just wish he would." But sometimes, we just have to swallow our pride.

• • •

Cousin Mitch stood waiting out on the porch. He checked his watch one more time before turning and returning to the kitchen. He smelled the aroma of dinner cooking and then decided to wait for him in the living room.

His cousin was clearly going through a rough patch. Mitch could see it on his face. Jason was tense and irritable. With his impending divorce, he needed a place to stay, some temporary refuge where he could clear his head, get back on his feet. So, once he cleared it with his wife, Mitch was happy to offer their guest room for as long as he needed. His logic was simple. There was no better place to ride out the storm.

Mitch happened to be three years older than Jason and one of his many cousins. A successful accountant who'd been married eleven years to his beautiful wife Laura. They and their two twin boys lived in a large well-appointed home in New Rochelle, New York, one of the city's tony bedroom communities.

• • •

After swinging his car into his cousin's double driveway, Jason popped open the trunk and pulled out the essentials, his battered suitcase, an old cardboard box, and his guitar. When he opened the front door, the intoxicating aroma of beef stroganoff filled his nostrils and Mitch's perfect wife Laura was standing in their grand foyer.

"Ah, Jason," she said. "How goes the war?"

"Well, I could say, as Zayde used to, that it's 99%," Jason replied. "But I'd be lying. Right now, it feels more like 43%."

"Well…," Laura said. "Come on in. Sit down. Maybe some comfort food will help. Everyone's already at the table."

"Oh, thanks." Jason head into their dining room.

"By the way, a woman called for you this afternoon," Laura added before she popped back into the kitchen.

"Really?" Jason said. "Did she happen to leave her name?"

"No, sorry. She didn't."

Jason shrugged. Seated in their usual places were his cousin Mitch and their twin boys, Peter and Sebastian. Jason took a seat opposite the boys.

"Hi, Uncle Jason," a spectacled Sebastian said.

He and his twin brother Peter were wearing matching striped bow ties. Their parents often made a point of pointing out that, while their boys were only eight years old, they were already at a third-grade reading level and were very precocious.

"Uh, hi, Sebastian," Jason said.

Laura placed a casserole dish of lasagna carefully down on the table and took a seat.

"So," she said. "Is the divorce moving ahead?"

Jason winced and put his fork down. He was just about to answer when Peter asked, "What's a diborce?"

"A divorce, stupid," his brother said.

"Sebastian, that is no way to talk," their mother said. "Many people divorce because they're no longer getting along."

Jason had helped himself to a wedge of lasagna.

"And current statistics show," Mitch interjected, "that 40.8% of people end up in divorce."

"Really?" the twins said in unison.

"940,000 people filed for divorce last year alone," Mitch said. "The numbers are really quite staggering."

Jason paused mid-bite and looked over to his cousin.

"Wow," Peter said, reaching for another biscuit. "That's a whole lot of people."

"Not everyone marries for love," Mitch added.

Jason's forehead furrowed.

"That's right," Laura said. "Some marry for honor. They feel a responsibility."

"Take our family," Mitch explained, looking over at Jason for acknowledgment.

"Our family?" Sebastian asked.

"Yes," Mitch said. "Zayde married Bubbie out of honor. He felt a sense of responsibility."

"Wow," the two brothers said.

"We didn't learn about this until much later," Mitch said.

"Yes, but getting back to the boys' question," Laura interjected. "Sometimes, two people marry and then, after some time, they no longer get along. They may try to work it out. Some may go to counseling... "

Jason slowly put his fork down and lowered his head while Laura continued.

"Then, after seeing a therapist for a while," she continued to explain, "where they've tried to discuss their differences. Maybe there hasn't been any progress, so they…"

Jason looked first at Mitch, then at Laura. He rose slowly from the table and pulled his chair back as quietly as he could. Then, he picked up his half-eaten plateful of lasagna and his utensils.

Mitch and Laura watched as Jason lumbered down the hallway and disappeared into the guest room. They turned to each other. "Did we say something wrong?"

CHAPTER 2

*"I couldn't sleep at all last night
Just a-thinking about you
Baby things weren't right
Well, I was tossin' and turnin'
Turnin' and tossin'
Tossin' and turnin' all night."*

Tossin' and Turnin'
Bobby Lewis

Saturday, May 11, 1966

> *"They're dancing in Chicago,*
> *Down in New Orleans*
> *In New York City*
> *All we need is music, sweet music..."*

Jason loved to wake up to New York City's WINS radio. That Saturday morning, it was playing *Dancin' in the Streets*, one of that summer's infectious hit songs. The morning traffic outside his bedroom window in Queens directly competed with the catchy tune. Jason slowly opened his eyes and looked over to his clock radio. Then, he remembered. *Oh, shoot. It's Saturday. I could have slept in.* He grabbed the blanket covers and pulled them up over his head. His reverie, however, was short-lived.

"Jason," his mom yelled from downstairs. She was making breakfast. "It's time to wake up. Life's passing you by."

Jason reached over to his radio and cranked up the volume, hoping it might drown out his mother's calls. *Maybe she'll get distracted and let me sleep another half hour.*

"Jason! Don't make me come up there."

Oh, gee. Sounds like she means it.

"Jason!"

"Okay, okay," he shouted back. "I'm up. I'm up." Jason threw back the covers with a groan. He rose out of bed and gave his poster of The Beatles hanging on his wall a mock salute. Then, he trudged down the hall to the bathroom.

• • •

Ten minutes later, Jason waddled into the kitchen. His mom was stirring a pot of oatmeal. "Here. Come. Have some," she said, motioning for him to sit down. Jason watched as his mother Sara spooned clump after clump of oatmeal into the bowl in front of him. When she was done, he reached for the bowl of sugar and began pouring heaping spoonful after spoonful onto his oatmeal.

"Don't be like your zayde," she said. "Too much sugar will rot your teeth."

What a nag. Jason begrudgingly put the last spoonful of sugar back into the bowl.

"Jason, you need to do something this summer," his mom said. "Find a way to make money."

Jason dropped his spoon and groaned. "M-o-m!"

"Don't be lazy."

"I'm not lazy."

"Look, Jason, you're sixteen years old." She put down her coffee and stared at him. "You need to be productive. It'll be good for you."

"My friends and I just want to hang out."

"Hang out?" His mother scowled disapprovingly.

Jason wished his mom understood how he felt.

"I wonder if your grandfather needs any help this summer?"

Jason cringed at the thought of working for his grandfather. Sara's crusty, but gregarious father, Harry, as his friends called him, operated a penny arcade in Coney Island. The arcade got very busy during the summer and Harry couldn't handle it all himself. Also, he hadn't been feeling very well lately. Whether he'd welcome the help was another matter.

"Why didn't I think of it sooner?" she said. "There's no harm in asking."

Wiping her hands on her apron, Sara walked over to the black phone mounted on the wall. While she dialed her parents' phone number, Jason pondered what it'd actually might be like working for his zayde. He leaned his head forlornly in his right hand and made swirling circles with his spoon in his oatmeal. His day wasn't unfolding as he'd planned. Jason secretly hoped that his zayde would say no.

"C'mon, pick it up, pick it up," Sara muttered as she waited for someone to answer the phone at her parents. Granted, her parents didn't always hear when the phone was ringing. After four rings, someone eventually picked up.

"Hello, Ma?"

"Yeah, Sara?" her mother Yetta answered in her singsong Yiddish accent. Sara angled the phone so Jason could hear.

"Yeah, it's me. Hi, Mom."

"Oh, hi, Sara."

No idle chatterer, Sara got right to the point. "So, Jason's looking for a job this summer. Any chance that dad could use him at the arcade?"

"Eh, I don't know. Maybe, bubbela. Jason could stay vit us and I could cook for him," she said excitedly. "Leave it vit me. I'll ask him tonight."

"Okay, Mom, thanks," Sara said. "See 'ya soon."

Sara hung up the phone and turned to see her son cradling his head in his hands.

"Oh, come on," she said. "You're assuming that it'd be hell."

"It would. Why do I have to work for Zayde?" Jason grumbled, knowing perfectly well that his grandfather would work him hard.

Sara then tried to appeal to his compassion.

"Jason, you never know what life has to offer. How much time people have left."

Jason gave her a quizzical stare. He hadn't considered that.

"And," she added, "he hasn't been feeling well lately. He could use your help."

• • •

Yetta was waiting up for him when Zayde returned home late that night. She knew her husband well. Knowing that he'd be tired and irritable, she waited for just the right moment to pop the question. She also knew that her husband Herschel always felt better after his favorite meal, her beloved moist beef brisket.

So, once she'd placed a serving in front of him, Yetta took the seat opposite him. She discretely watched him and waited for just the right moment. Eating was one of Harry's favorite activities, especially eating what his wife cooked for him. Yetta adjusted a strand of stray grey hair behind her ear and cleared her throat.

"So, uh, Herschel …"

"Yeah," he answered, not even looking up from his dish.

"Jason needs a summer job."

Harry had been totally consumed by the dish's wonderful aroma and taste. With her comment, he looked up with surprise. "Summer job?"

"Can he vork at de arcade?"

"Oy … uh, let me …" Harry reluctantly put down his fork and wiped his lips with the back of his hand. Yetta handed him a napkin and quickly launched into her next argument.

"It vould be a good ting," Yetta said, sitting up straighter. "A grandson to vork vit."

Harry looked at her. He took the napkin from his wife and wiped some gravy running down his cheek.

"Vee never know how much time vill haf vit our grandchildren. They grow so fast."

Yetta shifted in her chair. Then, she leaned over the table trying to meet his eyes. Her large bosom now rested on the table's edge.

"And you could use the help."

Initially, Harry had seemed cool to the idea. But, Yetta knew that with the right argument, he might concede. She also knew it was unlikely he'd go head-to-head with her at this hour.

Harry pondered it for another moment. After a minute, he said, "Oh … okay. But, only if he promises he'll get to vork on time and vork hard." He gave her a terse look and then dove back into his tasty dinner.

Yetta sat back in her chair and crossed her arms contentedly. She gave the tiniest of Cheshire smiles.

• • •

Friday evening, June 21, 1966

No sooner had the Steiner's car pulled up to the curb than Jason jumped out. He reached into the backseat and wrestled to pull out his suitcase and guitar case. Jason bent down to look back at his mother through the passenger window.

"Now, be good. Behave," his mom said.

"Okay, Mom," Jason said, rolling his eyes. "Talk to you soon."

Jason did not relish having to walk up three flights of stairs to his grandparent's apartment. While still panting for air, he knocked on their door. No one answered. *Gee, they're supposed to be home.* Jason knocked again. After a long wait, Jason could hear the shuffling of feet and the distinct sound of his zayde singing, "Hoy boy boy boy." Jason smiled.

When the door swung open, his grandfather was standing in his slippers smiling at him.

"Hello, boychik."

"Hi, grandpa."

Looking just over his grandfather's shoulder, Jason could see his grandmother, Yetta, praying in their kitchen, her head covered by a shawl. She lit two candles, then closed her eyes and began drawing little circles with the palms of her hands while she silently mumbled a prayer. Oblivious to this, Zayde leaned toward his grandson and said in a loud whisper, "Bet you didn't know your grandmudder vas such a religious woman."

Without missing a beat, from under her shawl his bubbie countered, "Drop dead, Herschel," and then continued on with her prayers for the Sabbath. Not missing a beat, Zayde turned to his grandson. "Nu, have you eaten?"

Jason shook his head.

"Come. *Essen.*"

Jason placed his suitcase and guitar case in the hallway and followed his zayde into the kitchen. A full Friday night meal had been laid out on their long kitchen table. Zayde hobbled back to his seat at the head of the table and plopped himself down. Jason's great grandmother, Jeanette, was already seated to Zayde's left.

While she was diminutive in size, registering 5'5" in height at best, she was a force to be reckoned with. For many years, the family assumed that she, or as they'd taken to call her Lil' Grandma, had been killed in the war, in the Auschwitz concentration camp, along with many of Jason's other relatives. But, it wasn't until 1947, two years after the war ended, that her daughter Yetta learned her mother was actually alive.

One cool September morning, Yetta happened to be standing in the neighborhood bakery when a woman she hardly knew turned to her and asked, "Is your last name Jacobovitz?"

"Yeah. Vy do you ask?"

"Vell, I saw your last name on a list of refugees. De're being held at Ellis Island. Maybe it's somevon you know."

Yetta shrugged. "Is dat possible?"

When she got home, she insisted that her husband Harry accompany her to Ellis Island the next morning to confirm whether her mother was, in fact, being held there. That night, she had trouble sleeping tossing and turning in anticipation. To her great joy and surprise, the following morning Yetta was reunited with her dear mother, a woman she hadn't seen in more than a decade.

Bubbie was overjoyed to see her grandson. She motioned for him to take his seat with his grandfather and great grandmother at the table. Then, she served the first course of dinner, cabbage soup and challah. Jason took the first sip of his soup and felt a warm glow spread through his body. His zayde turned to him. "So, you coming to vork tamarra?"

Jason simply nodded.

"I vant dat you should be dere no later den nine."

"Sure, grandpa. No problem."

Jason had visited his grandparents many times. But, this was the first time he'd ever witnessed one of their Sabbath dinners and it didn't take him long to realize that they were spectacles. Sure, the food was great. But, any meal at the Jacobowitz's was a symphony to his ears. A smorgasbord of languages. Depending on the topic and who was talking, Jason could be treated to a morsel of Yiddish, a smattering of German, a shmeer of Russian or an eclectic feast of broken English.

A typical conversation might go something like this, "So, you vant some we-ge-tables?" Yetta would ask. "A bissel," Zayde might typically reply. All the while, his diminutive Lil' Grandma would sit there silently. While she was fluent in five languages, she didn't speak a word of English. So, she and Jason were always forced to communicate in their own special brand of sign language. Jason would have to mime, "Please pass the pickles."

Jason quickly learned that his bubbie never sat during a meal. She was too busy serving, rushing about back and forth from the stove to the table and back, cooking, stirring, and serving round after round of food. That evening, Jason also realized that he'd never seen his Lil' Grandma in her element. Tonight, for example, just before the roasted chicken was served, his little grandma shockingly pulled her dentures out of her mouth and placed them smack on the table. Jason momentarily gagged at the sight. To counter his gag reflex, Jason instead visualized his favorite Yankee, Mickey Mantle, hitting a long home run to the left field bleachers. Despite using this tactic, through the meal he periodically wondered, *'Why would she do that?'* And then, it hit him. That must be the best way to suck the succulent meat off the bone.

Two hours later, when the dinner had ended, Jason politely excused himself from the table. Before his grandparents knew it, he was carrying his toothpaste and brush into the bathroom. Moments later, he reappeared and as he passed the kitchen table, he wished everyone, "G'night."

His bubbie was the only one who answered, "Gay schluffen."

CHAPTER 3

*"They say for every boy and girl
There's just one love in this old world
And I know I've found mine."*

Young Love
Connie Francis

The next morning, Jason awoke with a start. His little grandma was poking at his sprawled body with her cane. She loved watching television and the TV happened to be located in the living room. The problem was Jason was lying on her favorite spot on the couch. With his Lil' Grandma occupying the small guest bedroom, Jason had to sleep in the living room on the lumpy sofa bed. His long legs often draped over one arm of the sofa. Consequently, often he didn't sleep well.

Opera music blared from the kitchen and the acrid odor of Zayde's cigarettes hung heavily in the air. When Jason pulled the covers down, he was treated to an episode of the Three Stooges' blasting away on the small black and white Sylvania TV by his feet. That's the moment Jason realized he was in for one long summer.

With little grandma's next poke of her cane, Jason opened his eyes fully. He looked up only to see her stooped over him, staring down at him. Jason had never realized that she had a mustache.

"Okay, Lil' Grandma, okay. Good morning."

She grunted and gave his blanketed leg another jab of her cane, her signal for him to move over.

"Okay, okay."

"Morning, sleepy head," his zayde bellowed, his stocky frame looming in the doorway. Harry took a drag from his ever-present cigarette. "So nu. You got your beauty sleep?"

Jason chuckled and realized that there'd be no way that he'd get back to sleep. He flung the covers off him and stood up. Quickly realizing he was only wearing his pajama bottoms, he grabbed the nearest blanket and wrapped it around his body.

"Let's get de show on de road." Zayde barked.

"How much time do I have?"

"Time? You need time?" Zayde asked. By stepping in front of the TV, he was now blocking Lil' Grandma's view of the TV. "Did Einstein need time? Get dressed."

Jason shook his head and waddled off to the bathroom, but not before catching the sight of his little grandma swatting at Zayde's rear end with her cane.

CHAPTER 3

• • •

Even at that early hour, the sky was already a brilliant blue, the sun warming the sidewalk. As they strolled along Mermaid Avenue on their way to the arcade, Jason and Zayde were both lost in thought, in their own private worlds. Jason ruminated about the Yankees upcoming series with the Washington Senators. And Zayde, no doubt knowing the day was going to be a hot one, was probably glad he'd worn his pale green shorts. A voice suddenly brought them out of their daydreams.

"Herschel, vot's vit de cane?" a jolly looking older man, stooped under an awning called out.

Recognizing a familiar face, Zayde grabbed his grandson's arm and guided him over.

"If I tell 'ya my leg hurts, you'll call me a gimp," Zayde joked.

For the past several months, his grandfather had taken to using a cane. In fact, on that morning's walk, Jason found that he had to slow down several times so his grandfather could keep up with him. His zayde cringed with every step he took.

"Oyvink," Zayde said. "I vant you should meet my grandson."

Jason turned to face the stout man. "Nice to meet you, Irving."

Their conversation was cut short by the sound of a loud, prolonged honking of a car horn. Jason turned his head and spotted a snazzy black Buick LeSabre coming up the street. He took a moment to study the car's long, sleek lines. Jason had only recently developed a fascination for the new slick, stylish cars. He made it his business to know all of the current makes and models.

When he looked more closely, he realized the driver was none other than Nunzio Ricci, a fellow student at his high school. As well as being one of the stars of the high school's football team, Nunzio also happened to be one of the school's notorious bullies. When Nunzio honked his horn again, this time trying to get the attention of someone standing on the corner, Irving and Zayde both scowled.

"Dere goes dat god damn gonif," Zayde said. "He's nuttink but trouble."

"You're telling me," Irving said. "Ever since he got that car, oy, he tinks a big man."

When Nunzio pulled his car over to the curb, three young girls, their ponytails swaying to and fro, jumped out, giggling and chatting excitedly. Jason's heart stopped when he recognized one girl in particular, Anna Conti, a girl he'd been infatuated with all through the school year.

"Zayde, give me a minute," Jason said. Not waiting for a reply, he raced over to the girls. By the time he approached the car, Nunzio had the trunk open and the girls were reaching in to grab their bags.

"Need some help?" Jason asked breathlessly.

"Oh, no thanks," Anna said. "Nunzio's helping."

At that very moment, Nunzio was actually leaning against the car lighting up a cigarette.

"Where you headed?" Jason asked.

"To the beach," Anna said excitedly. "Wanna come?"

"Gee, I'd love to. But, I gotta work," Jason said, pointing back over his shoulder. He was ecstatic simply being in her company. *Heck, what are the odds she'd be here in Coney Island? There must be some divine reason for this chance meeting?* From the very first moment he'd seen her at school, he was smitten, taken by her classic Mediterranean beauty, her olive features, and her dark brown eyes. Through the school year, he developed a huge crush on her. They were both enrolled in the same Social Studies class and Jason ended up sitting behind her. During their many classes, he had gazed longingly at her, her long black hair, the slope of her long neck, often fantasizing about planting a soft kiss here and there.

Standing next to her now, he found himself getting lost in the deep pools of her eyes. Time seemed to stand still. He studied the tight tanned muscles of her neck and how they disappeared under the neckline of her summery blouse. It was the first time he noticed a small beauty mark at the base of her left ear.

"Jason," his zayde yelled. "Enough already. Let's go."

Jason roused himself from his reverie. "Well, I guess I gotta go," he said reluctantly. "See 'ya later."

"Guess so," Anna answered. "See 'ya."

Jason reluctantly rejoined his zayde. However, he couldn't resist taking one last look back. The girls were still chatting amongst themselves and Nunzio had removed the last bag from the trunk. Jason's only thought was of the long day which laid ahead. And it bothered him that he had no idea when he'd next get to see Anna.

After walking another block, Jason suddenly turned to his grandfather. "So, do I get a break during the day?"

"A break? Vat kinda break?"

"For lunch."

Zayde followed his grandson's eyes and saw that the girls were now heading toward the beach. He smiled. "Vell, I guess. Turty minutes. No more."

Okay. Thanks, Zayde."

Jason knew exactly how he'd spend his first lunch break.

• • •

"So, let me show you how to open up."

Jason and his grandfather were standing at the entrance to the arcade. Zayde reached over and swung the big accordion security gate to the side. It clicked into place with a loud clang and shuttered. Next, he unlocked the rusty padlock and wrapped its loop around one of the metal bars of the gate.

"It only locks ven you give it a good zetz."

Zayde slammed the padlock down. Then, he groaned heaving the corrugated metal barricade high up over his head. Grabbing the pole resting against the wall, he hooked one end of it into a notch on the barricade and using all of his strength, he pushed the barricade into a slot along the ceiling. Pointing to the metal barricade, Zayde issued his final instruction. "Make sure dis clicks into place. Udderwise, it could roll back and hit somebody. Got forbid."

"So, where do you keep the keys?" Jason asked.

"Ahh," Zayde answered, jangling the keys in front of Jason's nose for emphasis. "Ven I'm here, de keys stay vit me. Ven I leaf, I'll give dem to you."

Jason nodded. Then, he and Zayde both stared into the penny arcade's dark cavernous interior. Jason could just make out the glass tops of the multitude of games and machines. His senses were soon assaulted by a pungent odor of the sewer mixed with a buttery smell of popcorn. Zayde hobbled over to the wall to his left where there was a large panel of scuffed light switches.

"You ready for de magic?" Zayde asked, almost goading his grandson.

"Zayde, I already know the magic."

"Dat's vat you tink! Watch!"

Jason stared blankly back at him. He had no idea what his grandfather meant by that. Without any warning, Zayde launched into the opening bars of Strauss's Blue Danube Waltz. "Da dah da da dah, da dah, dah dah…" With the skill of a conductor, Zayde punctuated the end of each musical phrase with a flick of a light switch, and with the flick of each switch, first one, then another, and still another the many machines came to life. Little did Jason know that his grandfather was casting a spell. Slowly but surely, he was transforming the arcade into a symphony of bells and dings, pings and whistles. Jason's pulse quickened as the machines, some painted gaudily and all designed to excite and entertain the public, to woo the nickels, the dimes, and quarters from unsuspecting visitors, now sung and pulsated with their own throbbing, hypnotic energy.

Zayde waited until the waltz's rousing chorus to turn on the long strings of colored light bulbs hanging high overhead. With the skill of a magician, step-by-step, beat-by-beat, he brought what had been a dark slumbering penny arcade to life. All the while, Jason stood there motionless, mesmerized by the sights and sounds of the arcade, his eyes steeped in a child's sense of awe.

"Come vit me," Zayde said leading his grandson over to a row of pinball machines. Pawing the first one with his thick, bearlike palm, he said, "Dis is my favorite vun. De Big Casino." Zayde raised its glass cover. "Ven de players hit deese," he said, pointing at its five rubber bumpers, "dey can rack up lots of points."

Jason stood spellbound.

"Let me show you anudder vinner."

Zayde next guided Jason over to a large display case at the very center of the arcade. Sitting inside the glass case on a large platform was Esmeralda, a rather ornately painted gypsy doll holding court. Her brightly colored, gaudy outfit had a certain appeal.

"She's a fortune teller," Zayde explained. "For only two quarters, she can predict the future," he nodded knowingly. "Here, give it a try," he said, handing his grandson two quarters. Jason stared blankly at the coins in his hand. He plopped them hesitantly into the slot. Within seconds, Esmeralda came to life, turning her head first to the right, then sweeping her hand to the left. A moment later, the machine spat out a printed paper slip.

"Go ahead. Read it. Vat does it say?"

Jason plucked it from the chute. "You will meet beauty," he read.

Zayde raised his eyebrows. "Hmm . . . She's never wrong."

Jason looked at him quizzically.

"Now follow me." Zayde hobbled over to two smaller penny machines. A tall nondescript wooden booth sat between them. "Dis is the vun machine vit heart," he said mysteriously.

"With heart?"

"Ven people go into dis boot, dey speak their heart."

Jason had no idea what his zayde meant by that.

"Dey can make a record."

"Really?"

"Yup. They record a message and boom! Dey can send it anyvere. To anyvun around de vorld. To a lover, a soldier over de seas, a boyfriend, a gurlfriend." Zayde winked.

"Cool," Jason said somewhat hesitantly.

As his grandfather meandered on, continuing to give his tour of the arcade, expounding on each of the machine's special idiosyncrasies and features, Jason's mind wandered. His attention was drawn out on the street where a lone raven picked at a crust of bread. He nabbed it with its beak. At that same moment, Jason felt a slight tremor and the building began to shake with a deep, resounding rumble. Dust sifted from the rafters.

The rumbling was, in fact, the Cyclone roller coaster making its first run of the day. Jason could hear the cars rattle as they made their way up the track. There was a momentary silence. Then, Jason heard the frightful screams of its passengers as the rollercoaster roared down the track.

In utter fear, the raven took flight, carrying away its spoils. Jason imagined the bird soaring over the roller coaster, flying over the Steeplechase amusement park across the street and beyond, over the boardwalk's many shops and rides. Jason visualized that it eventually landed on the beach where Anna was sunbathing with her friends.

"Okay, enough of dat," Zayde abruptly said. "Here's vat you gotta do every mornink."

"Okay," Jason said obediently.

"Furst tink: You gotta clean de vashrooms. Den, you sveep de floors and trow out de garbage. I'll show you vere de supplies are." Zayde led his grandson over to a mysterious door which Jason had never seen before. It stood behind some of the machines and the word *Private* had been crudely hand painted on it.

"Everytink's in here." Zayde pulled out a set of keys from his pocket and unlocked the door. The small room consisted of a janitor's sink, several bottles of cleanser, a bucket, a mop, a broom, and some sponges.

Jason immediately noticed a dark green curtain at the back of the room.

Zayde grabbed the bucket and placed it in the sink.

"Furst, you put in de cleanser. Then, you fill it vit hot vaser," he advised.

"Uh huh." Jason studied the curtain again. "So, what's behind the curtain?"

"Nuttink you should vorry about." Without saying another word, Zayde turned and hobbled off to fix one of his ailing machines.

With no further instructions, Jason poured some cleanser into the bucket and turned on the hot water. While the bucket was filling, Jason took a moment to look around. He eyed the old curtain once again. *A little peek won't hurt.* Jason turned off the water and stepped closer. Drawing the curtain back revealed a small bathroom. When Jason flicked the light switch, he immediately noticed a dark blue suit hanging on a wooden hanger. An already knotted dark red tie was draped over it and a small bottle of aftershave and a bar of soap were sitting on a tiny shelf above the sink.

Just as he was about to leave, Jason spotted a postcard tacked to the wall to the left of the sink. The cover featured a faded black and white photograph, its edges now tan and faded. The photo depicted an attractive young woman with blonde hair. *Gee, that photographer sure caught her beauty.*

Jason carefully removed the tack and turned the postcard over. On the back was a simple handwritten message, *With my undying love, Gail. I miss you!* Jason racked his brain but he couldn't recall anyone having that name.

At that moment, Zayde unexpectedly pulled the curtain back. "Vat de …?" he yelled. "Give me dat." Zayde grabbed the card gruffly from Jason's hand. Then, he shook his head and stuffed the postcard into his shirt pocket.

Jason was speechless and embarrassed.

"Go," Zayde bellowed. "Clean de betrooms."

Jason grabbed the mop and bucket and carried them over to the public bathrooms. He plunked the bucket down on the ground. Jason then took one look in the men's room and backed away in disgust. The stench was overwhelming. Every urinal was plugged, reams of toilet paper were strewn all over the concrete floor and there wasn't a towel or a bar of soap in sight.

So much for the magic.

• • •

Jason couldn't wait for lunchtime to come. All morning, he had wondered whether he'd see Anna on the beach. When lunchtime finally did arrive, he raced as quickly as he could over to the boardwalk. All the way, he could hear his zayde yelling behind him, "Remember. Half an hour. No more."

Jason quickly climbed the wooden stairs and raced breathlessly over to the boardwalk's metal railing. He let his gaze extend beyond the beach to the Atlantic Ocean stretched out before him. Out on its horizon, he could make out a long train of barges hauling garbage out to sea. Hundreds of seagulls followed in eager pursuit.

Jason then lowered his gaze and took a moment to study the sunbathers on the beach. Within a minute, he spotted Anna, the object of his desire, sitting on a blanket wearing a light red bathing suit chatting with her friends. Suddenly, Jason heard someone whistling behind him. He turned his head. When he turned back, Anna was waving in his direction. Jason instinctively waved back. Then, out of the corner of his eyes he saw someone bounding down the stairs. Sure enough, it was Nunzio. *Damn him.*

Jason smirked as he watched Nunzio, holding three beaded bottles of soda in his arms, tiptoe gingerly across the hot sand. He seemed afraid he'd scuff his shiny black shoes. When Nunzio finally reached the three girls, he leaned down and handed a bottle to each girl. Before taking a seat on the blanket, Nunzio carefully removed each of his shoes and shook out any lingering, bothersome sand.

"Freakin' Nunzio," Jason cursed, slapping the railing in frustration. While he relished being able to see Anna, he quickly realized that his lunch break would soon be over. Jason strolled over to the nearby hot dog stand and was about to place his order when an older man sitting on a bench not ten feet away called out to him.

"You Herschel's grandson?"

"Uh, yeah," Jason said tentatively. "You know him?"

"Sure do. He's a regular at our card games. Beats us every time."

Jason and the older fellow laughed.

"I'm Yoseph," he said extending his hand. "Have a seat."

Jason shook his hand. "Uh … hi, Yoseph. Thanks. I'm Jason."

"Oh, I know," Joseph said. "He talks about you … a lot."

"Really?" Jason said, a little startled.

"Don't vorry. He says you're a good boychik."

An awkward silence followed.

"So, how is de old kaker?" Joseph asked.

"Um, good, I think."

"Mit his leg and everytink."

"Oh yeah. Well, he's been using a cane."

Joseph nodded. Another long silence followed. "Mit de sugar disease and everytink … "

"Sugar disease?" Jason answered. "I … When did…? I had no idea."

"Oh, sorry."

Jason was baffled by Joseph's news. Both were silent for a minute.

"Well, I better get some lunch," Jason finally said. "Nice to meet you, Yoseph."

"Nice to meet you too."

Jason walked backed to the counter and quickly ordered a hot dog. As he waited, Jason's mind reflected back to his year at school, particularly the first time he'd seen Anna. From that moment on, Jason couldn't take his eyes off her. From the moment she took her seat in class, he was captivated by her presence, her smooth olive skin, and her thin delicate features. Later that day, Jason told his friends, "I've never seen anyone so finely crafted." They looked at him as though he'd lost his mind. Social Studies soon became his favorite class.

What fascinated Jason most about Anna was not just her looks, but her intelligence. She was the only student he knew who could quote Wordsworth and Blake, Karl Marx and Darwin. Often, when Mrs. Mazur, their portly Social Studies teacher, posed a question in class, Anna or Jason were the only students who raised their hands. Even from that very first day, Jason knew they shared something special.

Throughout the school year, Jason longed for a chance to talk with her. It embarrassed him to recall the number of missed opportunities. The first one occurred in early September. Jason and his best friend Jeff had been chatting in the hallway about the Yankees-White Sox game the night before. While Jeff was prying a book from his locker, Jason casually leaned against the lockers.

"Boy, that was a close one."

"You bet. I didn't think the Yankees were going to come back."

"Yeah. The Sox played well."

At that moment, Jason turned and saw Anna strolling toward them. He gulped. *This is my chance. Don't blow it, Jason. Say something clever.* However, as luck would have it, the period bell rang and Anna rushed off to her next class.

Two weeks later, Jason missed another opportunity. All during the school year, he would fantasize about their conversation. *What'll my opening line be? What should I talk about?* One afternoon in late February, there was only a minute left in their class. When the bell rang, Jason grabbed his backpack and quickly hoisted it over his shoulder. In his haste, its entire contents, his books, pens, ruler, baseball cards, and rubber ball all flew out and fell on the linoleum floor. When Anna did stroll by, Jason was still down on his knees, sweaty and shaking, repacking his bag.

"Uh, hi, Jason."

"Oh . . . Hi, Anna." Jason felt his cheeks burn. At that moment, any hope he had of talking to her was dashed.

• • •

When Jason got back to the arcade, he found his zayde draped over the Flying Circus, fixing one of his prized pinball machines. For several days, customers had complained that the left flipper was sticky. Zayde, looking clammy and pale, was poking at the wiring and oiling the gears.

Jason watched as his grandfather took a momentary break, digging into his pocket and retrieving a roll of cherry Lifesavers. His zayde popped not one, but two Lifesavers into his mouth. Then, he dragged the stool closer and sat down. His face was unusually pale. He pulled a handkerchief from his back pocket and wiped his brow. Jason noticed a minute or two later that some color had returned to his zayde's face.

"You okay?"

Not missing a beat, Zayde said, "One hundred percent. Just needed some energy."

CHAPTER 4

*"Get out of that bed, wash your face and hands
Get out of that bed, wash your face and hands
Get in that kitchen, make some noise with the pots and pans"*

Shake, Rattle, and Roll
Bill Haley and His Comets

"So nu, vere ver you last night?" Bubbie asked.

"Oy, Yetta. Don't start," Zadye said. "Mit de kinder."

Jason, who'd been sleeping on the living room couch, couldn't help but hear his grandparents arguing in the kitchen in the next room. A few seconds later, Lil' Grandma shuffled into the room. Pointing her cane in the direction of the kitchen, she rolled her eyes and said, "Ah, feh." Lil' Grandma then pointed her cane at the TV.

Being the obedient great-grandson, Jason rose from the couch. With the covers still wrapped tightly around him, he dutifully turned the television on, patiently switching the dial from one channel to the next and then to the next.

"This?" Jason asked, pointing to the Captain Kangaroo show.

Lil' Grandma shook her head.

The next channel Jason turned to was a Sunday morning church service. "How about this?"

She shook her head again and kept shaking her head until Jason finally came to the Mighty Mouse cartoon show. Then, she eagerly nodded her approval. Thinking she was satisfied, Jason turned away and waddled into the kitchen as the show's catchy theme song began, *Here he comes to save the day*. "Tough crowd," he muttered.

That seemed to be the cue for his grandparents to start up again. "You ver out all night," Bubbie said. "Eating Got knows vat. Sugar and sweets."

"Don't vorry about me."

"Vere ver you?"

Harry sat tight-lipped.

"Mit your Time Square friends?"

"Look . . . Vee talk. Play cards."

"Oy, gutten you," Bubbie said, shaking her head.

Then, like the last tremors of an earthquake, just as quickly as they had started, they stopped. Jason swore he could feel the linoleum rumbling beneath his feet. Bubbie simply turned back to the sink and resumed what she'd been doing, that is, plucking the feathers off a chicken. It seemed to calm her nerves. As she pulled out each feather one-by-one, she sang the Al Jolson classic softly to herself.

"You made me love you
I didn't vant to do it,
I didn't vant to do it ..."

In the meanwhile, Zayde resumed wiping down the kitchen counters. As he reached for a beautifully cut-glass vase, it slipped from his fingers and crashed on the floor.

"*Oy gevalt,*" Bubbie muttered. She had had her back to him when it broke. Afraid to see what had broken, she waited a while before turning to assess the damage. The linoleum was now covered with shards of glass. Bubbie simply shook her head and sighed.

Unfazed by it all, with a half-smoked Camel cigarette dangling from his lips, Zayde grabbed a nearby broom and dustpan and began sweeping up the broken glass. When he'd emptied the remains into a nearby garbage can, he grabbed his coat and left the apartment.

• • •

'Roses are red, violets are blue.
It was a special day when I fell for you.'

No, no, no. That's terrible. Jason shook his head in frustration.
Bang! Bang! Bang!
The forceful banging of Bubbie's fist on the bathroom door interrupted whatever focus Jason had had.
"'You com-ink out?"
Jason rolled his eyes. "Yes, Bubbie. Just give me a minute." The problem was that space was at a premium at his grandparents' apartment. Jason was always searching for some quiet spot, some out-of-the-way place, a refuge, some place where he could do his writing without interruption. So far, the bathroom had been the only private spot that he'd found.

Up until a moment ago, Jason had been sitting on the toilet, holding a small spiral notebook in one hand, a pen poised in the other, beseeching the gods to send him some divine inspiration. Jason was trying to write a poem, a love poem to Anna.

"Just give me a minute." Jason repeated. He reluctantly pulled up his pajama bottoms and gathered his things, a clear sign that he'd been defeated. Then, he opened the bathroom door, nodded to his bubbie, and went to get dressed.

• • •

Several minutes later, now fully dressed, Jason walked in the kitchen. Before he even took a seat, Bubbie handed him a heaping plate of scrambled eggs, fried potatoes, and a toasted buttered bagel.

"Come. Sit. Eat," was all she said.

For a brief instant, Jason actually considered refusing the meal. But, the truth is he had never refused anything that his bubbie served and he didn't want to start today. Instead, he gave his grandmother a smile and picked up his utensils. Normally, his grandmother would turn back to the stove, attending to this or that, but this morning was different. After wiping her greasy hands on a small kitchen towel, Bubbie waddled over to the table and sat down beside him. Then, she crossed her stocky legs, rolled down her thick opaque stockings, and sighed.

While he was devouring the mound of food that she'd set before him, Jason did a quick bit of math. If his numbers were right, his grandmother had fed seven mouths, every day, two to three meals a day, for something like thirty years. Based on his calculations, he figured that in her lifetime she had served more than 150,000 meals! Even by his conservative estimate, Jason realized that it was a miracle that she ever made it out of the kitchen.

Out of the blue, his bubbie asked, "So nu, how vas your furst day of work?"

Jason took a moment to think about thought that. Yesterday, he'd been exposed to so much at the arcade, the bathrooms, the machines, the roller coaster, where the cash was kept. Jason also recalled the mysterious postcard that he'd discovered in the private bathroom. For a brief moment, he thought about mentioning it. Then, he wisely thought the better of it.

"Good," was all he answered.

Jason instead took his time studying his grandmother. He realized that he had rarely seen her at rest. Most of the photographs he'd seen of her, on the dressers or in the photo albums, were taken when she was in her prime, fresh-faced, her skin ruddy, soft, and clear, her arms contoured and slender, her eyes bright and inviting. With the morning sun now streaking in through the window, Jason observed a different woman, a woman now stockier, her face now etched with its first wrinkles around the eyes, her lips, and across her forehead. The flesh now sagged from her ample arms. Jason often joked to himself that that was a result of all of the schmaltz that she had handled in her life.

Jason considered the fact that perhaps Bubbie's many long years of service and unconditional love were only now catching up with her. He thought long about the life she'd led, first as a faithful daughter, then as a long-suffering attentive wife, and finally as a mother and grandmother. Bubbie had started working at the tender age of twelve, taking in sewing to support her large family. Later, when she married and was raising their children, she cooked, cleaned, and shopped for the entire family as well as for the boarders that they occasionally took in. It was remarkable that she never complained.

"So Bubbie, how do you do this day in and day out?"

"Do vat?"

"Clean and cook and serve?"

"Dis is vat I do. Since I vas little. Dis all I know."

Jason placed his knife and fork down. He used a thick cloth napkin to wipe the ketchup from his mouth.

"While you were doing that, what was your mother doing?"

"My faddeh vas a rabbi. He spent most of de day and night in shul."

"Yeah, but your mother?"

"She vas also religious. She vent to shul, to keep the tradition alife. ... in de home and in de community."

"That couldn't have been easy."

She nodded solemnly.

"I had to do vat she didn't haf time to do."

"That must've been hard."

"Dat's vy I came to de new vorld," she said proudly. "Mit tree dollars in my pocket."

Jason tskked and shook his head. He pushed his empty plate away and rose to leave.

Bubble leaned over and, reaching for a paper bag, handed it to him. "Don't fehget your lunch." Jason smiled. God only knows when she found the time to prepare his favorite sandwich, sliced turkey with lettuce, tomato, and Russian dressing on seeded rye bread.

"Thanks, Bubbie," Jason said, giving her a quick kiss on the cheek.

"Don't mention it."

Jason left for his second day of work.

● ● ●

A warm summer breeze greeted Jason as he strolled to work along Mermaid Avenue. He had a good feeling about today as he took a deep breath in and exhaled. *Ah, life is good.* Today, he felt, was going to be different, filled with surprise and great possibility . . . and he wasn't disappointed. When he reached the corner of 16th Street, he looked up. Overnight, someone had strung hundreds and hundreds of colored lightbulbs from telephone pole to telephone pole and it stretched all the way down the street. The odd thing was they were still lit . . . in full daylight. Jason smiled to himself.

Before he knew it, he'd arrived at the arcade. Still feeling unusually chipper, as he came through the entrance, he shouted, "Morning." The next thing he knew a dust cloth struck him square in the face. *What the . . .* With an embarrassed look, Jason took the cloth from his face and looked around to see who the culprit was. He should have known. His zayde was standing right in front of him.

"Hey, boychik," his grandfather laughed. "Nice of you to join us." Zayde fished around in his pocket and brought out a roll of Lifesavers. He quickly popped one in his mouth and asked, "Vant vun?"

"Sure. Thanks."

Zayde popped a Lifesaver into Jason's palm and put the roll back in his pocket. "Now, dust de machines."

Jason rolled his eyes and shook his head. *So much for fun.* The first machine he tackled was the Lucky Charm. While Jason began wiping the smudged glass surface in large sweeping gestures, he marveled at the design of the machine. The arrangement of the bumpers and its intricately painted images.

At that moment, he heard a commotion outside. Jason looked up to see a group of five young men. It was Nunzio and his cohorts horsing around. They appeared to be fake boxing, throwing punches and jabs at each other. After a minute, Nunzio glanced into the arcade and his expression grew serious. "Yo, follow me," he said.

His cohorts dutifully followed him into the arcade and over to the Grand Slam, his favorite pinball machine. Nunzio took a minute to study it's inviting playfield and colorful display as one would longingly study a lover. He smiled and dug into his pocket for a quarter which he promptly plunked into the slot. Out of respect, his buddies, who'd been whooping and hollering only a minute ago, quickly quieted down. With keen eyes, they followed his every move, cheering every flick he made with the flippers. "Go, Nunzio. Nice."

Once Nunzio's game ended, the boys, now bored and distracted, began whooping and hollering again. Jason watched as his grandfather's face slowly tightened and his eyes filled with anger. Zayde turned to Jason and gave him a wink. "Vatch dis," he whispered. Grabbing his cane, he hobbled over to the group. To get their attention, he banged his cane several times on the leg of one of the pinball machines. Then, he pointed emphatically to the sign hanging above the machines reading, *If You Pay, You Can Stay!*

Raising his voice above the din, Zayde warned them, "Boys, you got a choice. Vat's it going to be?"

One of Nunzio' cronies turned to Zayde and shot back, "You got a problem, old man?" Furious at the comment, Nunzio turned to the guilty party and, without warning, slapped him in the face. The boy cowered. Zayde grinned as he watched the drama unfold. Then, he raised his cane and shouted, "Get de hell out."

The boys looked sheepishly from one to the other. They were stunned, unable to move. Nunzio finally had to prompt them. "Come with me." As they slunk out of the arcade, Nunzio turned to Jason and pointed his finger at him as if to warn him. Jason wasn't sure what he meant by that, but he kept his eyes on the group, watching them cross the street and continue arguing amongst themselves. When they reached the far side of the street, Nunzio took another swipe at the fellow who'd been mouthy.

• • •

An hour later, Nunzio and his boys were sitting at the local diner. They had once again commandeered the round table at the back of the restaurant. Outwardly, Nunzio was quietly nursing his coffee. But deep down he was still fuming about his crew getting kicked out of the very same arcade he liked to play in. The memory of their earlier confrontation gnawed away at him. *Someday, I'm going to get the respect I deserve.*

After stewing over it for several minutes, Nunzio finally turned to his henchmen. "It's about respect. People should fear us when we walk into a place. Not see us as clowns."

"We could always rough 'em up," one of his cohorts fired back.

"That's not what I'm saying?" Nunzio said. "We shouldn't have to." He sneered at his cohort, picked up his coffee cup and gazed out the diner's large bay window, contemplating the kind of life he hoped to build; a comfortable life, with a beautiful home, a sleek car or two and adoring kids. And there'd be women in his life, beautiful, desirable women. A faithful wife who waited on him and a mistress or two. The bottom line being that women would respect him and his power.

Nunzio also reflected on the fact that his father never led that kind of life. His dad, God bless him, was a simple man, a humble man. But even from an early age, Nunzio sensed that his dad was not respected. For that, he had to look to someone else, chiefly Anna's father Sal.

For years, Sal had been a local capo in the mafia. His territory included parts of Queens and Brooklyn. And while Nunzio had just barely graduated the same high school that Jason and Anna were attending, he saw himself more as a soldier in training for the mafia, one of the many men who served Anna's father; collecting money, performing odd jobs and, if necessary, intimidating people. Two years ago, Sal had taken Nunzio under his wing. Nunzio sensed that he was grooming him for bigger things.

With his boss having three daughters, Nunzio suspected that Sal regarded him as the son he never had. If Nunzio worked hard, he could see the day, perhaps the following year, when Sal would welcome him in as a *made* man.

Sal was always respectful, careful to never interfere with the wishes of Nunzio's parents. But, he slowly and carefully taught Nunzio the business; how it operated, how to deal with people effectively and forcefully, how to lean on people and, most importantly, how to collect consistently. Sal, no doubt, envisioned that Nunzio, his daughter's boyfriend, might someday take over his business. But in Sal's eyes, Nunzio had to first prove himself, prove that he was a serious earner and not just any earner. Nunzio had to demonstrate that, after all of the effort and training that Sal invested that Nunzio would bring him a significant payback.

That's why the relationship between Nunzio and Sal's eldest daughter Anna was so important. When he and Anna eventually married, Sal likely envisioned that he'd be rewarded in many ways; chiefly that his business would remain in the family, that Sal would continue to amass money, and more personally, that he'd be blessed with grandchildren.

CHAPTER 5

"They're dancing in Chicago
Down in New Orleans
In New York City
All we need is music, sweet music
There'll be music everywhere ... "

Dancing in the Streets
Martha and the Vandellas

Zayde enjoyed starting his day with music . . . and not just any kind of music. He loved classical music. So much so that the radio in the arcade was always tuned to WQXR, New York City's well-known classical music station. Sure enough, when Jason arrived that morning Bach's Brandenburg Concerto #3 was blaring. Jason went about his chores unconsciously sweeping the floor in time to the courtly music.

The atmosphere, however, changed dramatically later that afternoon. Jason was restocking the shelves underneath the counter when a group of three teenaged girls, giggling and squealing, entered the arcade. Enthralled by their happy-go-lucky energy, he stopped what he was doing.

Jason was immediately drawn to the blonde-haired girl. She wore a flimsy white blouse which exposed her firm belly and her face was dotted with a sprinkling of freckles. Jason's eyes followed the contour of her long, sinuous legs. He watched as she leaned over one of the machines, her faded denim shorts riding up her tanned muscular thighs. His rapture, however, didn't last long.

"Jason," Zayde called. "I gotta go to de bank. To make a deposit."

"Okay."

"You're in charge."

Jason nodded dutifully. This being Friday, Zayde had to make his weekly deposit at the bank. The beige cash bag stuffed with the week's proceeds was typically kept under the counter. Zayde groaned as he reached for it. Then, he grabbed his cane and, giving Jason a quick parting whistle, he pointed behind the counter while mouthing the words 'baseball bat'. Jason returned a knowing nod.

"I'll be back in twenty minutes. No funny business."

Jason nodded again. As soon as Zayde left, he returned to his favorite pastime, watching girls. Before he knew it, the blond girl was standing directly in front of him. When she smiled, Jason gulped.

"This is a fun place," she said. "But it'd be a whole lot more fun if there was better music." She gave him a playful wink.

"Give me a sec," Jason said. Personally, he couldn't have agreed more. He knew plenty of music that was way better than what they were listening to at the moment. Jason prided himself on knowing every AM station in the city. So well, in fact, that if he switched the dial to WNEW radio at that very moment, he knew he'd catch his favorite DJ. Jason hopped off the stool. The radio in question rested on the top shelf behind the counter. Sure enough, when he tuned in the station, the manic voice of Mad Daddy filled the arcade. Jason took great pleasure in mimicking him.

"Hey, kids. Mad Daddy here,
A-rockin' and a-reelin'
A wallpaper peelin'
A-thumpin' and a-jumpin'
A wavy gravy pumpin'
From sponge rubber hall!"

Now, give a listen to The Troggs with W-i-l-d T-h-a-n-g!"

The arcade soon reverberated with the opening power chords of the current hit.

"Wild thing
You make my heart sing
You make everything
G-r-o-o-v-y ... "

The girls responded instantly by dropping their bags and dancing ecstatically in the aisles. Jason smiled in satisfaction. While they danced, Jason went about cleaning the pinball machines and emptying the garbage. From time to time, he looked over at the girls and took delight in watching them raise their arms above their heads and thrust their hips to the music. Jason was mesmerized by the young girls' shimmy and shake. *I wish this moment would last forever.*

In an instant, all of that changed. As Zayde came through the entrance and took in the scene, the muscles in his neck tightened and his face grew red as a beet. "Vat the hell is going on?" he shouted. Outraged, Zayde hobbled over to the counter and pointed vigorously at the radio. "Change de god damn station! Now!"

Jason gulped. "Okay. Sorry," he said, his tail between his legs. It seemed to take forever for him to find the soothing sound of WQXR again and when he finally did, the atmosphere changed instantly. It didn't take long for the girls to get the message. They quickly straightened their clothes and collected their things.

As they were leaving, the blond girl, his favorite, turned to him. "See 'ya. And thanks."

Without saying another word, Zayde disappeared into his own private bathroom. Jason desperately tried to find some meaningful task to do in the back to avoid his zayde's wrath. Moments later, his grandfather reappeared. This time, he was dressed in his blue suit, a faded white shirt and tie. Hobbling over to his grandson, he simply said, "Jason, go home. I'll lock up."

"Okay…" Jason couldn't understand why his zayde was wearing a suit and tie during the middle of the day. "Where you headed?"

"Out," Zayde said cryptically.

Still not understanding, Jason said, "Out? With who?"

"Vat is dis? De inquisition?"

And with that simple exchange, their conversation was over.

• • •

When Jason got back to the apartment, his bubbie and Lil' Grandma were waiting patiently with supper.

"Come. *Essen*," his grandmother said.

Jason joined them at the kitchen table. He, however, appeared to be distracted, in his own little world. When he was halfway through his mushroom barley soup, he suddenly stopped, his spoon suspended in midair.

"Bubbie... Where does Zayde go at night?"

His grandmother shrugged. "Got if I know. He says he meets his friends."

Jason thought that over for a minute. "And do you believe him?"

Bubbie was taking a roasted chicken out of the oven. She shrugged once again. Jason reached for a second slice of pumpernickel bread. "Don't you get lonely?"

"I keep busy. Zayde takes me to de movies fin time to time. Or for a valk."

Jason considered that. Then, he took another sip of soup. "Today, I noticed that Zayde didn't have much energy."

"On many days. I alvays tell him to eat bedder."

Jason nodded. When he'd finished his meal, he walked into the living room and took a seat in the easy chair. It wasn't long before Jason felt bored, not quite knowing what to do. Something was gnawing at him and he couldn't figure out what it was.

Before long, he reached for his guitar. While his little grandma watched the TV, Jason began playing his guitar, strumming one chord over and over. He added another chord... and then another. Then, he played the three chords together. *That works.* He repeated the sequence again... and again. Jason was surprised when a lyric came to him. *Hmm. I wonder if it'll work with these chords?* Jason sang the words softly accompanied by the chords. *Not bad.* At that moment, a second phrase arose in his head. *Let me try that out.* Through this process, Jason soon cobbled together a verse. Once again, he tried it with the chords and then repeated it again and again. From time to time, Lil' Grandma would look over at him and give him a quizzical look.

With sleep soon catching up with him, Jason got ready for bed. He hadn't been asleep more than an hour when he was woken by the sound of the front door opening. As he rubbed the sleep from his eyes, Jason saw Zayde shuffling past him.

His grandfather, looking tired and weary, plopped down into the easy chair next to Jason.

Zayde groaned as he leaned over to untie the laces of his boots. Then, he picked them up and, just before he disappeared into the bedroom, he dropped them with a *thud*. He looked over at his grandson. "Sorry, boychik. Go back to sleep."

At that moment, Jason noticed that his zayde was wearing different clothes than the ones he'd worn earlier in the day. "Zayde, where's your suit?"

"Oy. De qvestions. So many qvestions. I left it at the arcade. I didn't vant I should wrinkle it."

Just before Zayde opened the bedroom door, he turned back to look at Jason. "I need dat you should open up tamarrah. De keys are on de table." While he was puzzled by his request, Jason was so tired he simply nodded. His grandfather closed the door behind him.

With Jason now awake, he watched the reflection the headlights of the occasional car passing made on the ceiling and he thought about his grandfather. *I know so little about him. He's a god damn mystery.* Jason fluffed up his pillow and pulled the covers up over his head. He laid awake a long while as questions raced through his head.

• • •

On his very first day of work, Jason couldn't help noticing the small rifle range to the right of the arcade. A week later, as he neared the arcade, he spotted a short balding fellow standing outside. Jason could only assume that he was the owner. Being cordial, he waved at him. Jason wasn't sure whether the fellow grunted something back. He thought him odd.

He pulled the keys from his pocket and unlocked the arcade. After swinging the heavy accordion gate off to the side, he unlocked the rusty metal barricade. Then, using the pole, he pushed it up high overhead and into the ceiling. Jason felt a palpable sense of peace come over him as he stepped into the darkened arcade.

Heck. Maybe I can recreate the magic. Just as his grandfather had done, Jason flicked on one switch and then another and another. As the arcade slowly came to life, Jason marveled at the ease with which he could recreate the symphony of sights and sounds. It made him feel alive and his curiosity was aroused. At that moment, he realized there'd be no better moment to pull the arcade's curtain back and glimpse its true identity, see its inner workings. *Before any customers arrive, why don't I take a little tour around the place?*

As Jason strolled down the aisles, there were moments when he felt like a character in the Wizard of Oz. He first approached the Western Showdown, a machine which held a special place in his heart. From the time he was five or six years old, Jason felt strangely drawn to it. Western Showdown was the common man's version of High Noon, a classic face-off which featured, in this case, a large wooden cutout of a cowboy. As Jason stood before it, he spotted the imitation leather holster which held a fake 45 pistol just to his right and he smiled.

Pulling two quarters out of his pocket, he plunked them into the slot. Within seconds, he heard a familiar sound, the voice of the cowboy daring him, "Okay, partner. On the count of three, try to outdraw me. 1 ... 2 ... 3." Jason grinned knowing full well that that was his cue to pull the gun from the holster and fire it at the cowboy. He also knew that nine times out of ten the ornery cowboy would survive, only to taunt him, "You missed me. Try again." *Okay, partner. You want me to try again? Well, here goes.* Jason popped another two quarters into the slot. Once again, the cowboy survived. It took three tries for Jason to get lucky. He felt an indescribable joy when he heard the cowboy say, "Aw, shucks, partner. You got me." Jason had a broad smile on his face as he walked away.

Over the years, Jason had spent many happy moments at the arcade. However, there was one moment that stood out above all the others. On this particular occasion, his zayde behaved in a different way. Even at the age of five, Jason knew that his grandfather rarely took a break from working at the arcade. He constantly tinkered with the machines, polishing their glass surfaces, cleaning up after customers and that's what made the occasion all the more special.

That day, when Jason and his family arrived, Zayde stopped what he was doing. He swept Jason up into his arms and carried him over to the front counter. After hoisting him high in the air, Zayde then took a seat on the stool and placed his grandson squarely on his lap.

There was no mistaking that Zayde loved money. He loved the feel of dollar bills, fives, tens and twenties between his fingers. The way they looked, the way they felt, not to mention the cold, dispassionate feel and weight of coins as they jangled in his hand. In quieter moments at the arcade, he especially liked to stack the coins in neat little columns, building small edifices of quarters, dimes, and nickels on the counter.

On this occasion, his zayde leaned over and whispered into his grandson's ear. "Two nickels make a dime and two dimes and a nickel make a quarter." While Jason didn't quite know what his grandfather was getting at, he nodded in agreement. "Pay attention to money," his zayde instructed. Jason stored that nugget of advice in his five-year-old noggin.

As that memory faded, he grabbed the broom and dustpan and began his morning sweep. And only when he felt that the arcade was neat and tidy did he climb up on the stool. No sooner had he settled onto his perch at the front counter than he heard some rustling outside. When Jason looked up, he saw Nunzio crossing the street. A small thick manila envelope was tucked under his arm.

What the heck is he up to? Jason watched as Nunzio greeted the owner of the firing range. As soon as he handed him the envelope, the man immediately ripped it open and looked inside. The two of them then spoke rather heatedly to each other. Without any warning, the small wiry man slapped Nunzio across the face. "What do you take me for? You tink I'm a fool?" he yelled. Fearing that either of the two men might see him, Jason ducked behind the counter. He purposely waited a minute. When he lifted his head again, Nunzio was across the street rubbing his jaw.

CHAPTER 6

*"Candy on the beach, there's nothing better
But I like candy when it's wrapped in a sweater
Someday soon I'll make you mine
Then I'll have candy all the time."*

I Want Candy
The Strangeloves

For several days, Jason noticed some of the lightbulbs needed replacing. Now, with not a customer in sight, this was his chance. He lugged the ladder from the storeroom, opened it in the middle of the arcade and went to fetch a box of new light bulbs. Jason was perched high on the ladder when his grandfather arrived.

"Hey, Zayde."

His grandfather grunted.

From that vantage point, Jason could read his grandfather's face, see his milky eyes, his weary wrinkles. Jason was struck by how pale his zayde looked. *Is he taking care of himself?* Trying to be heard over the din of the machines' bells, whistles, and sirens, Jason shouted, "Where 'ya been, grandpa?"

Rather than having to yell across the room, Zayde hobbled over. "De docteh. He vanted I should see him."

"Oh? So, how you doing?"

"Ninety percent."

Oh, that man. Jason didn't know whether to believe him or not. Zayde was a proud man. The last thing he'd want is for someone to fuss over him. He was of a generation who toughed it out. Jason often wished that his zayde would reveal more about himself, talk about how he was really feeling, share his aches and pains. Zayde, however, remained a man of mystery, a man difficult to fathom.

• • •

Zayde took one look around the arcade and smiled. He had good reason to. The arcade was packed with people. All morning, they'd been playing the machines, buying snacks, and sodas. But with the arcade being so busy, Jason hadn't had a moment's break. Wave upon wave of customers kept coming up to him requesting change for the machines or armed with a question. So, it wasn't until late in the afternoon that Jason finally had an opportunity to lift his head and when he did, he was surprised to see none other than Nunzio and Anna standing at the skeeball machines.

Jason asked himself, why, of all of the penny arcades in the city, why did they choose this place? Jason had mixed feelings about them being there. On the one hand, he always felt nervous dealing with Nunzio. On the other hand, he longed to talk with Anna. But he never knew what to say. While he watched the two of them out of the corner of his eye, he rehearsed some possible lines he might use.

At the moment, however, he had to deal with two snotty youngsters.

"Hey mister. Wanna see my old nickels?"

"Uh, maybe some other time," Jason replied, dismissing him, and exchanging bills for quarters for other young customers. He wished that he, instead, could be left alone to just concentrate on Anna. He found himself gazing at her longingly as she strolled down the aisles. For the longest time, Jason resisted acknowledging her. But his emotions finally got the better of him and he gave her a quick wave when she happened to look over at him. Anna raised her hand, but then turned away, embarrassed and shy.

Nunzio saw her and quickly turned to her. "What the hell is going on?" Anna blushed. "Is that your boyfriend?" he asked sarcastically as he pointed to Jason.

Anna nervously didn't answer.

Without warning, Nunzio grabbed her by the collar and Jason's stomach clenched when Nunzio forcefully pulled her closer.

Jason was about to run to defend her but, surrounded by people, he quickly realized he couldn't leave his post. He was torn. The arcade's money was in clear view and there were too many sticky fingers around him. He felt so frustrated desperately wanting to know what Nunzio had said.

A moment later, Jason saw Anna lean over and whisper something to Nunzio. "Don't tell me how to be," Jason overheard him say. Then, just as quickly as their disagreement had flared up, it suddenly ended. The next time Jason had a chance to look over, Nunzio and Anna had apparently left. For the rest of the day, Jason agonized over what had prompted their argument and whether there was anything he could've done.

• • •

Later that afternoon, Jason was polishing the glass tops of the pinball machines when he heard, "Oy!" and then a loud thud. Racing back to the stockroom, he found Zayde lying on the concrete floor. His eyes were closed and his hand clutched his chest. His grandfather's face was milky white and he was sweating profusely.

Jason shuddered at the sight.

A moment later, Zayde opened his eyes and said, "Some candy. Get me some candy." Jason stood frozen in the doorway. He was conflicted. Should he honor his grandfather's demand for sugar or rely on plain old common sense? "You know Bubbie doesn't like that."

"Forget vat Bubbie likes and vat she doesn't like. Get me some God damn candy."

Jason's eyes searched the nearby shelves stocked with candies. Frantically rifling through the boxes of chocolate, he grabbed the first two Hershey bars he found and handed them to his zayde who quickly tore the wrappers open and gobbled them up whole.

Jason stood nervously over him. It took several minutes for the color to return to his grandfather's face and for his breathing to slow down. Two tiny streams of liquid chocolate ran down his cheeks. After he'd taken his first deep breath, Zayde grabbed a handkerchief from his back pocket and wiped his mouth.

• • •

That night, Jason was so exhausted when he returned to the apartment that he simply flopped on the couch. That didn't prevent his little grandma from settling in next to him. Even with the sound turned off, she sat in the easy chair and watched some wrestling on the TV. From time to time, Jason looked over at her and studied her features. The light emanating from the TV highlighted the many wrinkles on her face.

A lot of Lil' Grandma's behavior remained a mystery to Jason! *Even though she doesn't understand a word of English, she still watches hour after hour of television!* He had trouble understanding what she got out of watching Rocky and Bullwinkle, the Twilight Zone, Captain Kangaroo, and that modern Stone Age family, the Flintstones? However, the one show she invariably watched was wrestling. It didn't require any English. Night after night, Lil' Grandma would hoot and holler when her favorite wrestlers, Dick the Bruiser and Bobo Brazil appeared onscreen.

Lil' Grandma was a woman of few or, in Jason's case, no words. A woman who typically grunted or nodded to convey her wishes. On the surface, Jason's little grandma was a quiet, unassuming presence. However, all of that changed, her true persona emerged every hour, on the hour, when the bells of the church directly across the street, the Shrine Church of Our Lady of Solace, would chime. Then, as predictably as the sun rose in the east, Lil' Grandma would answer those chimes with a resounding spit, followed by the word, "Feh."

Jason knew that she spat as an expression of her hatred for what happened during the war. Though churches in France and Poland saved her life, the experiences of hiding in filthy basements and going without food seemed like nothing compared to how she'd been treated by just one or two nuns. Apparently, it was hard for Lil' Grandma to keep that in perspective.

Jason knew that it was one of those strange, curious things about being human.

• • •

What with the demands of work and his family, it had been a long week. And so, Jason was only too happy to get off work that day. With all that was on his mind, he longed for some diversion, something to take his mind off work. So, as he trudged along Surf Avenue, he pulled out his trusted transistor radio and plugged in his earphones. Then, he tuned his radio to WABC AM. Jason smiled when he heard the familiar, dulcet voice of Dan Ingram, one of his favorite announcers, introducing that week's No. 1 hit.

"Paperback writer, writer, writer . . . "

Despite its tinny sound, Jason retreated into his own private world. Oblivious to the outside world, he silently mouthed the song's catchy lyrics and bopped his head from side to side. However, as he crossed 16th Street, his attention was drawn upward. Steeplechase Park's famed Ferris wheel rose high above him in the sky. Its many gondola chairs dangled high overhead like jewels set around a circular ring swaying back and forth. Roughly half of the chairs were empty. The rest seemed to be occupied by couples. Jason immediately thought of Anna and studied the chairs. The gondola suspended at the highest point was unoccupied. *Boy, that must be quite the view. I wonder whether Anna would ever consider riding the Ferris wheel with me.* When he looked again at the gondola, he suddenly felt nauseous. He continued walking toward Surf Avenue. *Heck. There's no way you're going to get me up there.*

Not a minute later, he spotted the large colorful signs of Nathan's Famous Restaurant and felt his stomach growl. *There's always room for a hot dog. I haven't had one in weeks.* The logic made perfect sense. Jason stuffed his radio back in his pocket and walked over.

Two teenaged boys, one blond and one brown haired, were stationed at the white porcelain counter. Their pristine, freshly starched white uniforms and matching paper caps were only a shade darker than the restaurant's pristine white tiles. There was no need for Jason to study the restaurant's large menus posted on its walls. He knew them by heart.

"One hot dog and a small fries please."

"Sure thing. Coming right up," said the blond fellow who turned to the grill and, using a pair of tongs, rotated one of the hot dogs. Then, he removed it from the grill and placed it on a warm bun. Jason handed him a dollar saying, "Keep the change."

"Gee, thanks," the young man said.

Jason walked straight to the condiment table. Over the years, he'd developed his own special technique for dressing a frankfurter. The first item of business was nudging the hot dog to the side. Then, he applied a narrow gulley of relish along the spine of the bun and rolled the hot dog back into place. Jason's final step was zigzaging the mustard across the top of the dog. He took a quick look around the patio, spotted an empty table and took his seat.

• • •

Like clockwork, Nunzio predictably took Anna out for dinner every Saturday evening. That Saturday night, however, Anna found herself sitting in Nunzio's new Buick LeSabre as they drove up and down the streets of Coney Island with no seeming destination in mind. Having grown tired of staring out of the window, Anna started fiddling with the radio dial.

Oblivious to this, Nunzio took a puff on his cigarette. He turned to Anna. "I got to take care of a thing or two."

Anna rolled her eyes. Just once, she wished Nunzio would ask her what she wanted to do.

"I'm going to let you out here. I'll pick you up in half an hour."

Anna was floored, beside herself. Without saying another word, Nunzio pulled the car over at the corner of Stilwell and Surf Avenues. The bright neon lights of Nathan's Restaurant illuminated the car's shiny black vinyl interior. When Anna looked over at Nunzio, he was in a world of his own, staring out his window. She reluctantly got out and took a moment to summon up her courage. "What do you expect me to do?" she asked.

"I don't know," Nunzio replied offhandedly. Then, he peeled off a crisp twenty-dollar bill. "Here 'ya go. Get yourself something to eat."

CHAPTER 1

Anna stared incredulously at Nunzio and racked her trying to think of some appropriate response. But before even had a chance to, Nunzio sped off, leaving Anna alone on the street corner, shaking her head in disbelief.

With a sense of resignation, she stepped up to the counter and glanced up at the large billboard menu signs. One couldn't help being awed by the words *Sodas and Seafood, French Fried Potatoes, Frankfurters, Roast Beef and Hamburgers and More!* All were hand painted in large bright green and red letters against a bright yellow background.

"So, what'll it be?" the blond counterman asked. With so much to choose from, Anna took another look up at the menu board. After some deliberation, she finally picked the easiest.

"Can I just get a small fries?"

"Sure thing," the server answered a little too enthusiastically. He gracefully pivoted around to the fryer, scooped up some fries already drying in the metal basket and dumped them into a small cardboard boat. Then, he turned back to Anna and cheerfully handed them to her. "That'll be fifty cents."

Anna sheepishly handed him the twenty-dollar bill.

"Is that all you got?"

Vita nodded her head feeling embarrassed.

The fellow pressed the button on the cash register marked fifty cents, *Ka-ching!* and the till flew open. Handing her the change, he said, "Here 'ya go. Enjoy." Anna walked over to the condiment table and dabbed some ketchup on her fries, being careful not to drown the wooden fork. She found an empty table and took a seat. Then, glancing to her right, she spotted a familiar face.

Jason was sitting a few tables over. He smiled.

Anna withered and looked around for Nunzio. Then, she looked back at Jason.

Jason took a healthy bite out of his crunchy hot dog, got up, and sauntered over.

"What do you know?" he said.

"Uh, hi, Jason," Anna answered anxiously looking both to her left and right.

"Mind if I join you?"

"Um, no," she said nervously. "Maybe for a minute."

Jason slid into the seat opposite her.

Anna fidgeted with her flimsy wooden fork. "Nunzio will be back soon."

"Nunzio, eh?" Jason took another bite of his hot dog. "He sure keeps you on a tight leash."

"Well, he is my boyfriend."

"He doesn't seem to treat you very nicely."

Anna lowered her head and an icy silence followed. The two of them sat awkwardly across from each other for what seemed like an eternity. Then finally, trying to break the ice, Jason took another bite of his hot dog. Frankfurter juice trickled down his jaw. Embarrassed, he reached for a nearby napkin.

Meanwhile, Anna nibbled halfheartedly at her fries, still not saying a word. Anticipating her boyfriend's imminent return, she continued looking nervously up and down the street. Jason followed her gaze. Anna then rose unexpectedly out of her seat.

Jason got up as well. He looked embarrassed. "I'm sorry."

Anna didn't respond to that. "Well, I guess I'd better go," she finally said.

"I understand." Jason watched as she walked to the corner. He felt terrible, knowing that he'd blown it and made a fool of himself.

• • •

As Jason trudged back to the apartment, he replayed the conversation he'd just had with Anna over and over in his head. With each replay, he felt more and more depressed, wishing he had had more time to explain his feelings and express himself better.

Fifteen minutes later, when Jason got home, he went straight to the kitchen. His bubbie was wiping down the counter. When she turned, she could plainly see that her grandson was upset.

"Sumtink wrong?"

Jason thought about how he might answer that. "Yeah. Kinda." The last thing he wanted to do at that moment was have to explain how he felt.

"A gurl?"

Jason nodded and picked up a piece of cherry Danish which was sitting limply on a nearby plate. He chewed it abstractedly. After a minute or so, Jason roused himself out of his depression and asked, "So, where'd Zayde go this morning?"

"Oy. De doctor vanted to see him. Sumtink about his leg."

"His leg?"

Bubbie nodded nervously.

Jason frowned. Then, he reached out and gave his bubbie a hug. "It will be all right, Bubbie. You'll see."

"You're a good boy, Jason."

Jason turned and walked into the living room. To his great surprise, his little grandma wasn't parked in front of the TV. For that brief moment, he had the room to himself. He settled his bum into the lumpy couch and turned on his radio. Like many nights during the summer, Jason was thrilled to receive some distant R & B station out of Detroit, Michigan. He listened avidly while the announcer first pitched an all-night convenience store in downtown Detroit. However, his feelings were quickly soothed when the radio host announced the next song, Smokey Robinson and the Miracles' *Tracks of My Tears*.

> *"So, take a good look at my face*
> *You'll see my smile it looks out of place*
> *If you look closer, it's easy to trace*
> *The tracks of my tears."*

Minutes later, his bubbie shuffled into the room. Jason was still wiping away his tears. Just before she disappeared into the bedroom, she turned to her grandson and said, "Good night, Jason."

"G'night, grandma," he answered, choking on his words. Jason retreated into the warm comfort of the sound of his radio world. Only when the announcer started pitching another cheesy advertisement did Jason notice that his bubbie hadn't fully closed the bedroom door.

Through the opening, he could see his grandmother sitting on the edge of their bed. She held a framed photo in her hands. While Jason had seen it often on their bureau, he never actually knew the identity of the person in the photo. He had, however, noticed the strong family resemblance. When Jason looked more closely, he realized that his bubbie was in fact crying.

Suddenly, feeling the effects of the strange day catching up to him, he turned off his radio and drew the covers up over himself.

CHAPTER 7

*"They're creepy
And they're kooky
Mysterious and spooky
They're altogether kooky..."*

The theme song of
The Addams Family TV Show

Zayde was in fine form the following morning. He felt playful and mischievous as he rinsed his hands in the bathroom sink. While staring at himself in the mirror, he inexplicably made a funny face. Then, he began speaking in a high, squeaky voice, "Yippie ki yeah." Zayde laughed at himself. Then, he walked back to the counter, picked up a cloth and began polishing the glass surfaces. A moment later, he spotted Jason coming through the entrance. Zayde scrunched up his face and shouted gleefully, "Hi, Mickey."

Jason stared blankly at him. Ever since he'd been a toddler, Jason loved the cartoon character Mickey Mouse. He especially loved when his zayde would call him Mickey. "Uh, hullo," Jason answered.

"Hello? Dat's it? Dat's all I get?" Zayde stared at his grandson incredulously. "Whatsa matter? You don't remember me taking you to see Fantasia or the time I bought you those mouse ears?"

Jason didn't answer.

"Vat gives?" Zayde asked, hobbling over to him.

"Nothing," Jason murmured.

"Nuthink?"

Zayde tapped his skull a couple of times. "Ah. I get it." Divining his grandson's problem, he said, "It's a gurl. You got gurl trouble."

Jason sighed dejectedly. He didn't feel like talking. Instead, he walked over to the private bathroom and fetched the broom and dustpan. Jason went about doing his morning chores. Even after finishing, customers had fortunately yet to arrive. So, Jason pulled a small spiral notebook from his back pocket and took a seat at the counter. He opened his notebook and stared at it. Then, he raised his gaze and stared off into space. Jason was waiting for inspiration, some tasty phrase or perhaps a lyric to arise in his head.

Without him noticing, Zayde had hobbled up behind him and was now peering over his shoulder, curious as to what his grandson was up to. "So nu? Vat are you doink?"

"Oh ... Just trying to write a poem."

"A poem?"

Jason nodded.

"Ah … Let me guess. You're in luf."

Jason looked at his grandfather. He neither wanted to confirm nor deny it.

"Let me have a look," his zayde said, grabbing the notebook out of Jason's hands. He brought it within his eyesight, trying to decipher what his grandson had written. With much difficulty, he awkwardly recited,

Locked in a prison cell,
Her master holds the key.
What will her sentence be?
Only a starling can sing its own tune
and she yearns to sing.
Someday soon, she will find her voice.

Zayde nodded his head approvingly. "Not bad."

Jason raised his eyebrows.

"Is she vort it?"

Without hesitation, Jason said, "Definitely."

Zayde looked deeper into his grandson's eyes.

"Ahh … Let me guess. But she's not interested."

For a moment, Jason debated whether to answer that. Then, he revealed, "She's got a boyfriend."

"Ah." Zayde nodded in recognition.

As eager as Jason had been to write, with his grandfather now peering over his shoulder, his desire quickly faded. He put his pen down and closed his notebook.

"Don't give up," Zayde advised. "Tell her how you feel."

"But how?"

"Just like you're doink. Tell her your own vay."

Jason frowned, not convinced that that would work.

"Hey, vat's de vorst she can do?"

Jason weighed that over in his head.

• • •

Lunchtime couldn't come soon enough. As Jason raced over to the boardwalk, he hoped he'd once again get to see Anna sunbathing with her friends. With the beach packed with people, it wasn't easy to spot anyone. Jason's attention was first drawn to an older black man trudging along the sand. While he was dressed impeccably, in his white creased pants, his white short-sleeved shirt and the white paper hat of an ice cream man, with today's temperature in the 80's, he was sweating profusely. Despite that, he was undoubtedly the most popular person on the beach. The large white refrigerated box he carried on his back was packed with ice cream. Every ten yards or so, he'd stop and shout, "Get your ice cream here. Ice cold ice cream here. Tasty creamsicles and popsicles."

Before long, Jason spotted Anna sitting on a large beach blanket. She was once again with her friends. As Jason watched her rub some suntan lotion on her arms and legs, he imagined how silky and smooth her legs must be.

Seeing her excited him so much that he impulsively shot his hand up and gave her a wave. However, she failed to notice him. His passion finally getting the better of him, Jason shouted, "Hey, Anna. Over here." To his great joy, she turned in his direction. He hoped that she'd maybe smile or wave back at him. Instead, she gave him a pained, concerned look. Then, she simply turned back to her friends and whispered something. Undaunted, Jason smiled to himself, knowing that he had at least made contact.

• • •

The following morning, Bubbie was puttering around the kitchen. After slicing a few pieces of challah, she placed it back in the bread box. Then, she rinsed out a rag and used it to wipe down the counter. Jason was sitting at the kitchen table, his trusty notebook and pen by his side. From time to time his bubbie turned around and watched him scribble a word or two. Then, he'd stop and look up. It was as if he was trying to summon just the right words out of the air. Occasionally, he muttered to himself. Jason was in his own private world.

Curiosity finally got the best of her. Wondering why he was staring off into space, Bubbie stopped what she was doing and asked, "Dahlink, you okay?"

"Oh, yeah. I'm trying to write."

"I can see dat."

"A poem."

"Oh. Vat kinda poem?" Bubbie waited.

"To a girl." Jason looked once again at what he had written. He shook his head in frustration and put down his pen.

"Oh," she nodded. Bubbie thought it best not to ask any more questions. She turned back to cleaning the counter. Jason meanwhile continued writing.

A moment later, Bubbie asked, "So, you free dis Sunday?"

"Why? What's going on?"

"It's Zayde's burday."

"Oh, I know. You going to have a cake?"

"Good qvestion. Vit his new diet, he can't have anytink. No sugar, no salt, no nuttink."

"Hmm. So, who'd you invite?"

"De whole mishpocheh. Your parents, your aunts, your uncles, your cousins. Everyone."

"The whole family?"

Jason felt a sudden lump in his stomach. He knew full well that most family gatherings sooner or later turned into a three-ring circus.

• • •

All morning, Zayde had been repairing a machine at the back of the arcade while Jason was stationed at the front counter. With lunchtime quickly approaching, Jason was now getting restless. Hearing some rustling by the entrance, he looked up. To his surprise, his bubbie was standing there holding a large metal pot and a long loaf of bread. An apron was tied around the waist and a long knife jutted out of her pocket.

"Here 'ya go." Bubbie had somehow lugged a large pot of chicken soup and a fresh loaf of challah from the apartment six blocks away. Her husband, meanwhile, continued working. Being hard of hearing, Zayde had no idea that his wife had shown up.

"Here. Let me get that," Jason said rushing over to take the heavy pot out of her hands. Carefully placing it down on the counter, he walked back to the storeroom to fetch some bowls and spoons.

"Herschel, come," his wife yelled. "Haf some soup."

Bubbie took the bowls from Jason. Next, she sliced up freshly baked challah bread into thick slices and *schmeared* a wad of butter on each of them. "Come Herschel. Haf some soup," she yelled again. Then, she turned back to her grandson. "So, you comink on Sunday?"

"Yeah, sure."

"Dat mornink, I need you should pick up some tings. Some bread, some cookies."

"No problem."

By that time, Zayde had recognized his wife's voice. He lifted his head out of the machine, wiped his hands on a rag and slowly made his way to the front of the arcade.

"Here, Herschel," his wife said, offering him a bowl of soup. "Haf some."

Zayde took the bowl out of her hands and grabbed a spoon. He took a sip. Then another. "Dere's no taste." Zayde frowned.

"You know vat de doctor says," Bubbie said. "No salt for you."

"Oy, mein got. Dis is my life."

• • •

Mermaid Avenue was abuzz with people that Sunday morning. There were line-ups in most shops for freshly baked bread and pastries, meat and poultry, eggs, and cheeses. With his number in hand, Jason was waiting patiently in line at the local bakery. Once he'd been served, he headed back to the apartment, carrying two large paper bags and Zayde's birth[d] wasn't ready for the chaos in the apartment.

"Here 'ya go, Bubbie," Jason said placing the the counter. His younger cousin Barry suddenl[y] nearly hitting him.

"That's mine. Give it back," Barry yelled, chasing his sister Arlene who had just swiped his ball and wouldn't give it back. All the while, Lenny, their father, stood by nonchalantly chatting with several of Jason's other uncles.

After his two cousins had run past a third time, Lenny finally turned to his kids and yelled, "Stop your running, you two. You'll break your necks."

Barry and Stephanie stopped in their tracks. They looked at each other and rolled their eyes.

Feeling claustrophobic, Jason turned in the opposite direction. He was met with his Uncle Leo standing nose-to-nose with him.

"H-hullo, Jason."

"Hello, Uncle Leo." His uncle was notorious for having bad breath. At that moment, Jason felt like he was standing in a field of rotten eggs. When Jason tried to back up, he ended up bumping into his bubbie who was working at the stove. In desperation, Jason turned looking for an escape route.

At that moment, he sensed that his Aunt Sylvia was nearby. While he didn't actually see her, he smelled her. Known for using too much perfume, her nephews had taken to call her Aunt Stinky.

Generally speaking, Jason didn't care for these family gatherings. Too often, they turned into a three-ring circus and, in all likelihood, today would be no different. What bothered him most about these Jacobowitz family get togethers was his relatives' attitude. They still treated him like a child. While the adults got to sit comfortably like kings and queens at the long, rectangular table, Jason was relegated to sit with the kids, his many weird cousins, at a small folding card table. To make matters worse, because he had arrived late, all the chairs were taken. Looking around, the only remaining seat was a short stool. When Jason sat down, his chin barely cleared the top of the table.

Not a moment later, he heard someone grunt. Jason turned to see his cousin Bruce, breathing heavily, reaching desperately across the table for a bottle of Heinz ketchup. Bruce was groaning as if his life depended on it. Finally, after watching the drama for a while, Jason's sense of compassion kicked in. "Let me get that for you," he said.

"Aw, thanks," his cousin said, dropped his head and arm in exhaustion.

No sooner had Bruce taken his seat than his cousin Joanne spoke up. Pointing to a platter of sliced turkey, she asked, "Can you get me that?" She was a sweet girl who excelled at school and her parents never failed to remind Jason of her top marks. But God bless her, she was also an incessant talker and got on Jason's nerves.

"No problem," he said begrudgingly. Jason once again rose from his stool and reached across the table, this time being careful not topple any of his cousins' drinks. As Jason reached, his hand swiped Joanne's glass of 7-Up. Luckily, he caught it. While Jason was standing, handing the platter of turkey to Joanne, Bruce began palming the bottle of ketchup onto his sandwich. Not a moment later, *splat!* Jason suddenly felt something cold and wet on his crotch. Knowing only too well what it was, Jason resignedly looked down. Sure enough, his new chino pants were liberally doused with a glob of ketchup. He smiled benignly at his cousin.

"Sorry," said Bruce sheepishly.

When his cousin Kenny, who was also sitting at the table, took one look down at Jason's crotch, he guffawed sending pieces of the pastrami sandwich he'd been chewing flying across the table.

Jason quickly looked to the left and right. Then, he grabbed his napkin and used it to cover his crotch. He stood up and shimmied over to the bathroom. Turning on the faucet, he wet one of Bubbie's small white towels. Then, he furiously rubbed at the spot and wondered how much longer he had to endure this?

On the positive side, and there definitely was a positive side, Jason learned an awful lot about his family at these gatherings. For example, that day he learned his Aunt Felicia was going in for medical tests on Monday. And later, as dessert was being served, Jason's Uncle Alvin, his mouth stuffed with chocolate cake, revealed, "You know your cousin Eric lost his job . . . again." Over the years, Jason had come to rely on his Uncle Alvin for the most up-to-date family gossip.

At the very least, Jason knew that he'd never go hungry at these family gatherings. That afternoon, to the *oohs* and *aahs* of the rest of the family, his Aunt Leah had arrived with her multi-leveled, multi-colored Jello mold and a few minutes later, not to be outdone, his Aunt Esther walked in with her delicious chocolate Bundt cake.

When the meal was finally over, Jason, having sat through the entire meal on the stool, took the opportunity to stretch his legs. Having survived the meal, Jason breathed a huge sigh of relief as he settled into the couch. Then, he suddenly jumped as his older cousin Mitch plonked down beside him.

"So, you enjoying yourself?"

"Oh. I'm having a ball," Jason answered sarcastically. "You?"

"Listen, I thought you should hear this from me. Zayde just asked me to work at the arcade."

"Wha—?" Given the circumstances, Jason nodded as nonchalantly as possible. He desperately wanted to appear cool, calm, and collected. But deep down, he was shocked. He felt like a grenade had just exploded in his head. His mind was filled with questions. *What would make Zayde do that? Didn't he like my work?*

Out of respect, Jason waited until everyone had said their goodbyes and the apartment had quieted down before he approached his grandfather. His zayde was sitting at the kitchen table taking a last puff of one of his Camel cigarettes. Jason took several steps and sat down beside him.

"Hey, Zayde."

His zayde nodded briefly. Then, he snuffed out his cigarette and didn't say a word. So, Jason brought it up.

"So, how come Mitch will be working at the arcade?"

Zayde coughed twice bringing up some phlegm. Then, he spat into a nearby cup. "To pay for school," he bluntly answered.

Jason studied his zayde's eyes a long time searching for some further explanation. But none came.

CHAPTER 8

"Chains
My baby's got me locked up in chains
And they ain't the kind that you can see
Whoa oh, these chains of love gotta hold on me."

Chains
The Cookies

'An autumn harvest,
the trees heavy with olives,
luscious and green,
the wet fertile fields
surrounded by the deep Mediterranean' ...

"No, no, no. That's terrible," Jason said to himself. He slapped the top of his head.

Jason was sitting at the counter. His head was lowered and he was deep in thought. For the last few minutes, he'd been struggling to find just the right words for his poem. Jason looked off into space, but the elusive word was nowhere to be found.

Suddenly, he felt a subtle change in the atmosphere. When Jason looked up, he was face-to-face with Nunzio. Jason drew his head back. Staring intently at him, Nunzio was holding a large bill in his hand. His crew was waiting restlessly, but obediently behind him.

"Yo, Jason. Got change of a fifty?" he asked as if he relished the moment. Because Nunzio loved playing pinball, he often visited the arcade once he'd taken care of business in Coney Island. He loved to play a few rounds.

"Let me have a look," Jason said nervously. Nunzio waited restlessly, tapping his foot, while Jason first searched the bottom drawer. Not finding enough large bills, he bent down and searched the money bag underneath the counter. Once again, Jason came up empty. "Sorry," he said.

"No change?" Nunzio said derisively. "Gee. What kinda joint is this?"

"Sorry. We don't have that kind of change this early in the day," Jason said, feeling beads of sweat form on his forehead.

"Then, you should let me play for free," Nunzio said, slapping one of his crew members and laughing.

Seeing that Jason didn't have a comeback for that, Nunzio smirked. Jason recalled how cruelly Nunzio had treated Anna the last time he saw them together. The memory of that so upset him that he started unconsciously jabbing his pen on the counter. Hearing that, Nunzio turned. "You got a problem?"

Jason nervously looked away as Nunzio and his crew walked over to the pinball machines.

Then, Nunzio reached into his front pocket, found two quarters and plunked them into the slot. Jason furtively kept his eyes on Nunzio and his crew as they whooped and hollered their way through each game. In fact, Jason didn't take a deep breath until Nunzio had finished his last game and the words *Game Over* flashed on the machine's headboard

Jason mumbled the words, "Thank God," to himself. As if he'd heard his prayer, Nunzio turned to his crew and motioned for them to leave.

However, not before leaving, Nunzio turned back and pointed at Jason. "Keep your freakin' eyes off Anna."

• • •

Mitch arrived for his first day of work feeling quite chipper. When he entered, Jason showed him the ropes, where he could hang his jacket and where he could store his lunch. All that morning, Zayde had been working in the back. When he realized that both Jason and Mitch had shown up, he stopped what he was doing and called them together for a brief powwow.

"Okay, Jason," Zayde began. "I vant that you should show Mitch how tings vork around here."

"No problem." Jason nodded, feeling empowered by his grandfather's request.

"Bot of you vill vork five days a veek over da seven days. You two vork out who vorks vich days."

Mitch and Jason nodded to each other.

"De only ting. Saturday and Sunday are de busiest days. Bot of you vil need to vork den."

"Okay," they replied in unison.

Just before Zayde wrapped up his meeting, he added, "But tonight, Jason, I need that you should lock up."

"No problem," Jason said.

"So, show Mitch de ropes. How tings are done . . . and don't forget to mention about de lock."

"Gotcha."

"Now, let's get te vork."

With that, the meeting was over.

The first thing Jason did was motion for Mitch to follow him over to the private bathroom. After opening the door, he pointed. "All the cleaning supplies are kept here." Mitch innocently looked inside. Lining the walls of the small, windowless room were two brooms, a dustpan, a mop, a bucket, all sorts of bottles of cleaning supplies, a few towels, and other sundry items.

"Okay. Grab a broom."

Mitch reached for one while Jason grabbed the other.

"So, here's the routine. The first thing we do every morning is sweep. Then, we mop."

Mitch simply nodded.

"Why don't you start at that end," said Jason, pointing to the far end of the arcade. "and I'll start at the other."

Ten minutes later, their paths crossed in the middle of the arcade. Jason nodded to Mitch as if to say job well done. Then, out of the blue, he asked, "You ever notice that photo of a soldier on Bubbie's nightstand?"

"I think I do. The one that's in the brown frame?"

"Yeah, that one. The other night, I saw Bubbie looking at it. She was crying."

"Really?"

"Do you have any idea who that is?"

"I think that was one of Zayde's brothers."

"Oh yeah?" Knowing that their grandfather was working nearby, Jason put his forefinger up to his lips and whispered, "Sssh."

Mitch nodded.

"What do you know about him?"

Mitch cleared his throat and was just about to answer when a great unsettling rumble suddenly flooded their ears.

Jason raised his index finger again as if to say, *Wait, it'll soon be over.* He had worked there long enough to know that the roar was simply the Cyclone rollercoaster making its way up its long rickety tracks overhead and just as quickly as it had begun, the rumbling stopped. Jason knew that this was only short-lived. The rollercoaster ran every fifteen minutes and was only taking a brief pause at the very top of the track before it would come roaring down accompanied by the hair-raising shrieks of its riders.

Jason waited until the noise quieted down. Then, he bent down and, holding a dustpan in his hands, motioned for Mitch to sweep the dirt into it.

"According to Uncle Al," Mitch whispered, "His brother Aron served in the U.S. Army during World War I and he was killed."

This was the first time he'd heard that Zayde had a brother never mind learning that he'd been killed. Jason found it difficult to fathom.

He walked over to the garbage can and emptied the dustpan. When he returned, Mitch continued, "And that's the reason they married."

"Who?"

"Bubbie and Zayde."

"What?" Jason said, reminding himself to keep his voice down.

"Yup, it's in the Bible."

"What is?"

"That when someone dies, the other brothers are supposed to look after that brother's wife."

"Is that right?" Jason pondered that. A moment later, he shook off the thought. "Come with me." He guided Mitch back to the bathroom. Together, they put down their brooms and the dustpan. Jason then turned to Mitch. "Let me show you the rest."

Jason's logic was simple. He figured that if he showed Mitch the ropes and explained all of the various tasks that he'd be responsible for, that would leave him more time to write, to compose poetry when the arcade wasn't busy. So, over the next fifteen minutes, Jason showed Mitch where the cash was kept, where the candies and sodas were stored in the backroom, and

Jason spent the rest of the day trying to process what his cousin Mitch had just told him.

• • •

"What are you writing?"

Jason recoiled at the sound of Mitch's voice. He'd been so engrossed in his work that he hadn't noticed his cousin peering over his shoulder.

"A poem. At least, I'm trying to."

"What's it about?"

"A girl."

"A girl, eh?" Mitch stood silently for a moment. "Well, if you like her, you should give it to her. Carpe diem and all that."

"Thanks for the advice. I'll think about that."

Jason closed his notebook and put his pen away.

"Hey, speaking of girls," his cousin said, "I just picked up tickets to the Simon and Garfunkel concert."

"Cool," Jason said. Mitch's mention of the upcoming concert sparked the thought of Anna and, for a brief instant, he wondered whether she also liked the group.

"So far, I haven't found anyone to go with."

"Oh, that's too bad. Good luck." At that moment, the door to the private bathroom swung open and Zayde stood in the doorway wearing a suit, a starched shirt, and a tie. Jason and Mitch were both stunned. They looked at each other and shrugged.

After a moment, Mitch said, "Looking good, Zayde."

"Tanks." Zayde grabbed his cane and hobbled to the entrance.

Jason and Mitch were both curious where Zayde was headed but neither had the courage to ask.

"'Night, boys. Now Jason, make sure you lock up good."

"Will do."

Zayde hobbling out of the arcade seemed to be Jason's cue to reveal his evening plans.

"Hey, Mitch. I gotta ask you a favor. I got pla[ns] and need you to lock up. It's real simple."

"Oh, okay. No problem."

With his notebook in hand, Jason motioned for Mitch [to] join him over by the panel of light switches on the far wall. "Okay. First, you gotta turn off all the lights." Jason demonstrated by flicking each switch one by one. After a moment, he turned them back on. "That's how you start."

"Simple enough," Mitch said.

Jason then guided Mitch over to the front entrance. "Now, here's how you lock up." He pointed up to the ceiling. "You first gotta pull that metal barricade all the way down. It'll click into place."

"Okay."

"Then, you grab the gate over there and pull it over like this." Jason yanked the gate along its track until it was fully extended. Then, he took a set of keys out of his pocket. "This one …" Jason said, showing a large key he held between his fingers, "… will open the lock. Once it's open, you wrap the lock around the gate and …"

At that very moment, they both heard the delightful sound of girls' voices passing outside. Out of curiosity, they both turned to look. All that Jason could see were their backs. Entranced by the gentle bounce of one of the girls' ponytails, Jason somehow knew that it belonged to Anna. After spending a day at the beach, she and her friends were likely heading home. Mitch watched Jason do a double take.

"Is that her?" he asked.

"Yup." Jason gulped.

"Well," Mitch said. "Go. Go talk to her. Carpe diem."

Jason indecisively looked at Mitch, then he looked at the back of Anna disappearing. Mitch grabbed the notebook Jason was holding. Quickly opening the book, he ripped out the sheet of paper that Jason had been writing his poem on and thrust it into his cousin's hand.

"Take this. Give it to her. Now!"

Jason gave his cousin a confused look.

"Don't worry, Go. I'll close up."

Jason was conflicted, not certain whether he should stay or confront her. For a brief moment, he watched Anna and her friends continue down the street. Then, he quickly realized that the girls were about to turn the corner and would soon disappear from sight. "Ah, crap," he said and took off in pursuit.

"Anna! Anna!" he yelled.

• • •

When Anna heard someone calling her name, she stopped and turned around. She saw Jason running up to her.

"Oh, no. Not him again." Out of consideration, she motioned to her friends. *It's okay. You can keep walking.*

"Anna, please," Jason said breathlessly.

"What is it now?"

"Please. I just want to talk with you."

Anna looked once again at her friends who had crossed the street and were now waiting for her.

"I'm sorry." Jason dug deep and spoke from his heart. "I see how Nunzio treats you."

"That's none of your business," Anna said. "What is it with you men? You and Nunzio and my dad. You all think you know what's best for me."

"I'm sorry. I know I can treat you better."

"Jason please. Stop bugging me."

He stood with his mouth agape. When Anna looked again at her friends, they smiled. "Look, I gotta go."

Unable to think of anything else to say, he looked down at the sheet of paper he held in his hands. Anna was just about to leave when Jason suddenly thrust the piece of paper into her hand. "I-I-I wrote this for you."

"What the ---?" Anna said in exasperation as she looked down at the paper.

Suddenly, there was a flash of lightning and the evening sky rumbled. The skies opened and the streets were awash in rain. With Anna and Jason suddenly being pelted with driving rain, she said, "Sorry, Jason. I really have to go." Anna turned and raced across the street to rejoin her friends.

On the verge of tears, Jason watched Anna disappear from view. He was crestfallen and confused not knowing what to do and which way to turn. The only thing he knew for certain was he had no desire to stand there and be drenched by the rain. So, Jason began to walk, trekking aimlessly through the streets of Coney Island.

So much for carpe diem.

Oblivious to the downpour, Jason trudged through the darkened streets, past random shops and storefronts, neighborhood theaters, and parks. He obsessed about how awkwardly he'd handled their brief encounter. It cut deeply into him. By this time, he was drenched and realized that the boardwalk was nearby, that it might offer him some refuge from the rain. So, Jason sought shelter under the dark, broad wood planks overhead. A homeless man had also sought shelter under the boardwalk. Not seeing him bundled up under a grimy blanket, Jason nearly kicked him as he passed.

When he'd found a relatively dry spot where the sand met one of the wooden columns, Jason took a moment to burrow his bum into a hollow in the sand. He took off his soggy sneakers and socks and found momentary relief as he dug his toes into the cool envelope of dry sand. While he waited out the storm, Jason watched the rainwater trickle down a rusty drain pipe nearby. For some inexplicable reason, the sight of the narrow stream running to the ocean reminded him of the nape of Anna's neck, a spot he'd often studied during their class together.

As the rain eased off, Jason took his transistor radio out of his pocket and turned it on. Its static reception strangely mirrored how difficult his conversation with Anna had been. Sitting there in the dark, Jason suddenly had the feeling that nothing was truly certain in his life. Up until that moment, the love of his parents and that of his grandparents had been enough. Now, he was no longer certain of that. He knew that he wanted more and he was no longer certain that he'd ever find love. That he'd build a life together with someone. In that moment, he realized that he'd taken all of that for granted and now there seemed to be no safe refuge. Nothing he could rely on.

Huddled safely under the boardwalk and sheltered from the storm, the day's events soon caught up with him. Jason burrowed deeper into the cool, grainy bed of sand and, before he knew it, he had drifted off to sleep.

• • •

"Okay," Mitch mumbled to himself. "Here goes." He looked at his watch. At that late hour, he realized it was time to close the arcade. Mitch stepped off the stool and walked over to the exit. Then, just as Jason had instructed, he first flicked off the light switches one-by-one. As expected, all of the lights turned off. Then, he stepped over to the entrance and grabbed the pole. Though it took him three tries to find the hole, Mitch eventually pulled the heavy metal barricade down and it snapped into place. Next, he grabbed the accordion gate and pulled it all the way closed. Mitch removed the lock and fastened it around the gate. Then, he gave it a good slam and heard the click of metal on metal. At that point, Mitch's mind froze. *What did Jason say next?* While he remembered standing with Jason and listening to his instructions, he couldn't remember what came next. He remembered Jason saying that he should hear a click and he did. Mitch went through the instructions again. He swore he did it right. With that, he left for the night.

• • •

Several hours later, Jason awoke feeling cold and damp. The rain had thankfully come to a stop and Jason was still under the boardwalk. Feeling tired and soggy, he walked back to the sidewalk and trudged back to the apartment. After climbing the three flights of stairs, Jason opened the apartment door as quietly as he could. Then, he tiptoed down the hallway. In her weathered bathrobe, Bubbie met him in the kitchen.

"I vaz so worried about you. Vere ver you?"

Jason couldn't find the words. He was cold and wet and had no idea that his bubbie would still be awake, waiting up for him at 3:30 a.m.

"Everything okay?"

"I'm not sure." Jason waddled off to the bathroom and dried himself off. Then, he shuffled off to bed.

• • •

The following morning, Zayde arrived at the arcade. Jason and Mitch had yet to arrive and he was in an unusually chipper mood. As he was about to slip his key into the lock, he looked down and was shocked to see that the heavy lock wasn't locked. Rather, it was hanging idly on the metal gate.

"Vat de hell. Dis place vas open de whole night?" Zayde was furious. He looked around the arcade to confirm whether anything had been stolen or broken. Then, he hobbled over to the entrance and looked down the street. In the distance, he could see Jason. When Jason had gotten within thirty feet, Zayde screamed, "Vat in Got's name happened last night?"

Jason froze. He could see that his zayde was beside himself. "What do you mean?"

"It wasn't locked."

"That can't be. I made sure that Mitch knew how to lock it."

"Mitch? You asked Mitch to lock up?" Zayde said, his arthritic grip tightening around his cane.

"I had to go somewhere."

"Go somewhere? Vere de hell did you haf to go?" He could tell Zayde's blood was boiling.

"To speak to a girl."

"A gurl?" At that moment, Mitch came bounding through the door. Zayde turned on him.

"De lock vas open!"

"Really? I don't understand. I distinctly . . . It must've . . ."

"I swear I showed him," Jason said. "But—"

"Enough!" Zayde bellowed. "No excuses."

Zayde hitched up his pants and popped a Lifesaver into his mouth. Then, he took a long deep breath. Turning back to Mitch, he said, "Maybe Jason didn't teach you right. Maybe it didn't click. Vateveh. Dis von't happen again."

A long silence followed. Jason looked over at Mitch who looked back at him sheepishly.

CHAPTER 9

*"He stands like a statue,
Becomes part of the machine
Feeling all the bumpers
Always playing clean …"*

Pinball Wizard
The Who

The arcade, that day, was a madhouse. Jason was nearly run off his feet selling candy and beverages, answering customers' many questions and making change. So, he really welcomed the lull in the afternoon. It gave him a chance to write. While sitting at the counter and jotting in his notebook, Jason overheard an all too familiar voice coming from out on the street.

"Yo, Anna."

Jason looked outside.

Standing in the bright sunshine, Nunzio was saying, "Anna, come with me. Watch me play."

Seeing Nunzio and Anna together made Jason nervous. Jason found Nunzio pushy and he never knew quite what to say to Anna. So, as they passed by him in the arcade, he purposely kept his head down. Once they went by, he snuck a peek.

Out of the corner of his eye, Jason noticed Anna was wearing a rather chic dress which featured a Mondrian-like pattern of black, red, and white rectangles. Nunzio donned a dark blue suit, a crisp pink dress shirt, and a dark blue tie. Jason carefully watched Nunzio as he led Anna over to the pinball machines.

"Dis here is de Moulin Rouge," Nunzio proudly exclaimed, pointing to the pinball machine to his left. "It's my favorite."

"Really?" Anna said nonchalantly.

"Yeah. I kill on dis machine. I'll show 'ya."

Without waiting for her response, Nunzio plopped a quarter in the slot and the machine instantly came to life. Then, he drew the plunger back and *pop!* the first ball flew straight out of the gate arcing high up at the top of the field. As the metal ball fell, it bounced back and forth from cushion to mushroom bumper and back again, each bounce accented by a *ping*, a *knock*, or a *ding*. Nunzio nimbly fingered the flippers, tapping out a fervent staccato rhythm. Standing behind him, Anna watched as Nunzio used his whole body, his fingers, his wrists, and his hips to influence the path of the ball, periodically nudging the machine ever so slightly so as not to tilt it.

Distracted by the roar of the rollercoaster overhead, Nunzio mistimed one of his flips and the ball flew down the gutter. "Shit," he muttered. Eying the scoreboard, Nunzio was disappointed that he'd only scored 300 points. "Dese next balls bedder get me some points," he said to no one in particular.

With the grace of a dancer, Nunzio played the next four balls more deftly. Using his skill, the remaining balls hit more bumpers, ricocheted more frequently back and forth from the bumper to cushion to one of the flippers and back again. When his fourth ball finally sank down the drain, Nunzio could afford to smile. He'd scored 2,100. Knowing full well that the highest score ever recorded on that machine was 2,955 and that it was now numerically impossible to beat that score, he turned to Anna.

"Okay. Now you. Give it a try."

"Ah, no. I don't know, Nunzio."

"Come on. What are you afraid of?"

Anna hesitated.

"Aw, c'mon," Nunzio said, nudging her toward the machine.

Anna reluctantly stepped forward. After studying the field for a moment or two, she tentatively placed her slender fingers over the flippers.

"Alright," Nunzio said. "You ready?"

Without waiting for her response, Nunzio drew the plunger back and released the ball. Anna stood frozen as she watched the ball fly up out of the chute. It soon bounced back and forth from bumper to cushion and back again. Anna waited anxiously to use the flippers. She tried as hard as she could. But this was all new to her.

Jason couldn't take his eyes off the two of them. As Anna continued playing, he couldn't help noticing that Nunzio first placed his left hand and then his right hand firmly on top of hers. As the game continued, he inched closer, pressing his body against hers.

"Stop it, Nunzio," Anna said, "Don't do that."

Jason looked on nervously.

Nunzio soon had his arms around her and closed his eyes. His body was now mirroring the movements the ball was making, thrusting this way and that. Looking more and more uncomfortable, Anna looked nervously back at Nunzio. She wondered what he was up to.

Not knowing what else to do, Jason instinctively clenched his fists.

By this time, Anna had played four of her five balls. In a last-ditch effort, she tried everything, nudging the machine, double flipping and fingering the left flipper repeatedly. But, despite her best intentions, she mistimed a flip and the ball fell down the gobble hole. Anna watched as it disappeared from sight.

"Aw, shit," Nunzio said. "What's wrong wit you?"

Jason's ears flared when he overheard Nunzio speaking to her like that.

"Nunzio," Anna said, trying to defend herself. "Give me a break. This was my first time."

"Forget first time. You blew it."

"You're not being fair," Anna said, pointing her finger at him.

"Don't tell me how to behave." Nunzio suddenly grabbed Anna's lapels and violently pulled her body toward him. Seeing this, Jason's stomach clenched. He jumped off his stool and ran over to them.

"Nunzio, please. Stop," she pleaded.

Nunzio gripped her lapels even tighter and shook her.

"That's enough," Jason yelled. "Take your hands off her."

"You," Nunzio said, glaring at him. "Who do you think you're talking to?"

"C'mon, Nunzio. Take it easy."

"Mind your own freakin' business. Take it easy? I don't wanna take it easy."

"Yeah, but …"

"But what? You here to protect her?"

"Maybe. If you won't."

"I seen you looking at her."

"What? What are talking about?"

Nunzio let go of Anna and grabbed Jason's shirt, pulling him close. Standing only inches apart, they glared into each other's eyes. Jason tried to raise his hands hoping to free himself. But being so close, he found it impossible. Each of them, desperately trying to get a firmer hold, grabbed at each other. Jason's arms flailed about as he tried punching Nunzio. However, being so close, he couldn't land a punch. While Nunzio countered by kicking him.

Drawn to the melee, a small crowd gathered around them, among them members of Nunzio's crew. Quickly swept up in the fervor of the fight, his cronies shouted, "Do it, Nunzio. Give him what he deserves."

Nunzio grabbed Jason's arm and twisted it back. Meanwhile, Jason with his free arm desperately tried to put Nunzio in a headlock. However, before he even had a chance, Nunzio lunged at him. Stumbling backwards, Jason somehow got his left leg tangled up with one of the pinball machine's legs and the machine fell on him.

"Aw!" Jason screamed.

"Oh, my God!" Anna cried.

Pinned under the machine, Jason was now unable to move. He laid there helplessly writhing in pain. Towering over him, Nunzio glared angrily at him. Then, Anna bent down and tried to comfort Jason. Nunzio angrily glared down at her.

"So dat wimp is more important than me?"

"No, Nunzio, no."

When Nunzio looked down, he saw that his beautifully tailored shirt was now ripped and his tie was yanked to the side. Incensed, he turned to one of his henchmen and yelled, "Hey, Jimmy."

"Yeah, boss."

Nunzio pointed to the glass counter. "You know where the money is, right?"

Jimmy nodded.

"Don't you dare!" Jason screamed, desperately struggling to free himself.

"Take it," Nunzio said.

"You son of a ..." Jason shouted, watching helplessly as Jimmy reached under the counter and snatched the canvas bag.

Nunzio backed away from the machines and looked around. Seeing that a crowd had formed, he yelled, "Let's get out of here." Jason watched helplessly as Nunzio and his crew raced out of the arcade.

Fortunately, one of the customers ran to the payphone and called an ambulance. After a moment, he hung up and ran over to Anna. "They said they'll be here as soon as they can."

Anna nodded and continued wiping Jason's forehead. "Are you okay?" she asked repeatedly. Jason just grimaced in pain. Anna then looked up and motioned to the guys around them. "Someone please. Help me get this machine off him!"

At that moment, Nunzio ran back into the arcade and raced over to Anna.

"Come with me."

"No," Anna said. "I don't want to."

"I said, come with me!" And with that, he grabbed her by the wrist and pulled her out of the arcade.

It took three customers several attempts to lift the cumbersome pinball machine off of Jason's leg and reposition it back on its wobbly legs. Shortly after, they tried lifting him, helping him get back on his feet, but his moans made them back off and a few stayed, waiting for emergency services to arrive.

Zayde arrived just as the emergency services staff was carrying Jason out on a stretcher. With a concerned look, he looked down at his grandson and squeezed his hand. "You okay, boychik?"

Jason, still writhing in pain, nodded weakly.

"Vere you taking him?"

"Coney Island General," an attendant said.

Zayde waited until the ambulance had driven away. Then, he walked back into the arcade and took a long, slow look around, trying to assess the damage. Two pinball machines were damaged. Several other games stood in disarray and shards of glass were strewn everywhere. Zayde shook his head in disbelief.

Acting on a hunch, he hobbled over to the counter and reached his hand underneath. His chubby fingers felt here and there, desperately searching for the money bag. His expression dropped instantly when he confirmed that the bag was gone.

"Sons a bitches," Zayde said to no one in particular.

CHAPTER 10

*"Life is very short
And there's no time
For fussing and fighting my friend"*

We Can Work It Out
The Beatles

"How you doing, boychik?" Sara asked.

When Jason looked up, his mother was standing in the doorway of his hospital room, her arms filled with flowers and snacks.

"Not great." Jason was clearly in a foul mood. His left leg was now encased in a fresh white cast. A pair of crutches leaned against the wall and his bedsheets lay crumpled at his feet. Sara came over to his bedside and planted a kiss on her son's forehead.

"You look upset."

"What am I going to do now?" Jason began. "Zayde won't take me back and even if he did, there's no way I'll be able to do what I was doing at the arcade."

"We'll figure it out," his mother replied. "Right now, you need to rest. I'm here to take you home." Sara gently stroked her son's cheek. "You can recuperate there."

"Oh, jeez," Jason said, rolling his eyes. The thought of him having to recuperate at his parents' apartment only added to his misery. However, at that moment, Jason realized that there was no point in arguing. Instead, he reached for his sweatshirt and struggled to put it on. Sara came over and helped him into the shirt. Then, she bent down, slipped his sneakers on and tied them up. Jason sat forlornly on the side of the bed, shaking his head. He felt helpless. He reached over to grab his crutches and morosely followed his mom out into the hallway.

• • •

When Sara looked in on her son later that afternoon, he was snoring away. The TV was blaring and his leg was propped up on the ottoman. Having just prepared some chicken soup, she carefully placed a bowl of it down on the side table. At the same time, she removed a bowl of partially eaten Rice Krispies. Jason slowly opened his eyes and yawned.

"Need anything else?"

Jason shook his head, rubbing some sleep from his eyes.

"Anxious to get back to work?"

"Definitely."

"So, what's it been like at their apartment?"

"Well, pretty good. Bubbie always cooks and Zayde's out a lot."

Jason reached for the spoon. "So, where's he go?"

"Beats me. To his friends. To meetings. I have no idea."

Sara continued cleaning up while Jason remained silent, looking off into space. Then, out of the blue, he asked, "Do they love each other?"

Sara almost dropped the dish that she'd picked up. "What?"

"Do they love each other?"

"What kind of question is that? Of course, they do. They've got four kids."

Jason took another sip of his soup. "When were you going to tell me?

"About what?"

"About Aron."

"What do you mean?"

"That he's the reason they married."

Sara had difficulty finding her words. "I don't know," she finally said. "They never took the time to explain it to us."

His grandparents, like many grandparents, rarely talked about their past. Instead, they chose to keep their stories and their troubles to themselves, their attitude being, why burden our children or grandchildren? One can only imagine how many stories, how many events have been lost over time or have never seen the light of day, either being ignored or forgotten over time.

Finally, Sara said, "I guess Zayde felt obligated to do the right thing. Bubbie apparently followed Aron here to the States and stayed with him in Coney Island. He got drafted into the U.S. Army and was killed overseas."

Once again, Jason took time processing that.

"They just didn't talk about it," Sara shrugged. "Heck, we know even less about Lil' Grandma." Sara smiled at her son, picked up the tray and walked back into the kitchen.

• • •

Zayde purposely arrived early the following morning. With a cigarette dangling from his lips, he took a long, careful look around the premises, taking stock of the damage, surveying the debris from yesterday's fight; the pinball machine lying on its side, other machines in disarray, specks of blood on the ground, and shards of shattered glass which now glistened on the cold concrete floor. Zayde let out a sigh.

"Oy, vey ist mir."

Zayde resignedly grabbed the broom and dustpan and began sweeping up the mess. While tossing out the shards of glass into a nearby trash can, he heard some rustling directly behind him. Zayde turned to see Anna standing at the entrance, her slender silhouette shielding the sunlight. With a look of embarrassment on her face, she slowly made her way to the counter.

"So nu, you okay?" he asked.

"I could be better," she said meekly.

Zayde nodded knowingly. In the midst of the pings of the pinball machines, the incessant buzz of neon lights and the periodic rumbling of the rollercoaster overhead, Anna took a careful look around the arcade. The sight nearly overwhelmed her. After a minute, she summoned up the courage to ask, "You're Jason's grandfather, right?"

"Dat's right. And you must be dat jerk's gurlfriend."

Anna didn't answer. She waited for a moment. "How is he?" she asked.

"I don't know. Ve're going to see him tonight."

Anna nodded. The two of them shared a moment of silence.

Zayde sensed that Anna's heart softened at the mention of him. Anna studied all of the machines around the arcade. He could see that the recording booth caught her eye.

"How much does it cost to make a record?"

"For you?"

"Yeah, for me."

"Four shiny quarters."

'That's all?" she asked. She opened her purse and realized that she only had one quarter. Then, she dug her hand deep in her pocket and pulled out a dollar bill. She placed that on the counter.

"Can I get some change?"

"For you? Anytink."

Zayde methodically counted out four quarters, one-by-one, placing each of them in her palm. "Vun, two, tree, four."

Anna smiled. "Well, here goes nothing," she announced. She then walked over to the booth, opened the door, and placed her bag down on the floor. After giving it a quick look-over, she said, "Gee, it's tiny." Anna carefully plunked four quarters into the slot, one by one, and waited. The machine first made an odd whooshing sound. Anna gulped when she heard a strange whirring sound. A moment later, a green light appeared on the board. Anna quickly realized that that was her cue. She took another quick gulp and said, "Uh, hi, Jason. It's me, Anna. I'm thinking about you … I'd like to talk. And I'm sorry for what happened."

Anna then stood there waiting, not exactly sure what to do next. *Did I say too much? Was I clear?* Finally, after what seemed like an eternity, having not heard any more beeps or seen any other lights come on, she simply gathered her things and left the booth.

After five minutes, Anna watched wide-eyed as a shiny 45 rpm record slid down a chute on the side of the booth. Not wanting to smudge it, she used the tips of her fingers to carefully carry it over to the counter.

Zayde smiled. "So?"

Feeling shy, Anna didn't quite know what to say.

So, Zayde reached under the counter, a rat's nest of papers, books, work gloves, rags, and tools. After searching for a minute or two, he found a paper record sleeve. He gently took the record from her hands and slipped it into the sleeve. Then, he handed it back to her.

"So, nu?" he asked, raising his eyebrows

"Can you please give this to Jason?"

Zayde thought about this. "Vy don't you give it to him yourself?"

Anna hesitated and considered her options.

"Uh, thanks. Let me think about that." Then, giving Zayde a tiny smile, she turned and left the arcade.

• • •

Jason was bored out of wits. While he lounged on the couch, watching his umpteenth hour of television with nothing else to occupy his thoughts, he wondered when he'd get see Anna again. Eying his guitar leaning against the end of the couch, Jason reached for it and placed it in his lap. He reached for his guitar pick and gave it a few strums. Again, he thought of Anna. In the privacy of his parents' living room, he began strumming a few chords and hummed a simple melody.

• • •

That evening, Bubbie and Zayde paid him a visit. While seeing his grandparents wasn't at the top of his list of things to do, it did help to break up Jason's boredom.

Once they were done with the small talk, Zayde turned to Jason and, with a smirk on his face, said, "So, a gurl came by de arcade today."

"A girl?"

Zayde nodded. "De vun vit de mafia guy."

Jason's mood perked up. "Really? What did she want?"

"She made a record."

"Really?" Jason said, wiping the perspiration from his upper lip.

"Yup," Zayde said, drawing out the anticipation.

Jason's curiosity was now aroused. His mind reeled with the possibilities.

"What else?"

"She's quite a looker," his zayde added.

Jason felt his cheeks flush. Regardless of his feelings for his zayde, this was embarrassing talk. *Why would she want to make a record?*

"So, you vant to vork?"

Jason tried to sound cool, but he ended up blurting out, "Definitely. The doctor wants me to rest a week. But I could come back sooner."

"You could vould you?" Zayde asked playfully.

"If you're okay with me being on crutches," Jason said.

Zayde thought about that for a moment. "Vell, if you're okay vit me using my cane."

Together, they chuckled.

• • •

Just before dinnertime the following afternoon, the doorbell rang at the Steiner's apartment.

"I'll get it," his mother yelled while preparing supper in the kitchen.

"That's okay. I'll get it," Jason said. "The doctor wants me to use my leg."

Jason hadn't quite yet mastered the art of using his crutches. Groaning as he rose from his chair, he placed a crutch under each arm and hobbled awkwardly down the hall. Then, he opened the door. "Oh! Anna." Jason was surprised to see her standing there.

While Anna initially looked embarrassed, she grinned. Jason noticed there was a record tucked under her arms. Anna stared down at his cast.

"Uh . . . Why don't you come in?"

"Oh, no. I couldn't," Anna said. "What happened in the arcade, I'm so sorry. Are you okay?"

"I'm pretty good," Jason said, suddenly feeling more confident. "Here. Let me show 'ya." In the short time he had his crutches, he'd learned that when he bore down on the crutches, he could actually lift his feet off the floor. "See?" he said braggingly, nearly toppling while he swung his legs back and forth. Luckily, the wall was there to keep him from falling.

Anna giggled. "Here. Let me help you." She stepped up to him and put her hand on his back to lend support.

Hearing the commotion, his mom stuck her head into the hallway. Sara observed the two of them laughing.

"Invite her in," Sara said.

"It's okay, Mom." Jason turned to Anna.

"So, what brings you here?" Jason asked.

"I wanted to see how you're doing."

"Well, now you can see. I'm doing alright. You sure you won't come in?"

"Oh, I don't know," she said, looking shyly down at the hardwood floor. Suddenly, she remembered. "Oh, I did want to give you this." Anna extended her hand and offered him the record she'd made the day before.

Turning it over once or twice, he noticed that the labels on either side were blank. "What's on it?"

Anna blushed again. "Oh, it's just …"

"Don't just stand there, Jason," his mother interrupted. "Invite her in already."

Without turning his head to address his mother, he yelled, "Mom, I did. I did." Jason continued looking at Anna. Then, he took a breath. "Please. Why don't 'ya come in?"

"I couldn't."

"Oh, come on," Jason said.

Anna gave him a sheepish grin, then followed him down the hallway.

When they reached the living room, Jason said, "Mom, this is Anna." Then, pointing down at his cast, he added, "Her boyfriend's the one who did this."

"Jason. That's not nice."

Sara turned to Anna. "Come. Sit down," she said, motioning to the couch. While his mother and Anna took their seats on the couch with no problem, Jason had a bit more difficulty. After trying three different ways without success, he instead awkwardly eased himself into a nearby chair.

"It's not you who needs to apologize," Sara said. "It's your boyfriend who should."

"Well, that's definitely not going to happen," Anna said. "And I haven't spoken to him since the incident."

"Sounds like you're being smart."

"He works with my dad. Helps him with his business."

"What kind of business?"

"I've learned not to ask."

Jason and his mom quickly glanced at each other.

"Listen, why don't you stay for dinner?"

"Oh, really, I couldn't."

"I insist."

Anna seemed to consider that for a moment. "Well, okay. If you insist. I'd like that, Mrs. Steiner."

"Please, call me Sara."

"Whatever you say, Mrs. Steiner."

Jason smirked.

"So, how do the two of you know each other?" Sara asked looking from one to the other.

"From school," Jason said, smiling over at Anna.

Sara nodded. "Well, let me get some dinner ready."

As his mother got up to go into the kitchen, Jason looked over at Anna. She was once again studying his cast.

"Whatcha looking at?"

She pointed to his cast and said, "You don't have a single signature on it," she said.

"I know."

Anna thought for a second. "Can I sign it?"

At that moment, they heard the front door open. Jason's father Gary was just coming home from work.

"Is that you, Gary?" Sara yelled from the kitchen.

"Yeah, it's me, honey." He strode into the living room.

"Well, dinner's almost ready!" After a pause, Sara yelled, "By the way, we have a dinner guest!"

Gary looked over at Jason and then at Anna, his eyebrows raised.

"Uh, hi, dad," Jason said. "This is my friend Anna. Mom invited her to stay for dinner."

"Oh, great. Nice to meet you, Anna," Gary said.

"Nice to meet you too," Anna blushed.

Gary placed his briefcase down in the hallway and looked over to the couch. "Please excuse me." Jason and Anna watched as he headed to the washroom.

A moment later, Sara, ever cheerful, reappeared from the kitchen. "Come, you two. Take a seat at the table."

Jason and Anna walked over to the dining room table. Using one of his crutches, Jason pointed to where Anna might sit. "Why don't you sit here," he said. A moment later, his father reappeared, took his seat at the head of the table and placed a napkin in his lap. "So, how do the two of you know each other?" he asked.

Jason looked over to Anna and rolled his eyes. "We were in the same class together. She also knows the guy who did this," Jason said, pointing down at his cast.

Gary nodded. Then, he hemmed and hawed, not quite knowing how to ask the question. Finally, he ventured. "And how do you know him?"

Anna fidgeted in her chair. "Well," she said, looking down. "He's kinda my boyfriend."

Gary studied Anna, looking unsure of how he should respond. He shifted his weight in his chair. Then, trying the change the subject, he said, "Apparently, the police are looking into the incident."

Anna and Jason looked at each other with alarm. At that moment, Sara appeared again from the kitchen. This time, she was holding a steaming dish.

"Here we go," she said with a proud look on her face. "It's a new recipe. A variation on the classic Swedish meatballs but it's cooked in grape jelly." She grinned proudly. "Help yourself," she said, carefully placing the dish down on the table. Sara quickly ducked back into the kitchen and returned a moment later with two more dishes, one a serving of Uncle Ben's white rice and the other some limp green beans topped with butter.

After reaching for the casserole dish of meatballs, Gary turned again to Anna. "Forgive me for saying this, but it seems like you can do better than the guy who did that."

Shocked by his dad's appraisal, Jason quickly glanced over to Anna. She was once again staring into her lap.

After some deliberation, she explained, "My dad has it all mapped out. He wants us to marry, have kids, etc., etc."

Gary sat quietly for a moment. Then, he asked, "And what do *you* want?"

Anna didn't answer immediately. She took a moment and readjusted her posture.

"I'd like to . . . I want to study. Travel a bit and eventually teach."

Jason had never heard Anna open up before with such a degree of clarity and certainty.

"Well, don't let anything or anyone stand in your way," Sara said. "Follow your dream."

Anna blushed at the advice.

Gary openly studied Anna's face. "You seem like a smart person . . . Go for it." He reached for a serving spoon and served himself some green beans.

• • •

As nice as his parents had been, Jason couldn't wait for dinner to be over. He wanted to spend some time alone with Anna and ask about the record. So, when they'd finished dessert and the dishes had been cleared, he turned to Anna. "Can I show you my room?"

Anna hesitated. She wisely looked over to Jason's mother for some signal.

Sara gave her a tiny nod.

"Sure," Anna said. Then, she followed Jason down the hallway. And while there was no doubt that she was enjoying Jason's company, when they got to his doorway, she hesitated from entering.

Jason realized she didn't want his parents to get the wrong impression. "It's okay. I'll keep the door open," he smiled. Then, he made a grand gesture with his arms and said, "Come on in."

Anna smiled and stepped into the room. Before sitting down, she took a moment to study his room, gazing at the racing cars and the model airplanes on his shelves, the healthy stack of comic books splayed across his desk, and the posters of The Beatles, The Moody Blues and The Who which adorned his walls. While Jason hobbled over to his record player, Anna stood in the center of the room looking perplexed. She looked first at the straight-backed wooden chair at his desk, then over to his bed.

Jason only realized her dilemma when he looked back. "My bed will probably be more comfortable," he said. Anna hesitated a moment. Then, she put the record down and lowered herself onto his bed.

Jason looked longingly at the record. He would've given anything to hear it right now. But he thought it best that he wait for to suggest that. Perhaps she was shy about playing it in front of him. So instead, he turned to his record collection and began fishing through his many record albums.

"Do you like the Moody Blues?"

She looked over to him and shrugged.

"Nah, you probably like Simon and Garfunkel, right?" Jason gently slid the record out of its sleeve and placed it carefully on the turntable. Then he lowered the needle onto his well-played album.

"Hello, darkness my old friend,
I've come to see you once again…"

This time, when Jason looked over at Anna, she was smiling. Then, as suavely as he could, he tried joining her on the bed. Several times, he attempted lifting his leg and placing it on the bed, and each time, he failed. The rest of his body just wouldn't follow. Finally, he came up with a solution. First, he gingerly placed his bum on the edge of the bed. Then, he threw his right leg up and slowly jockeyed the rest of his body over. When he'd finally accomplished that, he gave a big sigh. Anna laughed. Sitting on the bed together, the two of them were soon entranced by the music's stark arrangements and inspired lyrics. Neither of them said a word until the first song had ended.

Anna then whispered, "I love Simon and Garfunkel . . . especially this next song. Their songs are just so, so . . ."

"Harmonic," Jason said. "Their voices intertwine so beautifully. And I love Paul Simon's lyrics."

"Absolutely," Anna said. A minute passed before she added, "Nunzio hates them."

Jason laughed at her observation. By all appearances, Jason was enjoying himself. But deep down, he was preoccupied. His overwhelming desire was to take Anna to see Simon and Garfunkel in concert. The problem was he didn't have tickets. But Mitch did. That, however, didn't prevent him from lying.

"You know, I can get tickets to the concert."

"You can?"

"Yup," Jason said, even though the concert was only days away and he had no idea how he was actually going to obtain tickets. "You wanna go?

"Well, I don't know. I gotta think about that," Anna said, her eyes darting about.

"Okay." A moment later, he added, "We could go as friends."

Anna nodded thoughtfully.

Jason snuck a glance at her while the next song, *Kathy's Song*, played. He was surprised when Anna seemed to summon up her courage and handed him the vinyl record that she'd made for him.

"When you get a chance, give this a listen," she said.

"Well, thanks . . . I will," Jason said. Then, trying to break the tension, he placed the record on his desk and picked up a Bic pen. He turned to face her. "Would you mind signing my cast?" he said, handing her the pen.

Anna gave a slight giggle. Then, she took a long, hard look at the cast and searched for the perfect spot. After a minute, she leaned over and, using her best penmanship, she wrote, *Get better. Love, Anna.*

Because he was looking upside down, he initially had no idea what she had written. After twisting his head this way and that, a light eventually went off in his head and he beamed. "Thank you."

After sitting through several more songs, Anna looked over at him. Jason realized that she was thinking about leaving "Please. Don't go," he said.

"Well, it is getting late. I think I've overstayed my welcome." She handed the pen back to him and hopped off the bed. She slowly began to gather her things.

Jason shifted his body to the edge of the bed and reluctantly reached for his crutches. Then, he struggled to his feet. When they finally looked at each other, they each gave each other a small smile before leaving the room. Walking out into the living room, they found Jason's parents chatting on the couch.

"So...," Gary said, standing to make room on the couch.

"I'd better get going," Anna said.

"Oh, that's too bad," Sara said. She stood up to face Anna and Jason standing by her. "Well, it was awfully nice meeting you, Anna."

"You too, Mrs. Steiner. Thank you for dinner."

"Please call me Sara and it was our pleasure."

"Will you be okay getting home?" Gary asked.

"Oh. yeah. No problem. I live close by. Thanks again."

"Well, goodnight," Gary and Sara said.

Jason escorted Anna down the hallway. As he opened the door, he turned to her and whispered, "Thanks for dropping by."

Anna returned the whisper, "My pleasure. Your parents are nice."

• • •

No sooner had Anna left the apartment than Jason raced to his room. That is, as quickly as anyone can using crutches. No longer able to contain his excitement, he quickly took the Simon and Garfunkel album off the turntable and tossed it on his bed. Then, he slid Anna's record out of its sleeve and placed it on the Victrola, carefully lowering the needle onto the record. Despite its scratchy sound, Jason was ecstatic when he recognized her voice.

"Uh, hi, Jason. It's me, Anna ... I'm thinking about you. I'd like to talk. Sorry for what happened."

Jason was barely able to contain his joy. He played the record over and over. Each time, he concentrated all of his attention on her voice, that meek tone of hers. He studied her nuances, her intonation, and the expression in her delivery. After playing it maybe ten times, Jason then looked over at his clock radio by the bed.

Realizing it was getting late, he reached for his crutches and hobbled down the hall to the bathroom. He quickly brushed his teeth and washed his face. Then, after gazing at himself in the mirror for a while, he quietly muttered, "Things are looking up." Jason then returned to his room. Just as he was about to get into bed, he had a second thought. Jason walked over to the Victrola and played Anna's record one more time.

CHAPTER 11

*"I can tell. Just you wait.
That lucky star I talk about is due!
Honey, everything's coming up roses for me and for you!"*

Everything's Coming Up Roses
Ethel Merman

"Ah, Madonna," Anna's father complained.

"What's the matter, Poppa?" Anna asked, raising her voice so she could be heard over the sound of pots and pans banging in the kitchen. Her dear grandmother was cooking in the kitchen.

Anna's father Sal was studying the silverware at his setting. Then, he looked up to the heavens shaking his head. "She forgota," he complained. "The woman forgota. She forgota ma espoon! Anna, be a good girl and get it for me."

Both her father's complaint and his request annoyed her. *Why can't he just get it himself?* Anna looked up while she mulled it over for a while. This was the first time, she recalled, that she'd noticed the rusty ceiling fan's repetitive *click, click, click.*

"Be a good girl, Anna," Lisa, her younger sister said, mimicking their father.

Anna gave her a dirty look. Then, begrudgingly pulling her chair back, she inadvertently bumped into her grandmother who was carrying a basket of warm crusty bread to the table. Several chunks of it fell to the floor. A dish of assorted antipasto was already sitting on the table.

To make a point before going into the kitchen, Anna turned to her father and said, "You know, Pop, next time you could get up and get it yourself."

Sal looked up from his salad. He scowled and shook his head.

Anna looked hard at her father. Sal, christened Salvatore Guiseppe Adamo Conti, had been born in Palermo, Italy and was the eldest of five children. His father, Anna's grandfather, Enzio Conti, was a local *mafiosi*. She had heard that he got his start as a security guard assigned to protect the property and holdings of a local aristocrat and that over the years, her grandfather worked his way up the ranks of the organization, the *Cosa Nostra*.

It was something she was not proud of ever admitting.

She also knew that her father had only gotten as far as the fourth grade. To make money, her father had begun shoplifting fruits and vegetables from the local grocery at the tender age of eleven. Anna recognized that it helped feed his family.

Her grandfather, Enzio, then brought her father into the business at the age of 15. At one of the family gatherings, an uncle once whispered to her that, as a petty thief, her father devised ingenious ways of making money. Her father was always proud to point out that local gangsters recognized his talent and enlisted him on their jobs. When he was hired, Sal told his daughter, they could be assured that their heist would come off without a hitch.

Anna had a very different way of looking at what one should be proud of. And her growing frustration was one of the reasons she decided to spend the summer with her nonna in Coney Island. As a rule, she and her family always went to her grandmother's house every Sunday anyhow and here they were now. Having supper. On Sunday night. But their presence intruded on the sense of peace she'd found at her grandmother's house and she craved that peace. She needed time to think. Something that was impossible to do in the presence of her boisterous family.

When Anna returned from the kitchen carrying his favorite spoon, her father stopped what he was doing and raised his head from his salad.

"What kinda wife you gonna be for Nunzio?"

Anna frowned. "I don't want to be his wife," she said, placing the spoon to his right.

"What'sa matta wit you? Nunzio's good for you."

"Good for me? Really?" Anna shook her head, secretly wishing she had the confidence to tell her father what she really thought.

"He'll give you a good life. He'll protect you."

"Well, he didn't protect me the other day!"

"Aww." Sal picked up his favorite spoon and seemed to study it.

Anna poked at her ziti with her fork while she vividly replayed the incident in her head.

"That day at the arcade when he attacked that boy? He was mean and violent. He wasn't being nice."

"Aw, Anna. People can't always be nice."

"For God's sake, he broke his leg!" Anna looked at her mother Maria imploringly who'd been standing in the doorway, drying her hands and listening to them. "Momma, what do you think?"

Maria didn't say a word. She instead looked nervously at her husband. Then, she looked back at Anna.

"Do you think what Nunzio did was right?"

Maria stared down at the floor. She shifted her weight from one foot to the other. Without saying a word, she stepped over to Anna and took her hand, leading her into the kitchen. Anna's younger sister Lisa followed eagerly behind them. In the kitchen, Anna's grandmother, her nonna, was busy stirring a large pot of marinara sauce.

"Momma, I don't want to live my life the way Poppa wants," Anna said. "I have no desire to be with Nunzio."

Her mother looked as if she was absorbing what her oldest daughter was saying.

"Life is not all about getting married and having babies," Anna said. "I want to study. I want to teach. I want to make something of myself."

Maria seemed to listen patiently. Then, she reached out and began gently stroking her daughter's hair. After a minute, she finally said, "It's a gonna be alright."

Anna looked skeptically at her mother.

"You like disa boy?"

"Jason? He's a nice boy. He defended me."

Lisa pointed at Anna. "Look, Momma, she's blushing." Lisa began singing in a sing-song style, *"Anna and Jason sitting in a tree, k-i-s-s-i-n-g!"*

Anna slapped her sister's hand.

"Basta, girls, basta," their mother said.

"Nunzio's nothing but a brute, Momma. He attacked Jason."

Maria patted her daughter's hand. "It was wrong. And you're right . . . Come wit' me."

Maria took her daughter's hand once again and together they walked back into the dining room where Sal was still eating. Maria looked plaintively at him. "Sal, what Nunzio did was a wrong. We owe disa Jason a someting."

"Owe him what?" Sal asked incredulously.

"Some kinda decency."

"Some decency? We don't owe nobody nuttin."

Maria then turned to Anna. "You invite a him to dinner disa Friday night. We'll show him what we're made of. Dat we're decenta people."

Sal shook his head and gave his wife a skeptical look. Then, he took an angry bite of his ziti and muttered under his breath, "Freakin' heeb."

• • •

Zayde was sitting reading the newspaper in his easy chair and listening to his wife clattering pots and pans in the kitchen. He knew she was pleased that he was home on a Saturday night for a change. On top of that, they were alone. Or, as alone as it ever got with his mother-in-law living with them. Zayde needed to speak with his wife. So, he had asked Jason to cover for him at the arcade tonight.

"Herschel," Bubbie shouted from the kitchen. "Come. Sit down."

Bubbie was what you would call a *balaboosta*. That is, she cooked, she cleaned and served anyone, anytime in her house. Tirelessly. There wasn't one day that Zayde had ever heard her complain. When he looked up from his paper, now saw her standing in the doorway. Her arms were crossed and, happy he was home, she was smiling.

"Okay," he said.

Zayde folded up the newspaper and reached for his cane. Then, he rose gingerly from the couch. With each step, he let out a little groan. After hobbling over, he took his seat at the head of their long kitchen table. Once he had taken his place, Bubbie carried the casserole dish to the table and sat down to the left of him. Lil' Grandma was already sitting to his right. Bubbie had made a point of preparing one of Zayde's favorite dishes, beef flanken.

"So," Harry sputtered nervously. He had trouble finding the right words.

"Nu?" Bubbie said, prodding him.

"De docteh, he vants I should see him."

"Again?" Bubbie asked. She blushed no doubt after realizing that she'd been too blunt.

"My leg. It still hurts."

"Does it?" Yetta said, responding this time with a bit more compassion.

Zayde was purposely using English so that his mother-in-law wouldn't understand what he was saying. While he continued struggling to find the right words, Zayde studied his plate of beef, the honeyed carrots, and mashed potatoes. Before he continued, he took a much-anticipated bite of the soft tender meat.

"He vants I should see him again dis Tuesday."

"So soon?"

"Yeah. He vants I should take more tests."

"More tests?" Bubbie shook her head and thought about it. "Vat kind?" she asked.

Zayde shrugged. "Who the hell knows," stabbing one of his carrots with his fork.

"Oy, Herschel." Bubbie shook her head again. Then, she glanced at her husband's plate, rose from the table, and walked over to the stove. A minute later, she returned with a serving dish filled with several more slices of beef. Using a large knife and fork, she placed two more slices on her husband's plate.

Zayde was suffering from diabetes. Unbeknownst to anyone, for several years he had experienced its symptoms. But he was a proud man and was perhaps ashamed to reveal it to anyone. Zayde was also a private man. He kept things to himself. Many years later, when his youngest daughter Leah was asked to describe her father, she simply said, "He was always a mystery. There were times we didn't know where he was. When November would roll around, he'd disappear, head to Florida for the winter. None of us ever knew where he went or if he went with anyone. Poof. He'd just disappear."

Six years earlier, a sore suddenly appeared on the bottom Zayde's left foot. Being on the heel of his foot, it was months before Zayde noticed it. And even then, once he did, he ignored it in the hope that it would somehow go away. Over time, however, it developed into an ulcer. The infection regularly discharged a clear ooze which would soak and eventually stick to his sock. Being the man he was, Zayde suffered quietly. At the end of a long day, he would close the arcade, leave for God knows where, and not come home until the wee hours. Only then would he take off his shoes. Over the years, he had more and more difficulty removing the sock from his foot. For whatever reason, Zayde never spoke to his wife about it. But, over time, she would find fewer and fewer of his socks in the laundry basket. This naturally aroused her curiosity. Until one day, she questioned him. "Vere de hell are your socks? Vy is dere only vone of each?"

Zayde merely shrugged. He never came up with a satisfactory answer. His foot progressively gave him more and more pain. To counter the pain and his increasing loss of balance, Zayde took to wearing work boots. And to ensure his balance, he tied the laces as tightly as they'd go. As the years wore on, he lost more and more sensation in his foot and used a cane more frequently. Over the years, he developed a noticeable limp.

Now, it didn't help that Harry liked his sweets. Through the day, Zayde would not hesitate to pop whatever candy was near him into his mouth, a Lifesaver, a piece of Bonomo Turkish Taffy, whatever. His favorite treat though was red licorice. He often carried a stick or two of it in his shirt pocket and it didn't help that the arcade stocked all of those candies.

• • •

"Come on, Mitch. Do me a solid," Mitch heard Jason shout into the phone.

"What'd you say?" Mitch shouted back. "I'm having trouble hearing you.

"I need your tickets," Mitch heard him say finally.

"My tickets? Tickets to what?"

"To Simon and Garfunkel."

At that moment, three beautiful girls walked past the entrance. Mitch spotted Anna and her two friends and put two and two together. He was also instantly drawn to Anna's redheaded friend.

"Aha! I get it." Mitch was onto Jason. "You want to take your poetry girl, Anna."

"Oh, well. You got me. Yeah, I'd love to take Anna."

"Oh, Anna. Sweet Anna," Mitch swooned mockingly. For a moment, Jason didn't say a word and Mitch wondered if he had teased too much. Finally, Jason spoke up, "She loves Simon and Garfunkel."

Mitch considered what Jason was proposing. "Do you have any idea how long I had to stand in line to get those tickets?"

"I know," Jason said.

"You owe me big time," Mitch yelled into the phone, as he thought again of Anna's redheaded friend.

• • •

The following morning, Jason showed up at the penny arcade with his guitar in hand. Before he even said hello to his zayde or his cousin, he turned to Mitch. "So, did you think about it?" he asked.

"Think about what?" Mitch said.

Jason knew that his cousin was toying with his emotions. "The tickets," Jason said in exasperation.

"Oh, the tickets." Mitch smiled. "Boy, you sure got it bad."

"Maybe I do. So, what do you want in return?"

"Okay," Mitch said. "I've thought about this long and hard.

"Yeah."

"The only way I'm going to give you the tickets is . . . if you can get me a date with Anna's friend, the foxy redhead."

"Laura?" Jason asked incredulously. Laura happened to be in the same grade as Jason and while admittedly she was very attractive, Jason also knew that she could be cool and aloof. "You're serious, aren't you?"

"Dead serious," Mitch said, folding his arms.

"Well ...," Jason thought hard about that. "It's not going to be easy." Jason quickly realized he had his work cut out for him. He knew that Laura could be very particular. "I'll see what I can do. Incidentally, thanks for covering for me while I was away."

• • •

That afternoon, Mitch was working the counter. He had just made change for someone when he heard a crash come from the back of the arcade. When Mitch got back to the stockroom, he stuck his head through the door. Dozens of packets of red Twizzlers were scattered on the floor and Jason was down on all fours, struggling to pick them up.

"What's going on?" Mitch asked.

"God, I'm clumsy. I tripped over my crutches."

Mitch appreciated how challenging it was for his cousin to have to rely on crutches. It was also the first time that he really studied the cast on Jason's leg. He quickly noticed that it only had one signature, Anna's, on it. "Hey, nice signature. Mind if I sign it?" he asked.

"Uh, sure. Got a pen?"

Mitch pulled a pen from his shirt pocket and held it in mid-air while he considered what he would write. After a moment, he cocked his head to one side and studied the cast once again. Then, he stepped closer and drew a simple figure with a large nose. Underneath it, he wrote, *Kilroy was here!*

Jason took one look at his cousin's drawing and laughed.

"You know you're one big turd?"

Ignoring his cousin's comment, Mitch asked, "Hey, you wanna go to Nathan's after work?"

"I'd love to, but I got plans."

"Plans? What kind of plans?"

Jason gulped and turned a shade of pale. "I'm having dinner with Anna."

"Isn't that a good thing?"

"Yeah. Except that it's at her parents . . . I feel like I'm walking into a lion's den."

Mitch chuckled, then looked down at Jason's crutches and considered his cousin's dinner plans. "How the hell are you going to get there?"

"I'll take the subway," Jason said matter-of-factly. "The walk over is nothing."

Considering the route and the herculean effort that it would involve, Mitch said, "You're kidding, right? It'll take you forever. I'll tell you what. I'll drive you there."

"Aw, that's not necessary."

"I know. You owe me big time," said Mitch grinning.

• • •

Later that day, Jason and Mitch stood beside Mitch's parents' red Ford Fairlane. Just before they got into car, Jason turned to his cousin and said, "I really appreciate this." He may have spoken too soon. One look inside the car's cramped quarters should have convinced him that, with his crutches and the cast on his leg, getting into the front passenger seat was not going to be an easy task.

But Jason quickly came up with a solution. He first hobbled around the back of the car and opened the rear door. Then, he plopped his behind on the edge of the back seat. Slowly, he shimmied his way over cheek-by-cheek. Jason then took a deep breath and draped his crutches across his body. As a final gesture, he lifted his left leg up and straddled it over the front passenger seat. "Whew."

Mitch turned and took a quick look at his cousin now in the backseat. He laughed. "So, where are we going?"

"Kew Gardens ... Just off of Queens Boulevard. I'll show you."

Mitch turned onto Surf Avenue and headed over to the Belt Parkway.

That day, the weather in Coney Island had been hot and hazy. Having to wear a cast and use the crutches made it especially difficult. So, the first thing that Jason did was roll down his window. The cool evening breeze was a welcome relief. When they stopped at their first red light, Jason looked out the window and smiled. Some kind soul had opened a fire hydrant. The neighborhood kids were now happily dashing in and out of its forceful spray. Before he knew it, the light turned green and they sped off.

"Mind turning the radio on?" Jason said.

"No prob," Mitch said, reaching for the dial.

The syrupy sounds of the Association's current hit song, *Cherish*, quickly filled the car. Jason initially welcomed the music. But, his cousin was soon singing along and tapping the rhythm on the steering wheel. Jason rolled his eyes. It was a little more than he had bargained for.

"Say, Mitch, do you mind changing that?"

Mitch flashed his cousin a quick, questioning glance in the rearview mirror. But he acquiesced and soon switched to another station. Suddenly, the Beatles' catchy tune, *We Can Work It Out*, was pouring out of the car's tinny speakers.

"Now, that's more like it," Jason said, beaming. The two of them were soon bopping their heads in rhythm and singing, *"Life is very short and there's no ..."*

Thirty minutes later, they were in Anna's parents' neighborhood and the traffic was heavy. Even at that hour, the local shops along Queens Boulevard were teeming with people. Jason made note of every passing street. *72nd Drive, 72nd Road.* Shortly after they'd passed 71st Drive, he advised Mitch, "Take the next right." And halfway down the block, Jason pointed to a house on the right and said, "Here it is."

When Mitch had pulled into the driveway and turned off the ignition, he looked into the rear-view mirror. "You ready for this?"

"Not really."

Both of them laughed heartily. At that moment, Jason began to realize that family was perhaps something wonderful to have.

CHAPTER 12

*"Well, my hands are shaky and my knees are weak
I can't seem to stand on my own two feet
Who do you think of when you have such luck?
I'm in love
I'm all shook up."*

All Shook Up
Elvis Presley

Anna must've been watching from her bedroom window. No sooner had Mitch turned the ignition off than she'd opened the front door and was standing on the front porch smiling. Jason, stuck as he was in the backseat, wasn't even sure that she could see him. Despite that, he gave her his best smile. Jason thought Anna looked lovely in her lacy light green dress.

"Hi," she yelled.

While Jason struggled to extract himself from the backseat, he noticed Mitch and Anna looking nervously at each other. Clutching his crutches, he carefully lifted his left leg back from the front seat. Then, he opened the back door and leaned back precariously. He next shimmied his bum inch-by-inch over to the edge. From time-to-time, Jason looked over at Anna and then at Mitch at the wheel. He saw them nodding politely to each other. Eventually, he lifted himself out of the car. Jason then took a deep breath. Just before he hobbled up to the front porch, he looked back at his cousin in the driver's seat and mouthed the words, "Thank you."

"No problem," Mitch yelled. "I'll pick you up later." After waving at him, he backed out of the driveway.

When Jason turned to face Anna, he noticed she was smiling. He draped his arms over the crutches and slowly hobbled up to the porch. Anna leaned toward him and whispered, "I should warn you about my family."

"Warn me? About what?"

"Well, they're, uh . . .," Anna searched for the right word, "different."

"How so?"

Anna shook her head and laughed. "You'll soon see."

They were both giggling when the door suddenly swung open and they found themselves standing face-to-face with Anna's dad, Sal.

"What's so funny?" Sal asked.

Anna nervously searched for a comeback.

"Nothing, Poppa." Without skipping a beat, she said, "This is Jason."

"Hello, Mr. Conti," Jason said cordially.

Sal simply nodded and motioned for them to come in. The dining room table was already set and Jason could hear someone busying in the kitchen.

"Sit down," her father said bluntly.

Without saying another word, Sal took his place at the head of the table and poured himself a glass of his homemade wine. He then poured a second large glass and placed it in front of Jason. Anna shot him a quick glance.

"Thank you," Jason said. He couldn't help but notice that her father hadn't poured any wine for either Anna, her two sisters or for his wife Maria.

Jason raised his glass and took a hearty sip. A moment later, he coughed it back up. Anna's two younger sisters giggled. *Wow. That's some powerful stuff,* he thought to himself. Jason suddenly felt light-headed. He giggled for no apparent reason and began to feel unusually confident. It dawned on him that he had never sampled any homemade wine before. The only other wine he'd ever tasted was Manischewitz, the sweet, almost candy flavored wine his father traditionally served during the Jewish High Holidays.

Feeling his face flush, Jason wisely put his wine glass down and took the opportunity to study his surroundings, noticing immediately that the two couches in the nearby living room were covered in plastic. The rose-colored walls were accented with ornate circular patterns of white molding while gilded statues of warriors stood on various shelves and if Jason listened carefully, he would swear that he heard opera music playing in a nearby room. The Conti home even smelled differently, a earthen aroma of garlic, tomato, and peppers. At that moment, Jason realized he was in a new world, experiencing an abundant palette of new sights, new sounds, and tastes.

Anna's mother Maria entered the dining room carrying a plateful of *caponata*. Their youngest daughter followed behind her, holding a basketful of crusty bread. Before putting it down on the table, she turned to Jason and politely said, "*Buona sera.*"

When Jason cordially answered, "*Buona sera,*" Anna smiled.

As soon as Maria had placed her dish down on the table, she quickly turned and disappeared back into the kitchen. Reappearing only a minute later, this time carrying a dish of *pasta e fugal* with *escarole*. Jason sat wide-eyed at the table taking in the wide variety of dishes. Anna turned to Jason to explain, "We eat a lot of vegetables." Her mother nodded eagerly in agreement.

"Northern Italians typically eat a lot more meat," Anna proudly continued. "We Sicilians are farmers. We grow vegetables, zucchini and tomatoes, garlic, and grapes and we eat them all."

Jason nodded and gladly accepted the heaping casserole dish of eggplant stew that Anna was holding. While serving himself, it occurred to him that since Anna's father had initially greeted him, Sal had not made any further eye contact or said one further word.

At that very moment, Sal turned to Anna and asked, "So, when are you and Nunzio going to get togedder?"

Anna flinched at the sound of her boyfriend's name and put her fork down. "Nunzio and me?" Her eyes filled with anger and she hesitated before answering. "Dad, I'd rather not talk about Nunzio. We have company."

"You and Nunzio . . .," her dad began, but quickly thought the better of it. Sal placed his fork down and reached for his wine glass. Then, he methodically began to circle his forefinger around its edge. From that moment on, Sal didn't say another word.

Anna and Jason somehow survived the dinner. After the dishes were removed, Anna turned to Jason and gently touched his hand. "Come, let me show you our backyard," she whispered. Jason couldn't have been more relieved. He followed her out into the early evening. With the sun setting, the clouds' underbelly was turning a warm rose. For several minutes, he and Anna stood silently in the backyard, Jason marveling at its beauty. He heard crickets chirping and a yellow moon was rising above the back row of cedar trees. When Jason raised his gaze, the stars seemed to be appearing one by one. There was a general late summer buzz in the air.

Jason and Anna both took a long breath in. The air carried a woody evening fragrance. Finally, after a long silence, Anna turned to Jason and said, "Well, we made it." They both laughed. Jason gazed into Anna's deep brown eyes. He felt unusually happy and content though he wasn't sure if his giddiness was from the wine or from her company.

Anna stepped closer and studied his face. "You know you've got peach fuzz above your lip," she said.

"I do?" Jason asked. Anna nodded. At that distance, he noticed for the first time a smattering of short dark hairs between her eyebrows.

"Sorry about my dad," she said.

"Don't be."

"He's dead set on me marrying Nunzio."

"That's obvious."

"And that's the last thing I want to do."

After considering that for a while, he asked, "Anna, what do you want to do?"

"Well, as I told your parents, I want to go to school, to university. And eventually, I want to teach English in college or at the university level."

"Wow. That's pretty ambitious."

After another long silence, Anna added, "Marrying Nunzio is the last thing I need."

"Then don't."

Anna gave a tiny nod and then looked back at the house, peering through the dining room window to see what her parents were up to. While she was doing that, Jason studied the garden's many trees and shrubs. The Conti's garden was beautiful --- a healthy mix of well-maintained flower beds as well as sturdy tomato plants, heads of purple radicchio and earthy vines of zucchini.

When he turned to look back, Anna was staring at him. He gazed into her eyes and his mind went blank. Suddenly, he couldn't find any words. After a lengthy silence, he finally blurted out, "Nice garden."

"My father's pride and joy."

A car honked on the street.

"Oh, that must be . . .," Jason said, suddenly remembering that Mitch was going to pick him up. "That must be my ride."

"Aw … Too bad."

"Hey, before I go, can I ask you a favor?"

Anna gave him a quizzical look. "What kind of favor?"

"My cousin wants to ask Laura out."

Anna laughed. "The guy who brought you, who works with you at the arcade?"

"Yeah. That guy."

"He's cute."

"Cute?" Jason shook his head in disbelief. "Can you ask if she'll go out with him?"

"Well, I'll give it a try," Anna said, giggling.

Jason smiled broadly. "Anyway, I gotta go. Is there any chance we can meet tomorrow after work?"

Anna nodded.

"How about under the boardwalk?"

"It's a deal."

Jason felt a warm glow sweep over him. "Well, goodnight, Anna."

"Goodnight, Jason." She took another quick look into the dining room window as if to confirm that the coast was clear and that no one was looking. Then, she leaned in toward Jason and planted a small kiss on his cheek.

CHAPTER 13

*"You never close your eyes anymore
When I kiss your lips.
And there's no tenderness
Like before in your fingertips."*

You've Lost That Lovin' Feeling
The Righteous Brothers

You were right, boss," said Enzio, one of Nunzo's henchmen. "So, this son of a bitch drops that heeb off and he walks straight into Sal's house." Enzio was reporting on his surveillance the night before. Nunzio and his cohorts had again commandeered the large corner booth of the diner.

Nunzio was nursing a second cup of coffee. Clenching his jaw tightly, he said, "I figured something fishy was going on." Nunzio was about to take another sip, when the cup slipped from his fingers and splattered in his lap. "Son of a bitch," he shouted. When he looked down, he spotted a large coffee stain on his crotch.

"Get me a rag, will 'ya?" Nunzio bellowed. "And a new pair of pants."

"From where, boss?" Enzio asked.

"Where do you think? The trunk of my car."

Nunzio tossed him the keys and Enzio ran out to fetch it. Five minutes later, he returned with two sharply creased pairs of pants, holding each of them out for inspection.

"Forget that one," Nunzio said, pointing to the ruby colored pants. "I'll take the blue one."

Nunzio rose from his seat and Enzio handed him the pants. Then, Nunzio walked straight into the men's room. While slipping off his stained pants, he remembered the advice Sal had once given him. *It's all about dignity and patience.* Nunzio took a deep breath. He slipped into his dark blue pants and fastened his belt. Then, he let the hot water run and, reaching for a paper towel, he wet the crotch of the stained pants and started dabbing at the spot.

Minutes later, he took a wire hanger from over a steam pipe overhead and hung his pants to dry. He knew no one working at the diner would mind. It was part of his territory.

On his way back to the booth, Nunzio turned to a passing waitress and said, "Honey, get me another cup of coffee, would 'ya?" Then, he settled back into his seat, but not until he had checked that the seat itself was dry. Spotting a couple of drops of coffee, he turned his head and stared pointedly at Enzio.

After a brief second, Enzio jumped up, took out his cloth handkerchief out of his pocket and dutifully wiped away the offending drops.

"That's more like it," Nunzio muttered, as he hitched up the knees of his pants before finally taking his throne.

• • •

Anna studied herself in the mirror. "No, no, no. That doesn't work," she mumbled after trying on a pink blouse. Anna tossed it on her bed on top of her other discarded tops. She then slipped on a fuscia one. Once again, she looked at herself in the mirror. "Oh, no. Not that one either." It was the fourth one she'd tried on. "Oh well. Guess I'll go with the peach one."

In the privacy of her room, Anna couldn't hide her excitement. In twenty minutes, she'd get to see Jason again. She couldn't wait to tell him that Laura had agreed to go out with Mitch. Anna slipped her delicate lavender sandals on and bounced down the stairs. At that moment, the front doorbell chimed. She threw open the door.

Nunzio was leaning against the brick wall. He straightened up and said, "Hey, babe."

"Uh, Nunzio? What are you …?" Anna said, fumbling for words. "What are you doing here?"

"What do you mean, what am I doing here?" Nunzio stared at her up and down. Then, he pointed at her clothing. "Why aren't you ready?"

"Ready for what?" Anna had no idea what he was doing here at this hour. Suddenly, her eyes grew wide. Her blood began racing as all the pieces came together.

"For dinner. At my parents. C'mon, Anna. It's Wednesday." Nunzio leaned forward to give her a kiss. But she turned her head. In all of her excitement, Anna had somehow forgotten their weekly routine, that every Wednesday they had dinner at his parents' home and she had to go dressed up. Nunzio leaned back against the doorframe and a quizzical look came over his face. "Were you going somewheres?"

"Uh, no," she stammered.

"Then, what are you waiting for? Go get changed. Put on something nice."

Anna rolled her eyes. "Why don't you come in?"

Nunzio sauntered into the living room. As she climbed the stairs, Anna turned and could see Nunzio standing by the phone. She felt a pang in her stomach. She only wished she could call Jason and let him know that she wouldn't be able to meet him. Anna sighed and ran up and into her room. She grabbed another outfit from the closet as panic rose into her throat. She could taste the bitter misery of her seemingly impossible situation.

• • •

Mitch was in the storeroom restocking the sodas and candies his cousin stood by the counter. Jason looked at his watch.

"Hey, Mitch. I gotta head out now."

Mitch stuck his head out of the stockroom. "Okay. Well, have fun."

Jason reached for his crutches. He was excited. He would soon get to see Anna again. He had watched the time all day and swore that there was something wrong with his watch. But finally, the golden hour had arrived. He looked back over the counter. "Remember to watch the counter, Mitch."

"I'm almost finished here!" yelled Mitch impatiently.

Jason hobbled and swung on his crutches out of the arcade. With the evening air cooling down, Jason fastened the top button of his shirt. He turned and made his way to the ocean. When he reached the boardwalk, he took a long moment to study the last die-hard sunbathers. Then, he hobbled down the long wooden stairs and ducked underneath, following the many narrow slats of light over to an old burnt-out log in the cool sand. In the safety of that spot, he happily and excitedly waited for Anna.

• • •

"Come in, come in," Nunzio's mother said, motioning son and Anna to come into the house. Anna couldn't notice the dining room table was set for four.

"Poppa's gonna be late," his mother Tina explained. "He got some business."

No sooner had they sat down than Nunzio picked up the salad tongs and began serving himself. Anna meanwhile sat quietly.

"So, Anna, how's it going?" his mother asked.

"Not bad, thanks for asking," Anna said. She felt that Tina always seemed to stare at her critically, no doubt sizing her up as marriage material, a future daughter-in-law. It turned Anna's stomach.

"Not bad?" Nunzio, between bites of food, interrupted. "That's not what I hear. From what I hear, it's going good. Real good."

Anna shot him a look of concern. She wasn't sure what he was getting at.

"Seeing all of your friends," he continued. "All of your new friends."

Anna eyed him critically. Nunzio unexpectedly put his hand on her knee. Shocked by this, Anna pushed his hand away as gently as she could without his mother noticing. Nunzio stubbornly put his hand there again.

This time, he began slapping her knee slowly and repeatedly while he deliberately said, "Yeah, all…of…Anna's…new…friends."

"Nunzio. Please. Stop," she whispered, this time pushing his hand away a little more forcefully. Then she turned to Nunzio's mother and with a forced smile said, "Your son has got quite the imagination."

• • •

While he waited for Anna to show up, Jason took out his transistor radio and turned it on. At that very moment, WINS radio station was playing that week's Top Forty Hits. Jason would normally have found it entertaining. However, at that moment, his mind was elsewhere. He checked his watch one more time. *What in the world is keeping her?*

To make matters worse, with the sun quickly setting, Jason was getting cold and an annoying sand flea had crawled up his leg and under his cast. He tried scratching here and then there with no relief.

When Jason checked his watch a third time, he realized he'd been waiting twenty minutes. Fumbling with his cast and crutches, Jason managed to get back to his feet. He couldn't decide how much longer he should wait. When he looked at his watch ten minutes later, there was still no sign of her. He couldn't fathom what might be holding her up. As the evening light faded, Jason took one last look at the ocean and shook his head. Dismayed, he began his long slow trek back up the stairs of the boardwalk. He didn't feel like going back to the arcade so he simply went straight to his grandparents' apartment.

• • •

The following morning, Nunzio had to take care of some business back in Coney Island again and thought that while he was there, he'd check in on Anna. Last night's dinner was stilted and he wasn't happy with her. He expected a problem finding parking near Anna's grandmother's house because it was a perfect beach day but he got lucky. He found a perfect parking spot on her grandmother's tree-lined street just a little way up from the house. After backing into the spot, he turned off the ignition. Then, he settled back into the driver's seat and tapped a Kool cigarette from the pack. He lit it and waited, keeping his eyes peeled on her nonna's front door.

Fifteen minutes later, Anna appeared. After locking the door, she turned and headed toward the beach. Nunzio snubbed out his cigarette, got out, and, keeping a safe distance, followed her on foot. For the first little while, he had no problem, that is, until she picked up her pace. Then, no matter how quickly he walked, he couldn't keep up with her. And it got worse once she started running. Granted, Nunzio was an athlete, but he was overdressed for this much exercise in the direct sun. By the time Anna got to the arcade, Nunzio was sweating and simply out of breath, huffing and puffing.

When Anna ducked into the arcade, Nunzio finally hid behind a truck parked only twenty feet away. From that vantage point, he could plainly see anyone coming or going. Nunzio pulled out another cigarette and waited.

• • •

When Anna entered the arcade, Jason was stacking coins into neat little columns and any customers who'd been playing were in the process of leaving. He did a double take and then took one last look down at what he was doing.

She waited until she was sure no one would overhear. "I'm sorry about last night," she said.

Jason remained quiet. He thoughtfully began to play with the coins.

"I owe you an apology."

"Well, I suppose." He shrugged. After a moment, he said, "So, what happened to you?" He didn't know how to look at her.

"I'm embarrassed to say this. But every Wednesday night, Nunzio and I usually go to his parents for dinner. I completely spaced it out."

"Wow," Jason said, not knowing what else to say.

"Nunzio showed up just as I was about to leave and he insisted that I go with him."

Jason seemed not to know how to respond. Anna was afraid that perhaps he was very angry. Or hurt.

"I'm sorry I stood you up."

Jason took her hand. "Well, I guess we'll have to arrange a rain date."

Anna chuckled. "That's very sweet."

Jason finally smiled. "I mean it."

"Oh, before I forget. Laura agreed to go out with Mitch."

"Really?" Jason brightened up. "That's amazing!"

Anna looked around. "Where is he now?"

"He'll be in at 2:00. You have no idea how happy he'll be."

"I can only imagine."

She relaxed as she watched Jason continue to brighten up and take a quick look around the arcade. She looked around as well. There was no one there amidst the singing, dinging machines.

"Listen. I've got an idea," Jason said.

"What kind of idea?"

"Let's take some photos."

"Photos?" Anna answered nervously. "You want to take photos of me?"

"No, no, no. The two of us."

"The two of us?" She felt herself grin.

"Yeah. C'mon"

Jason grabbed Anna's hand and led her over to the photo booth. He pulled back the curtains. "We gotta do this quickly. So, c'mon in." Anna noticed there was barely enough room in the photo booth for one person, never mind two. Jason quickly took a seat on the small adjustable stool. Then, patting his lap, he motioned for her to join him.

Her heart skipped a beat. She stared at his lap, then down at his leg in the cast and how it stuck out the door. She smiled and carefully stepped over his leg. As she entered, she was thrilled when he placed his hands on her hips and gently guided her down onto his lap.

She watched as Jason reached into his pocket and pulled out some change. One-by-one, he plopped four quarters into the slot. *Plop. plop. plop. plop.* "Okay, here goes. We get four photos."

Anna nodded.

"Let's make each of them different."

"Uh, okay," she smiled warily.

"You ready?"

Anna nodded nervously. Just before Jason pressed the green button, he said, "For the first one, let's do happy."

Anna looked quizzically back at Jason. He was already flashing a big plastic smile. So, she too turned to the camera and mimicked him just as the light flashed.

"Okay. Now, a serious one," he directed her. Both of them dropped their smiles and took on grim faces just as the light flashed again.

"Let's put our heads together," Jason advised, "For this one." Anna gave him a quizzical look. A moment later, each of them instinctively tilted their head toward the other and the third light flashed. When neither of them suggested a final pose, Anna simply leaned over and planted a kiss on his cheek seconds before the last light flashed.

He giggled. "Okay," Jason said, "Let's see how they turned out."

Given how tiny the photo booth was, getting out of the booth was more complicated—between rearranging their clothes, standing up together, Jason grabbing his crutches and Anna picking up her bag. Jason took a quick look out before they exited the booth. Only when he was sure there were no new customers, he motioned for Anna to join him.

For what seemed like an eternity, Anna and Jason waited for their finished photos to appear. Then, in what seemed like an underwhelming climax, the booth simply spat out the strip of four photos. Holding them by the edges, Jason removed them from the slot and held them up for both to see. He laughed.

A smile came over Anna's face. "I like this one," she said, pointing to the first one.

"How about that one?" Jason asked, pointing to the last one.

Anna giggled.

For several moments, they both stood basking in the moment. Jason suddenly turned to her. "Okay. Let's make a pact."

"A pact? What kind of pact?"

"You take the first two and I'll take the other two. Twenty years from now, we'll reattach them."

"Hmm, interesting."

Jason quickly folded the strip of photos in half and tore it in two. He handed Anna a strip with the first two photos and slipped the other strip into his shirt pocket. Then, he extended his right hand and mockingly shook Anna's hand.

"You've got a deal," Anna said.
"A deal, it is."
Anna looked at her watch and frowned, "Oh, sorry. I gotta go. My nonna's expecting me."
"Okay. And I should get back to work." His eyes danced as he smiled at her. Finally, they gave each other a brief hug.
"See 'ya," Anna said.
"Yeah," said Jason, "See 'ya."

• • •

Nunzio was still hiding behind the truck when Anna exited the arcade. He noticed that she was smiling and looking down at something in her hand. In disgust, Nunzio snubbed out his cigarette on the side of the truck and scowled before turning around and making his long, arduous walk back to the car.

CHAPTER 14

*"And the most important thing of all
It makes a boy and girl, oh
Say they feel so fine, now (feel so fine)"*

Love Makes the World Go 'Round
Deon Jackson

"You are one lucky guy," Jason shouted as he entered the arcade the next morning.

Mitch had been on his knees stacking the shelves under the counter with various candies. At first, he had no idea where the voice was coming from. When he raised his head, his cousin was standing there. "Lucky guy? What do you mean?"

"Where you gonna take her?" Jason demanded happily.

Mitch knew right away Jason was having fun drawing out the suspense.

"Who?" Then, the light suddenly went on in Mitch's head and his pulse quickened.

"Do you mean …?" Mitch asked nervously. "Did she …?"

Jason gave him a nod.

"Did she actually say yes?"

"Yup," Jason said, smiling broadly.

Mitch began dancing ecstatically around the arcade. "She said yes? Really!?"

Jason continued nodding his head. Then, he pointed his finger at him and said, "Now, don't blow it."

Weak-kneed and hands quivering, Mitch bounded over to Jason and gave him a big bear hug.

"So … What do I owe you for the tickets?" Jason asked.

"Oh, we'll figure it out." Mitch waved at him happily. "I'll bring them in tomorrow. I like her. She's worth it." He shook his head in disbelief and then grinned, staring into nothing. He could hear his heart beating hard.

"Well, then, it's a win-win."

Mitch shook himself out of his reverie and continued cleaning up behind the counter. "Say, did you hear there's going to be fireworks at the boardwalk tonight?"

"Really? What's the occasion?"

"Beats me. The local retailers are putting it on. Wish I could go," Mitch frowned.

"Why don't you go?" Jason asked.

"My parents. They organized something."

"Too bad."

Mitch looked up at him. "You and Anna should try and catch them."

"I don't know." Jason looked at his watch. "It's kind of short notice."

Mitch grinned and shrugged. "Too bad, so sad."

Jason motioned to throw something at him and Mitch ducked. They both laughed heartily and felt as if they had the world in their hands.

• • •

Jason had no idea what he was going to do when his shift ended. His only thought was that he needed to get out into the fresh air and the boardwalk was calling to him. As he approached, a gentle breeze was blowing in off the ocean. Jason had no idea how busy the boardwalk would be. Even at that early hour, people were milling about; young parents pushing strollers, couples walking their dogs, and children darting playfully in and out of the crowd. With his clunky crutches and cast, Jason found it particularly challenging getting through the crowd. He must've said, "Sorry" fifty times as he jostled along. As careful as he tried to be, he still ended up tripping over the wheels of a baby stroller and then later got his legs tangled up in the leash of a large German shepherd.

It didn't take long for Jason to wear himself out. So, the first chance he got, he made his way over to the railing to take a breather. Moments later, he was surprised to see Anna standing not thirty yards away from him talking to another girl. Stacy was a fellow student who had sat beside Jason that year in their Social Studies class. Stacy and Anna seemed to be deep in conversation. Jason waddled a little closer and was beginning to hear what they were saying.

"So, this coming semester," Stacy said happily, "I'm going to study in France."

"Wow. Lucky you, Stacy."

"Yeah, I can't wait." Stacy looked up as Jason approached and casually waved. Then, she turned to go. "Well, let's keep in touch, okay?"

Before answering, Anna turned to see who Stacy was waving at and realized Jason was there. She smiled. "Hey, Jason." She leaned over to whisper something into Stacy's ear and then motioned for her to walk toward Jason.

"Hey," said Jason, happy to see some familiar faces.

"Hi, Jason," Anna and Stacy said in unison. They giggled at that.

Jason couldn't take his eyes off of Anna. "You look nice."

Anna blushed and cast her eyes downward. She searched for something to say.

"Going to stay for the fireworks?" Jason asked.

"I'd like to," said Anna.

"It'd be great to catch them with both of you."

Stacy frowned and looked at her watch. "I wish I could. But my mom's expecting me."

"Aw, that's too bad," Anna said.

There was a long pause.

"You don't mind if I stay, do you?" Anna asked, looking over to Stacy.

"No problem. You guys have fun," Stacy said with a coy smile. "Wish I could join you. But I gotta go."

"Oh, okay," Anna said. "Well . . . See ya."

She and Jason watched as Stacy disappeared into the crowd. When Jason finally turned to look back at Anna, she was smiling up at him. "So."

"Looks like everyone's here for fireworks." She looked around at the growing crowd and Jason followed suit.

"Looks like the world's come out to watch them." Jason turned and looked at her. "I was hoping you were around. Want to watch them together?"

"I'd love it," she smiled.

Jason looked around to see if there was space enough for them to watch comfortably. "Where should we watch it?"

"Good question," Anna said.

When they both looked out over the crowd, there didn't seem to be any available space.

Anna suddenly took the initiative. "Follow me."

"Sure thing," Jason said, shaking his head as he realized that his last comment likely sounded a little too eager. But he was exactly that. Very eager. Jason was elated to find himself with her again so soon. He followed Anna dutifully as she guided him over to the wide wooden stairs which led down to the beach and, forgetting that Jason had to use his crutches, she bounded down the stairs, only looking back when she'd reached the bottom. Anna blushed in embarrassment when she saw Jason gingerly descending the stairs one slow step at a time. "Oops. I'm sorry," she yelled, giggling.

"No problem."

Jason finally reached the bottom worn wooden step and took the first few steps when Anna stopped and, seeing some open space near the water, she pointed to a nearby jetty. "Why don't we sit there?"

"Good idea."

With the sun setting and the sand cooling down, Anna led the way. As they neared, she raced over and plopped herself down on a spot.

Jason giggled at her spunk. Stymied by his cast and crutches, he followed slowly behind her. Dragging his left leg through the sand, he left a furrow behind him. With each step he took, his cast dug deeper and deeper into the sand. At some point, Jason failed to see a rock buried beneath the sand and, as his cast banged against it, he went tumbling face first.

Anna gasped loudly and then couldn't help but stifle a laugh at the hilarious sight. She quickly bolted over to him. Then, she bent down and grabbed his crutches to move them off to the side.

Jason dizzily lifted his head and Anna laughed as she watched him spit out bits of sand.

With great effort, she bent over and helped him get back to his feet. Then, she retrieved his crutches and carefully guided him over to the spot. There, Jason gently lowered himself down on the empty patch of sand. For several minutes, they sat there not saying a word, preferring instead to gaze out at the ocean. The waves were now gently lapping not very far from their feet. With the sun setting and reflecting in the water, it was all awesome and brilliant.

After taking in the mesmerizing sight, Anna eventually spoke up. "Lovely, isn't it?"

"It sure is." When Jason looked at her, she was flicking a windswept lock of her hair from her eyes. *I must be the luckiest guy on earth.* Then, he readjusted his posture and cleared his throat. "So, how are you able to come to the beach so often? I don't see Nunzio anywhere. I mean, don't get me wrong. I love seeing you." He looked around to see if Nunzio was hanging close by. "Queens is a long way from here."

"Well, my nonna lives nearby. I'm staying with her this summer."

"Oh, wow. I didn't realize. That's why. Where does she live?"

"On 16th Street."

"Geez. Close to my grandparents on 18th."

She nodded. "Yup." She looked down and played with the sand around her feet.

For a while, Jason mulled over the dinner he had at her parents' place the other night. Jason suddenly recalled a moment from his youth. He turned to Anna and said, "You know, I remember you from way back. When I was eleven years old, I had this stick that I'd whittled into a point and was dragging it along those black wrought iron fences on the street you live on. I looked up at one point and saw three girls dressed in Sunday clothes. That was you and your sisters. I guess you'd just got back from church. You guys were giggling and playing in the front yard. A man, I'm guessing your dad," he giggled, grinning. "He was standing watering the garden. His hair was greased back and he wore a lime green golf shirt and matching shorts. He yelled at me."

"No way," Anna giggled.

"Yup," he laughed. "He shouted, 'Donna you touch da fence. Keepa dat sticka to yourself'!"

Anna laughed and squinted. "That's my dad alright." She wrapped her arms around her legs and rested her little chin on her knees.

Jason nodded and grinned. "Yup. That must've been your dad. He scared the shit out of me. I dropped the stick and ran away."

They both laughed.

He looked over at Anna's beautiful tanned face. "To this day, I can still see you in your Sunday best playing in your front yard."

"Really?"

"Really. I never forgot you."

Anna smiled sweetly and reached over and placed her hand on his. He looked down. His heart skipped a beat. Afraid of being too forward, Jason, in the darkening light, lifted his thumb to lightly caress the top of her hand. He studied her hand until she withdrew it to pull some hair out of the corner of her mouth.

Jason smiled and kicked off his sandals. He dug his heels into the cool sand and moaned with delight. Then, after sitting silently for a minute, he took his transistor radio out of his pocket and turned it on. "Let's listen to some music," he said, fine-tuning it to his favorite station.

Several bystanders looked over as the gravelly-voiced Wolfman Jack loudly announced, "Hey kids. This next song's going out to all you cats and kitties hanging out at the beach tonight. Dig this. The Lovin' Spoonful with *Summer in the City*."

Jason and Anna glanced at each other and grinned.

> *"Hot town, summer in the city*
> *Back of my neck getting dirty and gritty*
> *Been down, isn't it a pity*
> *Doesn't seem to be a shadow in the city . . ."*

When the song was over, Jason turned to Anna. "You free this Friday night?"

"Why? What do you have in mind?" she grinned, her eyes twinkling at him.

"I've got a surprise for you."

Anna's eyes widened. "A surprise?"

"Yeah," he grinned.

"What is it?"

"Guess?"

She pushed his shoulder. "Tell me!"

"Well," Jason smiled, noticing the light fading on her face. "I got tickets to see Simon and Garfunkel."

She sat up and slapped his shoulder. "No way!"

He giggled and leaned away for a moment. He was happy he could surprise her with the news.

"You didn't!" Anna exclaimed, barely able to contain herself. "Oh, my goodness." She covered her mouth and shivered with delight.

Suddenly, light warmed her face. Jason turned to look back toward the ocean and saw the darkened sky light up with fireworks. The explosions almost immediately shook the beach, the ground below them vibrating under the sand.

"Ah!" the crowd collectively sighed. For the next ten minutes, the sky erupted in a series of dazzling bursts of color. Reds and silvers, and blues. A celebration of light. Jason and Anna sat transfixed by the brilliant spectacle which unfolded over the ocean. She inched her bum closer to his. He put his arm around her and the fireworks seemed to never end. Consumed by the moment, Jason slowly turned to look to his left and then to his right.

Then, he leaned over to Anna and whispered into her ears. "I've never experienced a more perfect moment."

CHAPTER 15

"Slow down, you move too fast
You got to make the morning last
Just kicking down the cobblestones
Looking for fun and feeling groovy ... "

49th Street Bridge Song
Simon and Garfunkel

Friday night couldn't come soon enough. As soon as his shift ended, Jason hurried back to the apartment, almost tripping over his crutches. He quickly washed up and changed into his clothes, putting on his favorite plaid cowboy shirt and snapping up all of its snazzy mother-of-pearl buttons.

Jason, however, found it especially difficult getting into his grey bell bottom pants. Pulling them up and over his cast was no easy task. Also, in his excitement to leave the apartment, he thought he'd lost the concert tickets or left them behind at the arcade. He panicked, until finally he remembered that he'd put them in his jacket pocket.

Rather than picking Anna up at her nonna's house, she and Jason agreed that they'd save time if they met instead on the subway platform. Not the most romantic of meeting places, but it was efficient and easier on him.

"There you are," Anna said warmly as he finally reached her side out of breath.

Jason had just climbed the train station's four flights of stairs. Not easy with crutches and a cast. "Whew. Remind me not to do that again in a cast," Jason said while giving her a hug. "You ready for this?"

"Absolutely." Anna beamed from ear to ear.

An unexpected gust of air ahead of the subway train suddenly swept through the station causing her to squeal in surprise as her dress blew up over her face. Anna had decided to wear a full skirted pale green knit dress and a matching scarf. Jason thought she looked stunning and she noticed him stealing a glance at her underskirt before she was able to flatten the material down again.

"What?" she asked defensively. "What are you looking at?"

"You. You look beautiful."

"Oh my gosh. Thanks." She blushed just as they heard the roar of the oncoming train. And when, a minute later, the clackety train pulled into the station, another gust of wind swept past them, playing havoc with Anna's hair. Jason laughed as she squealed and then very carefully followed her over to the slowing subway car.

"Here you go," said Anna, graciously holding the doors open. Her biggest fear was that, with Jason having to use a cast and crutches, the subway doors would suddenly close and he'd be left standing on the platform. Jason safely hobbled a few steps onboard and, before the train unexpectedly lurched, Anna quickly grabbed the leather strap overhead and waited until Jason had taken his seat. Then, she snuggled next to him on the subway's unforgiving laminated thatched straw bench.

After stowing his crutches to the side, he reached for Anna's hand and she gave his hand a momentary squeeze in return. For the next little while, they sat together in silence and watched as station after station passed by their window. Several stops later, a homeless man boarded the train and took a seat just two rows in front of them. Jason and Anna quickly glanced at each other as if to acknowledge his odd, shabby appearance.

She leaned into Jason. She covered her mouth and spoke in a loud whisper, "I wonder if that guy's eaten anything today?"

Jason looked first at her, then at the homeless man and shrugged his shoulders. He reached over and caressed her hair for a moment. He leaned in to her and whispered loudly, "You have a very big heart."

He looked over at the man again and took a moment to study him. Wrapped in a long ratty blanket and wearing a grubby moth-eaten sweater, soiled baggy pants and fingerless gloves, the man looked like a longtime resident of the streets. Jason grinned. Then, he turned to Anna and whispered, "My zayde looks like that first thing in the morning."

Anna giggled and gave Jason a playful jab in the ribs.

Before long, their train hissed into the busy 42nd Street station. When the doors opened, Jason and Anna sat contently in their seats. They watched as people rushed about here and there, some exiting, others boarding, many running to meet trains on other platforms. At one point, Jason took the opportunity to stretch in his seat as he continued studying his surroundings. He spotted a newspaper stand not thirty feet away on the platform festooned with the day's newspapers and magazines. Boxes of various candies were stocked on shelves. And on both sides of the stand, several plastic buckets held bouquets of fresh flowers.

As Jason studied the scene, he wondered aloud, "How can a business like that possibly survive down here when it has to rely only on the people just getting on and off the trains?" Anna simply shrugged.

With that same curiosity, Jason studied the people clustered around the newsstand. He leaned over to her. "Who are they? Where do they come from?"

She looked over to where he was looking and shrugged.

An older, dapper gentleman wearing a dark blue suit, a white shirt, and a tie suddenly caught Jason's attention. There was something frightfully familiar about him. Jason was struck by the sight of a younger woman nestled in the older man's arms. The gentleman turned to the woman and puffed up his chest. Jason couldn't take his eyes off the couple. Then, he suddenly bolted forward in his seat.

"What the —?"

Anna looked over at him and then again followed his eyes. "What? What is it?"

Jason remained silent. Instead, he studied the couple more closely. "Could that be . . .? Is that my . . .?" Jason was confused and his mind searched for answers. But the subway doors shut and the train slowly began to move out of the station. Jason's eyes were still fixed on the couple as the train gathered speed. He strained his head to look back until they were out of sight. Then, he turned to Anna saying, "I think I just saw my zayde."

"Really? Your zayde? Where?"

With the train now at full speed, Jason could only point futilely behind him. He was haunted by the image of someone who may very well have been his grandfather with a younger woman in his arms. At this point, Jason could do nothing but sit silently and be rocked by the movement of the train for the rest of their journey. After a while, the hypnotic clickety-clack of the train gradually lulled him back into the present. All the while, Anna sat patiently beside him.

After some time had passed, she leaned in closer to him and gently tugged on his sleeve. "Are you okay?" she asked.

All that Jason could say was, "Man, that was weird."

At every stop, more and more apparent concertgoers boarded the train. So that by the time they pulled into Forest Hills station, their subway car was packed. And when the doors opened, everyone excitedly jostled off the train. Jason grabbed his crutches and rose from his seat. With Anna by his side, he exited the train, hobbling slowly along the platform and struggling up the stairs.

The gentle late summer breeze refreshed Jason as they escaped the subway out into the summer night. The surrounding happy milling crowd and the sight of Anna's excitement made him finally look forward to the concert once again.

• • •

Though the stadium was quickly filling with concertgoers, Anna and Jason found their seats quite quickly. They were only nineteen rows up from the stage. As they sat there expectantly, Jason marveled at how quickly the production crew had transformed the space from what was primarily a tennis stadium into a concert hall.

"Did you know they play the U.S. Open here?"

"Sure did," Anna said. "One day, I'd like to see Billie Jean King play here."

They looked around and took in the sights. A crew had constructed a large rectangular stage where center court normally stood. A mountain range of amplifiers, microphone stands, and guitars dotted the stage. Jason sat with his mouth agape as he took in the number of acoustic and electric guitars which were lined up in a row. Each was propped on their own stand and miles of electrical cords snaked out from the mixing board.

"I am so excited." Anna beamed.

"That makes two of us." Jason was in his element. He leaned toward Anna. "I feel so at home when I go to a concert of one of my favorite groups or performers. When I hear a particular group or solo artist is coming to town to perform, I make sure I'm standing in line the day tickets go on sale. And I've seen some great concerts. I got to see Ray Charles and Dr. John, the Steve Miller Band, and many more."

Anna rubbed her hands and grinned. "That's wonderful."

"And that's not all. I follow any kind of news I can about them. You know, their exploits, their lives, the loves of each singer, each band and its members. I devour the Village Voice, Rolling Stone and a bunch of other magazines." He was just about to go on and share a memory of going to a Mad Dogs and Englishmen concert at the Filmore East when the lights suddenly dimmed and an expectant hush came over the audience.

Jason and Anna turned to each other and smiled in eager anticipation. In the darkness, Jason could see the outline of four musicians walking onstage. Knowing popular music as well as he did, he immediately recognizing the girth of Cass Elliott, one of the group's storied singers. Jason leaned over to Anna and whispered, "Oh my god, it's the Mamas and the Papas."

Anna's jaw dropped. Neither she nor Jason had known that the currently hot California group would be the opening act for the top-billed Simon and Garfunkel. Moments later, the lights came on and the group's ebullient leader John Phillips yelled out, "Good evening, New York City!" The expectant crowd gave them a warm, enthusiastic reception.

Then, the group launched into their current hit, California Dreamin'. The Mamas and Papas followed that with a long string of their hits; Words of Love, Monday, Monday, I Saw Her Again and many more. Anna and Jason couldn't resist singing along to all of them. Both of them found the group's four-part harmonies infectious and their playful banter onstage delightful. After an extended, inspired set, the lights came up.

During the intermission, Anna and Jason opted to stay put and sit quietly in their seats, basking in the afterglow. They watched wide-eyed as the production crew reset the stage for the next act.

To Jason's surprise, Anna suddenly began mimicking Cass's spirited vocal style, quietly singing the first verse of the Mamas and Papas', Go Where You Wanna Go, in his ear. He smiled, grateful that he was being treated to his own private mini-concert. They laughed and giggled and at one point, he stretched his arm over her shoulders and squeezed her. She rested her palm on his chest. His heart fluttered. At one point, he was close to tears.

When the house lights dimmed again, Simon and Garfunkel walked onstage. Anna and Jason turned to each other once again, their eyes wide with anticipation. She reached for Jason's other hand and squeezed it affectionately.

Simon and Garfunkel did not disappoint. For over an hour, they treated the audience to all of their current hits; Homeward Bound, I Am a Rock, and of course, their current chart-topper, Sound of Silence. Anna and Jason sat spellbound, awed by the duo's intricately woven harmonies. Despite them performing for over an hour, Anna and Jason weren't prepared for the concert to end. The two groups had amazingly played for almost three hours and it all went by in a flash.

When the lights came up all too soon, Anna and Jason remained in their seats. Rather than get up and jostle with the crowd, they sat transfixed and transported and watched the rest of the audience make its way to the exits. They deliberately resisted the urge to make idle chatter, electing instead to let their many memorable moments of the concert wash over them. Only when a handful of people still remained, Jason leaned over and suggested, "I guess we should probably go." As they rose out of their seats, Anna clutched Jason's arm and whispered, "I can't think of a more perfect evening. Thank you, Jason." She stretched up and kissed him on the cheek.

Jason felt his heart soften.

In the magical hush of that summer evening, they walked back to the subway station. Not until their train had pulled out the station and Jason had taken his seat did he elaborate.

"What an amazing evening." He thought for a moment. "Paul Simon is one amazing writer."

"He sure is," Anna said. "and I love Garfunkel's sweet tenor voice. It's like listening to an angel soaring in the heavens."

They spent much of their journey in contented silence. Several times, one of them would start, trying to describe the evening, to faithfully convey their feelings about the concert. But the words escaped them and it wasn't until they were finally standing on the front porch of Anna's nonna's house that Jason felt like talking again. There, in the glow of the overhead light, Jason leaned in and quietly said, "Thank you."

"And thank you, Jason."

"May I kiss you?"

Anna nodded her head shyly. Jason slowly bent over and planted a warm delicate kiss on her lips. Then, he drew his head back. "Sweet dreams, Anna."

She watched him hobble off into the night.

CHAPTER 16

*"Sugar and spice and all things nice,
Kisses sweeter than wine.
Sugar and spice and all things nice,
You know that little girl is mine."*

Sugar and Spice
The Searchers

The following morning, Jason almost bounded down the street. He was still riding the high he felt, savoring his evening with Anna. How he got to sit beside her, hold her hand, laugh with her and, of course, share last night's fantastic live music with her. When Jason walked into the arcade, Mitch, who'd been polishing the glass tops of the skeeball machines, looked up.

"So?" he asked, "How did it go?"

"What?"

"What? . . . C'mon. How was it? Did you kiss her? I want to hear everything."

Jason blushed. He needed a moment to compose himself. Finally, he gushed, "It was fantastic. She was beautiful, the music was unbelievable, and you'll never guess who opened the show."

"Who?"

Jason wanted to milk it for all it was worth so he took a moment before he answered. "Would you believe the Mamas and the Papas?"

"No way!" Mitch simultaneously dropped his rag and his jaw. Then, he simply shook his head and turned to his younger cousin, saying, "You are one royal turd."

Jason laughed. Then, he remembered their deal. "So, have you contacted Laura?"

"You betcha," Mitch glowed. "We're going to see each other this weekend."

"Cool," Jason said. Then, he added, "No need to thank me now."

Both of them laughed.

Jason rode on a cloud that whole morning, replaying last night's concert and the wonderful time he'd shared with Anna over and over in his head. But then, as the day wore on, something started to bother him. The memory of what he saw on the subway platform came back. *Was that really Zayde? And if it was, who was that young lady?*

At 11:30 am, Jason looked at his watch. Then, he turned to his cousin and asked, "Where do you think Zayde is?"

Mitch simply shrugged. It was very unlike their grandfather to not show up for work.

After a couple of hours, Jason turned to his cousin and asked, "Do you think he's okay? Did he have an appointment or something today?"

Mitch simply shrugged. All sorts of questions raced through Jason's mind.

• • •

Just after 1:00 p.m., the phone rang at the Steiner house. Jason's mom was vacuuming the master bedroom at the time. She ran to the phone to answer it. "Hello."

"Sara?" It was Bubbie. Her daughter could hear the nervousness in her voice.

"Mom. What's up?"

"Zadye's back in de hospital."

"The hospital?" Sara asked with some trepidation, "What's wrong?" while she fiddled with the phone cord, wrapping it first around her index finger, then unwrapping it.

"He fainted. Again," Bubbie reported. "Dey say a voman found him. Tank got. She called an ambulance."

"Really?"

"An angel, she vas. Didn't even leaf her name."

"Is that right?"

"Dey vant he should take more tests."

"That's good, Mom."

Bubbie suddenly got unusually silent. After a minute, she said, "I'm vorried."

"Don't be, mom. Listen, I'm leaving now. I'll be there in half an hour."

As soon as Sara hung up the phone, she dialed the arcade phone number and waited. After ringing three times, someone finally picked it up. "Is that you Mitch?" Sara could hear the unmistakable pings and bells of the arcade in the background.

"Hi, Aunt Sara. Yeah, it's me."

"Can you put Jason on?"

Sara listened to the background noise while waiting, her heart beating hard. Finally, Jason got on the phone. She said, "Your zayde's back in the hospital."

"Oh, no. What is it this time?" Jason clutched the phone.

When Mitch heard the worry in his cousin's voice, he began pacing back and forth. "What's going on?" he mouthed to Jason. His cousin raised his finger, signaling for Mitch to wait a moment.

"Oh my god," he said, "he fainted?"

Mitch stood in front of him, wide-eyed. He leaned in to listen to both ends of the conversation.

"Should we go see him?"

"Jason, you need to stay there," his mother answered. "Your zayde would want that." Her voice was loud enough for both to hear.

"Aw, Mom."

"Don't worry. It's probably nothing. I'll call you when I learn something more."

"Uh, okay." Jason hung up the phone and looked at Mitch, who was staring at him intently.

"So?" Mitch asked.

"All I know is that Zayde fainted and that he's now in the hospital," Jason said.

"We should go there, right?" Mitch said.

"I know … But my mom said we should sit tight. She said she'll let us know."

For the rest of the afternoon, the two cousins waited anxiously, periodically looking over at each other. Each of them had a nervous look on their face.

Several minutes later, Jason sighed. He, at least, found some solace remembering the cherished moments he had had with Anna the night before.

• • •

Being a good cousin, Mitch took the shift the following morning while Jason and his mom visited their zayde in the hospital.

When they entered his room, Jason first noticed that Zayde was lying in bed, gazing distractedly out the window. There was an IV machine by his bedside, a dense thicket of tubes protruding from it. Jason couldn't help but notice a bulge underneath the sheets at the foot of his bed. Bubbie was pacing nervously back and forth in the room. The tension in the room was palpable.

As they entered the room, Sara, in her most positive tone, said, "Hey, Mom. Hey, Dad." Looking weak and frail, Zayde said, "Come in, come in."

While Sara approached and kissed her father's forehead, Jason kept his distance.

"So, Dad, how's it going?" she asked.

"Fine."

Sara turned to her mom. "So, what did they say?"

"De doctors come. They look at de charts. Den, they go."

"Don't vorry, my meidelah," Zayde interrupted.

"I'm not worried, Dad," Sara shot back as she looked around the room. "I'm going to find a doctor. I'll be right back."

As soon as she stepped out into the hallway, Zayde turned weakly to his grandson. "So nu? Who's looking after de arcade?"

"Mitch."

"Oy vey." Zayde muttered, giving his head a slight shake.

Jason suddenly felt weak and felt like he needed to sit down. When he looked around the room, he saw that his Lil' Grandma was occupying the only chair in the room. The only other available spot, Jason realized, was on the bed. So, he hobbled over to the bed and lowered himself onto the rumpled hospital sheets.

"Ow!" Zayde howled, recoiling away from Jason. "Oy, boy-chik. Be careful."

Jason wasn't sure what he'd just done. But he lifted himself off the bed as quickly as he could.

They could faintly hear his mother in the hallway. She had buttonholed the doctor outside of Zayde's room and the doctor led her back in. He nodded at Jason and looked back at Sara.

"So, what happened?" asked Sara.

"Apparently, he passed out on the street. Luckily, some woman found him and called an ambulance."

Sara shuffled from one foot to the other, twirling her hair in small loops around her forefinger. "So, what's his condition?"

The doctor lowered his voice and led her into a corner. Jason hobbled closer. "Your father's not well. He likely has an advanced form of diabetes."

"Oh," Sara said apprehensively.

Jason's mind raced through a whole host of possible complications.

The doctor looked down at his clipboard. "We'd like to do some more tests."

"And then what?"

"We'll know better when the results come back."

Jason watched as Sara nodded pensively and nervously turned to look at her father, who was now resting with his eyes closed.

• • •

With Bubbie insisting on staying with her husband around the clock, Sara quickly realized that her mother was exhausted. Several times, she offered to drive her home. But, her mother refused, electing instead to stay day and night by her husband's bedside. So, Sara and Jason reluctantly said their goodbyes.

They took the elevator down to the first floor and walked out to the car. Jason slipped into the passenger seat. He sat quietly gazing out of his window while his mother drove. Both reflected on Zayde's life, the recent turn of events and how quickly he'd be back on his feet.

After twenty minutes, Jason turned to his mother and said, "Tell me more about Zayde."

Sara, who no doubt had been consumed by her own web of hopes and fears, was roused by her son's request. "What do you want to know?"

"Where did he come from? And how did he get here?"

Sara let the questions percolate in her head. Then, she took a deep breath. "Well, the little I know is, Zayde was the oldest of seven children. His family was from a little village outside of Warsaw. What we Jews call a shtetl."

"A shtetl?"

"Yeah, a ghetto, a district. Because his family was poor and he was the oldest, he had to go to work when he was very young. So, he started working in a factory when he was only fourteen."

Jason thought about that as he studied the cars around them. "That must be where he learned to fix stuff."

A light summer rain had begun to fall. Sara eased off the gas pedal and turned the windshield wipers on. "When he was nineteen, he and his youngest brother tried to emigrate to the United States. But they weren't let in. They had to go elsewhere. They instead went to Argentina."

"Argentina? Wow. That's quite a distance."

"Sure is," Sara said, "and to make money, Zayde supposedly sold water on the streets of Buenos Aires."

"Really? That's bizarre."

"Two years later, the U.S. agreed to let them in."

The rain was now falling more heavily. With his window open, Jason had started to get wet. He adjusted his position and rolled the window up.

"Those first years, your zayde took a lot of odd jobs. He was able to make some money and, somehow, he saved some money. After six years, he was able to make a down payment on the penny arcade."

"Cool. So, how'd he and Bubbie get together?"

"Well, as you know, Zayde's brother Aron and Bubbie were childhood sweethearts. Shortly after Aron came over, he got drafted into the U.S Army and was killed in the First World War. As the eldest brother, your zayde felt responsible to look after Bubbie. So, he took her in. Two years later, they were married."

For the remainder of their drive home, Jason pondered the many fascinating twists and turns in his grandfather's life.

• • •

With their zayde in the hospital, Jason and Mitch were forced to pick up extra shifts. So, Jason was now working a fifty-hour week. By the end of that first week, he was exhausted. He needed a break and was looking for some way to reward himself. So, he asked Anna out to dinner. He wanted to take her to a nice restaurant, but didn't have a clue where to take her. So reluctantly, Jason called his mother for advice. With no hesitation, Sara suggested, "Take her to Catalina's. The food's good and it's reasonable."

"Yeah, but it's Italian. She eats Italian all the time."

"Trust me. She'll love it."

• • •

That Friday evening, Jason made extra sure he was presentable, wearing a freshly laundered light blue Oxford shirt and dark grey pants. And just for good measure, he actually ironed them himself. They turned out better than they were so he felt quite proud of himself.

When he and Anna finally arrived at Catalina's Restaurant later that evening, he made a point, like any good gentleman, of holding the door open for her. As they stepped in, he quickly surveyed the restaurant looking for an empty table.

"There seems to be one toward the back," Jason whispered to Anna. At the same time, he noticed four impeccably dressed gentlemen sitting around the large round table at the very back of the restaurant. Each of them wore a well-tailored suit, a crisp wide collared dress shirt, and a tastefully patterned tie.

One of the gentlemen who must've been distracted by their entrance turned from his conversation and looked at them.

At that moment, Jason heard Anna gasp. He turned to her. Anna looked horrified.

"What's the matter?" he whispered.

She turned to him. "That's my father."

He looked up and recognized Sal.

Sal caught sight of them and scowled. The guys at his table also looked back at them.

Anna quickly turned to Jason and said, "Let's go."

"You sure?"

"Yup. Follow me. Now!" They filed out of the restaurant with Anna walking six feet in front of him. And they didn't stop walking until they'd gone half a block. Only then did Anna seem to take her first breath. She turned to Jason and said, "Oh, God. Not good."

"Really? That bad?"

"Trust me. I won't hear the end of this."

"You still want to go out for dinner? I mean, this didn't put you off or anything?"

"Are you kidding. I'd love to. You're a kind and considerate person. Why shouldn't I want to still have dinner with you?"

Jason smiled and nodded, then looked around. "So, where should we …?" For a moment, Jason stood frozen on the street. He was at a loss for where they should go. Not being from Coney Island, he knew of very few restaurants, never mind any fancy ones which were good enough for Anna.

Fortunately, she rescued him. "It's such a nice night," she said. "Why don't we just stroll through the neighborhood?" Anna seemed to be content with just spending time with Jason.

He was very happy about that. "Okay. Well, let's walk up to Mermaid Avenue. We should be able to find a decent place."

"Sounds good to me." Anna took his hand.

Jason had spent so many mornings and evenings on Mermaid Avenue walking back and forth from the arcade, that he could easily have served as its unofficial ambassador. As they strolled along, Jason decided to give Anna a walking tour of the neighborhood and its many shops.

"Now, this place, if you haven't been here before," Jason said, pointing to Saperstein's, "has the best egg creams in town."

"Really? Want to stop there?"

"No, no, no." Jason realized that his reaction had been quick. "Well, maybe later. After we eat something." After walking half a block, Jason said, "Now this place," pointing to a rundown establishment. "This is Veinish's Tobacco Shop."

"You want to stop here?" They both giggled at the thought of them stopping for tobacco.

"Of course not," Jason laughed. "I just wanted to point it out. If it weren't so late, good old Mr. Veinish would be sitting right there," Jason said, pointing to a cluttered desk at the front of the shop. "rolling one thick, fat cigar after another."

Anna and Jason continued strolling along the avenue, taking in the ambiance. A weather system had apparently stalled over New York City making the air unusually damp and heavy. After walking another block, Jason said, "And here's Bubinsky's." He quickly ushered Anna over to their display window which featured an array of freshly baked desserts, babkas and macaroons, pinwheel cookies and black and white cookies as well as poppy seed and honey cakes.

"Oh, yummy," Anna said. "Everything here looks delish."

"You gotta try their rugelach."

"Their what? Rugelach? What's that?"

"It's like a small cinnamon roll. But it's made with chocolate."

"Yummy. Maybe we should go inside."

Jason considered that for a minute. "Why don't we find something a little more substantial."

"You're probably right," Anna said, placing her hand on top of his as he gripped his crutches. For some inexplicable reason, the longer they strolled down the street, the more animated Jason became. Perhaps it was the joy that Jason felt showing her the neighborhood.

"Now, these guys," he said excitedly, pointing out a local dairy restaurant, "they make the best soups in town."

"Really? Like what?"

"Well, for starters, they make a great cabbage soup."

"Yummy. Do they make a mushroom barley soup?"

"One you could die for. And you can't beat the price. You can get a delicious bowl of soup and a thick slice of challah for only seventy-five cents!"

"Challah?" Anna asked, pronouncing the word as if a dry wedge of wood was stuck in her throat.

"Egg bread. With a shmear of butter."

"A shmear?"

"Oh . . ." For a moment, Jason considered explaining it, but realized that it might be easier to just move on. "Just follow me," he said, laughing. Once again, he made certain to open the door for her and they quickly found a table near the door. Before they were even seated, a waitress was hovering over them. She dropped the menus on the table.

"What'll it be, honey?"

"Uh," Jason said, a little stunned. "Can you give us a minute?"

The waitress frowned and turned to leave. Undeterred, Anna asked, "What's your special today?"

"Mushroom barley soup."

Anna's eyes lit up. "I'll have one of those."

Jason was shocked by her decisiveness. "Uh. Can you make that two please?"

Not saying a word, the waitress turned, rolled her eyes and walked into the kitchen.

• • •

When they'd finished their simple meal, Anna suggested that they continue strolling along the bustling Mermaid Avenue. As they made their way amongst other pedestrians to the next corner, Anna suddenly turned to Jason beaming. Out of the blue, she said, "Why don't we stop for ice cream?"

"Ice cream?" Jason said. "You got room for that?" Jason laughed, pleasantly surprised by her appetite.

Jason and Anna moved on and soon found the popular neighborhood ice cream shop, Scooper Dooper, half a block down. Both of them were so enjoying their evening, they decided to get their cones to go. Neither wanted the evening to end.

With cones in their hands, they walked on. Each of them licking their cones quickly to prevent them from dripping. With the sun quickly fading, they came to a dark alley on the next block. Jason peered down it. "Looks scary, doesn't it?" Suddenly, the back door of the local deli swung open and they both stood frozen staring at the interior of its cramped kitchen.

There, they saw a thick, stout Slavic-looking fellow standing behind a long metal table. Thick heads of cabbage, bunches of carrots and industrial-sized jars of mayonnaise were dumped on the table beside him and he was making reams and reams of coleslaw. Intrigued by this, Jason and Anna took a few steps closer to watch. They quickly became fascinated by his technique. Using great sweeping, circular movements with his muscular arms, he blended the mixture together. Jason watched as he dug into the mixture with his stubby, gnarled fingers. When he drew his hands out, he couldn't help but notice that shredded cabbage and carrots and globs of mayonnaise still clung grotesquely to the hair on his arms.

Jason suddenly felt a bit queasy. Turning to Anna, he saw that her face was unmistakably drained of color. "Well," Jason said, "on that note." They both burst out laughing.

CHAPTER 17

"The roots of love grow all around
But for me, they come a-tumblin' down
Every day heartaches grow a little stronger
I can't stand this pain much longer"

What Becomes of the Broken Hearted
Jimmy Ruffin

"How about a nice cuppa tea?" Bubbie asked.

Zayde nodded.

"Vant some cherry danish mit dat?"

Her husband grunted. Bubbie had come to know that that meant *yes*. She went to the stove and put on a pot of tea. Then, she cut the pastry into four smaller wedges and lovingly placed the plateful of danish on the table in front of him. After a long, monotonous week in the hospital, Zayde was happy to be home.

But domestic life wasn't his cup of tea. He could never understand all the fussing and fretting that Bubbie made over him. Asking whether he was wearing clean clothes? Had he had eaten something recently? Did his nails need cutting? What was all the fuss about?

Bubbie placed a fresh pot of tea down on the kitchen table and took the seat beside him.

"So, who vas de young woman?"

"Young voman?"

"De voman dat found you?"

"Vat voman? I tolt you I vas vit my friends."

"So, she vas dere?"

"For de turd time, dere vas no voman!" he insisted. Zayde then raised the cup to his lips and took a sip. Suddenly, he clutched his stomach. "Oy!"

"Vat's wrong?"

"My stomach. It hurts."

Bubbie shook her head. "Vant some prune juice?" she asked, searching his eyes.

Zayde shook his head. "Da qvestions. All de qvestions."

Bubbie rolled her eyes and went back to the stove.

As the days wore on, Zayde grew grumpier and more irritable. It seemed the longer he sat around the apartment with nothing to do, the crabbier he became. He secretly longed for the day that he'd be able to return to work.

Over the next few days, he plotted his escape and when Friday finally rolled around, he made his move. That afternoon, after getting dressed, he walked into the kitchen. Bubbie was peeling potatoes for the evening meal when Zayde announced, "I need some fresh air."

She shot him a surprised look. "Vere you going?"

"Out."

Bubbie gave him a look of concern. "Vill you be okay?"

"Don't worry. I'll be fine."

Zayde grabbed his cane, limped through the hallway and down the stairs. Despite his pain, he was on his way to the arcade.

• • •

Mitch and Jason were each helping customers at the arcade.

"Hello, boys!"

Recognizing a familiar voice, his grandsons looked to see their zayde standing in the doorway of the dusty, noisy arcade. He got a certain kick out of knowing that Mitch and Jason were shocked to see him. They quickly gathered around him.

"Welcome back, Grandpa," said Jason, beaming.

"Didn't think we'd see you so soon," Mitch said.

Zayde shook his head. "So, how'd you ever get along vitout me?"

"Oh, somehow we've managed," Jason said, smiling.

"It's good to have you back," Mitch added.

"Yeah, yeah, yeah. Now, bring me a chair already."

Jason and Mitch looked at each other questioningly. Then, Jason ran past some arcade players to the stockroom and found a folding chair. He then struggled to carry the chair through the crowd to the front of the arcade.

"Put it right dere," Zayde said, pointing to the very center of the arcade. Jason hadn't even set it down before their zayde plopped his weary body down. "Oy." From that vantage point, Zayde took a long look around, eying all of the machines, the many games of chance, every corner of his domain. The few players who were there continued playing, minding their own business.

At that point, Zayde closed his eyes and visualized the arcade once again, its sights and sounds, its frenetic energy, the invigorating pings and dings and rings of the pinball machines, the percussive knock a machine made when someone won, and the metallic jingling of coins in someone's hand. In his reverie, he could smell the sweet fragrance of cotton candy from the street, the thick pungent odor of the bathrooms, and he could actually feel the crush of customer's bodies jostled together.

Zayde could almost sense his grandsons glancing over at him. At some point, he heard Jason whisper, "He seems content."

"I am," Zayde yelled, "So, leave me alone, gotdammit!"

Half an hour later, they both looked over at their zayde. He was still sitting in the chair in the middle of the arcade's ongoing noises and music.

Mitch walked over to Jason. "There's still a smile on his face."

Jason saw it clearly. The arcade was without a doubt his Zayde's home, his refuge.

Then, something suddenly caught Jason's attention across the street. At first, he thought it was just the shade caused by the sun slipping along the pavement. He quickly realized it was, in fact, a young woman walking back and forth. As he moved to the entranceway and on closer examination, he realized that she bore a striking resemblance to the woman he'd seen two weeks earlier in the train station nestled in his grandfather's arms.

Jason stepped back. He hesitated. The last thing he wanted to do was wander into territory he wanted nothing to do with. He quietly walked over to where Zayde was sitting, leaned down and gently tapped him on his shoulder.

Zayde jumped. "Vat!?"

Jason pointed at the entranceway. "I think someone's waiting for you outside."

Zayde frowned. Jason helped him to his feet and walked with him to the entranceway. They both peered out in her direction.

"Is that her?"

"Who?" Zayde asked, straining his eyes to see who Jason was pointing at.

"The woman who saved you?"

"Feh. Dat's crazy talk," Zayde scoffed at his grandson's suggestion, turned away from the door and returned to his chair. He sat down with a grunt, lowered his head and shut his eyes again. For a minute, Jason continued watching the woman and mulled over the situation. Then, he went over and placed his hand on his grandfather's shoulder. It didn't happen immediately but after a while, Zayde simply sighed in response. But, he stubbornly continued to sit smack dab in the center of the arcade, oblivious to any of the customers who came and went.

Jason shook his head in exasperation. His grandfather obviously did not want to talk about it. Jason walked back to the counter and climbed back onto the stool. The young woman was no longer pacing back and forth across the street.

After ten minutes, Zayde finally raised his head and looked over at his grandson. "Life is short, Jason," he bellowed. "Enjoy it." Then, he closed his eyes again. Not knowing exactly how to respond, Jason simply nodded at his zayde even though he knew he wasn't looking anymore. Jason decided to take the opportunity to study his grandfather's face. Looking carefully, he thought he detected a certain sadness and resignation around his eyes. As though an electrical plug had been yanked from its socket. Jason suddenly noticed that in a very short time Zayde had somehow aged in some strange way. As if life had finally caught up with him. His grandfather had always exuded energy, a certain spunk. But now, as Jason looked at his grandfather's slumped shoulders and his tired face, he observed a distinct world-weariness. Jason's biggest fear was that his zayde would now regard his life as one long inevitable slide toward oblivion.

• • •

A short time later, Zayde opened his eyes and checked his watch. "Oy vey." He suddenly remembered the main reason he'd come to the arcade. Bank deposits were typically made on Fridays and it'd been more than a week since anyone had made one. With his bank closing in half an hour, Zayde needed to get going. He rose slowly from the chair and ambled over to the counter.

"You been putting money in de bag?"

Jason nodded and reached under the counter. He handed the beige money bag to his zayde. "It should all be there."

Zayde opened the bag and took a quick look inside. He was happy to see the week's receipts. "Not bad for a week. De bank is closing soon. I better get goink."

"They'll be happy to see you."

"Ve'll see about dat."

Jason smiled when he heard a bit of his grandfather's old spunk return.

Zayde then began his long arduous trek up to the bank on Mermaid Avenue and he arrived not a moment too soon. A young female clerk was just about to lock the door.

"Hello, Mr. Jacobowitz," she said.

"Hello, dere, sweetheart," Zayde said, feeling a sharp jabbing pain in his left leg.

Zayde generally liked banking at the Dime Savings Bank of New York. The staff was generally helpful and he especially liked its spacious, dignified interior. Zayde hobbled over one of the isolated high counters where customers could complete the forms in relative privacy. He had always been sensitive about filling out forms. Because he'd never finished grade school, it took him a long time to complete their forms. He labored over each one, having to print out each letter of his name in large block letters.

While standing there, Zayde suddenly didn't feel quite right. Even though it hadn't been a particularly hot day, he noticed that he was now sweating. He wiped his brow twice with his handkerchief and dropped it the last time. Zayde groaned reaching down to fetch it. When he got back up, he felt lightheaded.

"Oy gevalt," he muttered, feeling faint. Out of habit, he patted his breast pocket in the hopes of finding a piece of red licorice. He quickly realized that he'd forgotten to pop some in his pocket that morning.

At that moment, his vision became blurry. "Vat de hell is going on?" he muttered. To keep his balance, Zayde grabbed the counter and leaned against it. Then, he reached for his pencil again. As he printed the last letter of his last name, the tip of the pencil broke and his left hand shot out from under him in a wide sweeping arc causing the forms to fly off the counter.

Zayde collapsed on the tile floor. Seeing him fall to the marble floor, one of the tellers yelled, "Call an ambulance."

• • •

"Yuck. This is so gross," the young emergency nurse said.

"Shhh. That's about enough," the older resident doctor said. "Just do your job."

The nurse had been trying to remove a sock from Zayde's left foot. Stuck to the bottom of his infected foot, it took all of the nurse's patience and training to peel it away. A minute later, the nurse looked over and saw a middle-aged woman rush into the emergency room, her eyes darting this way and that, searching for someone. By this time, Zayde was lying on a gurney in the far corner of the room. He weakly looked over and raised a hand. The woman caught sight of him and rushed over. When Bubbie finally reached him, she choked.

"Oy. Not again," she cried.

• • •

Sara answered the phone on the second ring. It was a tearful Bubbie. Sara remained pensive while her mother relayed the news. Then, she promised she'd come to the hospital as early as she could that evening. As soon as Sara got off the phone with her mother, she placed a call to her son at the arcade to brief him on his grandfather's condition. She took a deep breath and dialed the number.

"Hullo."

Sara immediately recognized her son's voice. "I just wanted to let you and Mitch know that your grandfather's back in the hospital."

"Again?" Jason put his hand over the receiver and turned to his cousin. "Zayde's back in the hospital."

"Again?" Mitch asked.

Jason took his hand away from the receiver. "What is it this time?" Mitch leaned toward his cousin and the phone. Jason looked over at Mitch. "He fainted." Then, returning to the conversation, he said, "I want to see him."

"Me too," Mitch blurted out.

Jason listened to his mother for a few more moments and then said goodbye. He slowly hung up the phone.

"What should we do?" Mitch asked anxiously.

"Well, someone has to keep the arcade going. We can't both go to the hospital."

"Okay, then. Who's gonna stay?"

When Jason thought about it, he realized there was really no easy solution. He turned to his cousin. "Why don't we flip a coin?"

"Sounds fair."

Jason quickly reached for a quarter sitting on the counter and started juggling it in the palm of his hand. "Okay, call it," he said, tossing it in the air.

"Heads," Mitch yelled. Jason caught it in mid-air and smacked it down on the counter.

"Ooh, sorry. Tails, it is."

"Ah, shit. You lucky duck."

Jason grinned. "You okay looking after the arcade while I'm gone?"

"Sure. No problem. Just keep me posted."

"You got it."

• • •

Jason wasn't prepared for the scene in Zayde's room when he arrived at the hospital. The tiny hospital room reeked of cigar smoke, perfume, and body odor. His bubbie sat in one corner crying uncontrollably while Jason's mother and her two sisters did what they could to comfort her. Various uncles milled about.

Zayde, however, was in a foul mood. With his hospital gown gaping in the back, he stood in the center of the room, his hairy bum exposed for all to see. The once proud man was embarrassed. He had just wet himself and he was ashamed.

"Vy didn't you help me?" he yelled at his son-in-law. "I told you I had to go."

"I'm sorry," Gary said. "I didn't realize it was such a rush!"

"Didn't realize?"

Hearing the frustration in his voice, Bubbie rushed to his side and tried fastening the back of his gown.

"Vat de hell," he yelled, swatting at her.

When Jason looked over at the bed, he spotted the wet sheet. Jason's dad had apparently tried to lift his father-in-law off the bed but wasn't quick enough and Zayde had soiled himself and the bed. Jason's aunt Esther came over and removed the stained sheet while his dad carried in two fresh towels from the bathroom. He placed the first one on the bed. The second he offered to Zayde.

"Now?" Zayde shot back irritably. "Now you give it to me?"

Jason found all of this too much to bear. He desperately needed some air. So, he left the room to gather his senses. Not knowing what else to do, he started pacing back and forth in the hallway. A moment later, his mom joined him.

"Jason, I know this is difficult."

"You said it."

Sara, as if feeling her son's frustration, said, "There's really nothing for you to do here. You don't have to stay. Why don't you go back and relieve Mitch? Maybe he'll want to come"

"Is Zayde going to be alright?" Jason suddenly blurted out.

Jason watched as his mother struggled for the words. He thought he saw tears in her eyes. "I'm not sure. But, go back to the arcade. Your zayde would want that."

• • •

Mitch happened to be standing outside the arcade when he spotted Jason coming down the street. He rushed over to his cousin, asking, "So, how's Zayde?"

"Not great. He had an accident."

"An accident?" Mitch said, fearing the worst.

"Yeah. He wet himself just before I got there. Peed in his bed, in front of everyone, your mother, your father, my parents. Everyone."

"Oh, geez. That must've been embarrassing."

"It didn't help that with those damn hospital gowns, his bum was hanging out for all to see. He was one angry, humiliated dude."

"I'll bet."

"Do you want to go and see him."

Mitch frowned and looked around before answering. "Nah, I guess not. I'll stay, too."

"My mom promised that she'll call us when she knows something more anyway."

"Oh, good," Mitch said, looking relieved.

• • •

One hour later, the attending physician walked into Zayde's hospital room. Sara rushed over to him. "So, what's the prognosis?" she asked nervously.

"We need to talk about your father's care." Motioning for everyone to join him, he said, "Please follow me so we can talk."

The doctor led the family into a conference room down the hall. Everyone quickly took a seat, that is, as many as the chairs would allow. Bubbie and her daughters formed a circle around the doctor while the others waited on the perimeter. The silence was deafening with everyone waiting for the doctor to speak. Sara was sitting next to her mother. Everyone looked at each other as they waited.

As the physician cleared his throat, Sara took her mother's hand.

"Your husband has an ulcer on the bottom of his left foot."

"Oy," Bubbie said.

"It's been there for some time. He's lost significant mobility and sensation in the foot." He paused. "Gangrene has set in."

Some members of the family gasped.

"Gangrene?" Bubbie asked, "Vus is dus?"

"The skin has decayed," Sara explained.

"Oh, mein got. Guttenyu," Bubbie cried.

Sara looked anxiously to her husband, then back at her mother who was now crying.

"If it's left untreated, it's quite dangerous."

Shocked as they were by the news, no one said a word. After a minute, Sara finally spoke up. "So . . . What do you recommend?"

"Well," the young doctor took a moment to gather his thoughts and seemingly his courage. "We need to operate."

"Operate?" Sara said. "What are you suggesting?"

The doctor took another moment seemingly to consider how best to explain what was necessary. "Your father's leg needs to be amputated."

"Amputated?"

Bubbie howled. Sara instinctively placed her arms around her mother to comfort her. Her eyes welled up with tears.

"Time is critical. The surgery's been scheduled for this Thursday morning."

CHAPTER 18

*Walk like a man, fast as I can
Walk like a man from you
I'll tell the world "forget about it, girl"
And walk like a man from you.*

Walk Like a Man
The Four Seasons

CHAPTER 18

Later that afternoon, there was a momentary lull in activity at the arcade. As bits of verse and the odd phrase came to him, Jason scribbled them into his small spiral notebook. When the phone suddenly phone rang, he pounced on it immediately.

"Jason, is that you?" his mother asked. She sounded frazzled.

"Hey, Mom. What's going on?" Jason asked. He looked up and motioned for Mitch to join him.

"Well, we just had a meeting with the doctor."

Jason felt his stomach tighten. Mitch came over and, leaning in, hovered over Jason and the phone.

"His news wasn't good."

"What'd he say?"

"Zayde's going to need an operation."

"An operation?"

When Mitch overheard Jason say the word *operation*, he asked, "What kind of operation?"

Jason held up his hand and motioned for Mitch to wait until he got off the phone.

"Sorry, mom. What were you saying?"

Sara took a breath. "They need to amputate Zayde's leg."

Jason tried to speak but the words didn't come. The wind was knocked out of him. After a moment, all he could manage to say was, "Geez. "

"What!?" asked Mitch.

Sara paused a long time allowing Jason to soak in the information. Then, she quietly said, "I'll call you later, okay?"

The next thing Jason heard was a click. He was left stunned and silent, still holding the phone. His mind was reeling. He turned to Mitch and simply repeated word for word what his mother had just told him. Mitch took it in and said, "I don't know about you, but I want to see him. Now."

"I do too. Let's both go."

"When?"

"Let's lock up at 6:00 and go. We've got a pretty good reason to lock up early, don't you think?"

Mitch frowned and nodded. "Yup." He looked at his watch. "In an hour."

Jason nodded slowly and suddenly felt unwell.

• • •

Two hours later, Jason and Mitch stepped off the hospital elevator and were struck with how quiet Zayde's floor was. When they leant their heads against his door, they didn't hear a sound. "He must be resting," Jason whispered. Rather than barging in, Jason opened the door just a crack. Both were taken aback by what they saw. Perched on his bed, Bubbie was leaning over her husband and putting a bib around his neck. She then picked up a spoon with one hand and a plastic container with the other.

Jason and Mitch watched as their grandmother spoon-fed her husband some homemade soup. The only sound the boys heard was that of their zayde slurping and smacking his lips. "Oy, schmek git," he said.

They slowly let the door slide shut and stepped back. They looked up and down the corridor and spied some chairs off to the side.

"Let's give them a moment, okay?" Jason suggested.

Mitch nodded. "Good idea."

• • •

Not a day went by that Sara didn't visit her father. Three days after the operation, when she was visiting, tending to her father and helping him dress, her father, out of the blue, asked, "So nu, vere's my grandson?"

Sara gulped. She debated about whether she should tell him the truth. "He's nervous about seeing you. Afraid to see what your leg looks like."

Zayde mulled that over. Then, he shook his head. "Doesn't a grandfadder have a right to see his grandson?"

Sara searched his face. Something tugged at her. And it didn't feel good. "Dad, he'll come. He's never experienced anything like this before. He doesn't know what to expect."

"I vant I should see my grandson!"

Sara nodded. "You'll see him, Dad. I'll arrange it with Mitch and him so that both can come and see you."

Zayde grunted and turned to look out the dirty window at nothing.

• • •

Jason was sitting in the passenger seat feeling nervous and scared. Before his zayde, there had never been any reason to visit any of his relatives in the hospital, never mind know anyone who'd lost an appendage. Jason squirmed at the thought.

"How will he walk? How does he get dressed? Heck. How will he get to work?" Jason's head spun from the many questions that arose.

"We all will have to take this one step at a time," his mother said, as she pulled into the hospital parking lot. She parked the car and got out.

Jason didn't move in the passenger seat. His mother walked around the back of the car and opened the car door. Then, she tucked her head in. "You coming?"

It was impossible for him to say *no*. He had agreed to come visit his grandfather and was now sitting outside in the hospital parking lot. "What am I going to do? Refuse to come up?"

"You have to go up and see him."

He manically began fingering the part in his hair.

His mother reminded him, "Your zayde wants to see you."

Jason sighed and reluctantly got out of the car fretting over what awaited him.

• • •

When Jason and his mom stepped off the elevator, they encountered a disorienting spectacle; the disturbing sight of an elderly man disrobing in his room, his flesh sagging in unwanted places. Then, they heard the disconcerting groan of a patient in the next room. As Sara and Jason got to the door of Zayde's room, they heard the unmistakable sound of two people bickering.

"Vat do you mean I can't smoke?"

"Mr. Jacobowitz," his attending nurse said as patiently as possible. "It's dangerous. Not to mention, unhealthy."

"I lost my leg and you von't even let me have a cigarette?"

At that moment, the door flew open and the nurse, red-faced and upset, swept past them. Sara shook her head and tiptoed into the room. She placed her purse down on the windowsill.

"Dad, she was only trying to help," she said.

"Dat vas trying to help?"

Sara took a deep breath and tried to change the subject. "So, Pop, how you doing?"

"Ninety-nine per cent. Top shelf."

Sara smiled. "I can't believe it. You're so positive!"

Her father waved her away.

Jason watched as she took a quick look around the room and spotted a tray of uneaten hospital food.

"Have you eaten anything?"

"You expect me to eat dis dreck?"

"Okay, okay. I'll get you something."

Jason paced nervously back and forth, his eyes darting about. He was looking at everything and anything so long as he didn't have to look at his zayde's leg. Meanwhile, his grandfather casually reached for a stick of red licorice that he'd hidden under the pillow which he promptly popped into his mouth.

"Dad, that's why you're here," said Sara accusingly, pointing to the stick of licorice he was chewing.

"Enough already," Zayde barked. "I need a smoke." Turning to his grandson, he pointed to the wheelchair in his room and said, "Jason, be a good boy. Grab my cigarettes and matches. We're going out."

When Jason looked over to his mother for approval, she rolled her eyes.

Jason went over, grabbed a package of Camel cigarettes he saw over on a cabinet and stuck them and matches in the breast pocket of his shirt. Then, he hobbled over to the wheelchair and paused. He quickly realized that taking his zayde out wouldn't be easy. While holding his crutches in one hand, he clumsily had to push the wheelchair over to Zayde's bedside with the other. He and his mother then lifted Zayde awkwardly off the bed and lowered him into the wheelchair.

Undaunted, Zayde pulled his bathrobe across his chest, looked up at his grandson and said, "Let's go."

As they got to the door, his mother called out, "Jason." She raised her fingers to her mouth and mimed as if she were smoking. Then, she pointed at him. "Don't get any ideas."

• • •

Stymied by his crutches, Jason had to use all of his force to get Zayde's wheelchair across the street. *How am I going to get over that curb?* Twice, he tried tipping the heavy wheelchair back to mount the curb and twice he failed. The third time, the chair unexpectedly rolled back and slammed him in the knees.

"Aw, shit," he grimaced.

Jason's next hurdle was getting the wheelchair over a small hill. After making several unsuccessful attempts, he gave the wheelchair an especially aggressive push. With the extra momentum, the wheelchair sailed up and over the hill. However, Jason lost control of it as it careened downhill and it smacked into a stone footer.

"Gotdammit," Zayde howled as he lurched forward in the wheelchair.

Hearing Zayde's curse, several bystanders turned to look. One of them laughed.

"Sorry," was all Jason could say.

Unperturbed, Zayde, spotting an empty bench, not twenty feet ahead of them. He pointed to it and said, "Take me dere."

With great difficulty, Jason jockeyed the wheelchair over to the waiting bench. Feeling lucky that he got there at all, Jason bent over and let out a huge sigh.

"Give me those," Zayde said, pointing to the pack of cigarettes in Jason's breast pocket.

Jason handed Zayde his cigarettes and matches. Then, gazing down at the matchbook his grandfather was now holding, he inadvertently caught sight of the mound of gauze wrapped around what remained of his grandfather's leg. Jason nervously averted his eyes, not knowing where to look.

Seeing his grandson gawking at what was left of his leg, Zayde said, "Jason, don't even look dere."

His grandson tried to look elsewhere. Seemingly trying to break the awkward silence, Zayde joked. "Vell . . . now maybe your grandfadder is only fifty percent."

Jason laughed in spite of himself.

"It's not de end of de vorld."

"I know I know."

"Now, Gotdammit, give me a light."

Jason clumsily ripped one of the paper matches out of the book. He struck it so hard against the friction strip that it bent out of shape. Jason realized that this was the first time he'd ever tried lighting a match.

"Try anudder."

Jason ripped a second match out of the book. This time, the match burned all the way down to his fingertips. "Ouch," he winced. Instinctively, he stuck the tips of his fingers into his mouth and sucked on them.

After watching his grandson try to light it twice unsuccessfully, Zayde took the cigarette from his lips and handed it to his grandson. "Here, give it a try."

Jason looked nervously at his grandfather. "My mother would kill me."

"Aw, be a man."

Jason stared at the cigarette. Then, he awkwardly stuck it between his teeth. Zayde quickly struck a match and brought it to the end of Jason's cigarette.

"Now, suck it in."

Jason looked nervously to his zayde. After taking a tentative puff, he erupted in a huge cough.

"Dat's my boy," Zayde beamed. Then, he quickly yanked the cigarette from his grandson's mouth, stuck it between his lips and took a deep, satisfying drag. "Ahhh," he exhaled. "Now, dat's more like it."

For the next few minutes, as the lunchtime crowd strolled by, Jason watched as his grandfather sat in his wheelchair savoring his smoke. No sooner had he butted out his much-needed smoke than he barked, "Take me back."

Obeying his grandfather's wish, Jason backed up his wheelchair and turned it around. As they sailed through the sliding glass doors of the hospital, the same nurse who Zadye had earlier had the run-in with sailed past them.

Completely unfazed, Zayde smiled and greeted her. "Hello dere, sweetheart."

The nurse deliberately ignored him, electing instead to look the other way.

"Geez," Zayde said. "Not even a smile."

"What do you expect?" Jason countered, "You yelled at her."

"Eh, feh!"

CHAPTER 19

*"So take a good look at my face
You know my smile looks out of place
If you look closer it's easy to trace
The tracks of my tears."*

Tracks of My Tears
Smokey Robinson and the Miracles

Zayde was discharged from the hospital five days later. When Jason and his mom went to pick him up that morning, Jason was immediately struck by his grandfather's cheerful mood. Completely out of character, Zayde greeted every single nurse they ran into, even waving to his fellow patients, patients he had never previously said one word to. In fact, as they were leaving, Zayde spotted the nurse he'd previously had the run-in with and made a special point of greeting her, saying, "Deep down I know you're going to miss me."

She smirked and shooed him away.

His buoyant mood, however, didn't last long. As they rode home, Zayde grew sullen as he stared idly out the window. Jason could see that the painful reality was hitting home. When they pulled up to the apartment house, Zayde waited impatiently while his grandson pulled and prodded at the wheelchair, trying to remove it from the trunk. The new reality was also dawning on Jason. *How the hell are we going to get him up the stairs?*

Jason looked to his mother questioningly as they stood by the open passenger door about to help Zayde out. Without waiting, Sara took the initiative and grabbed her father's remaining leg. Seeing this. Jason put his arms around his grandfather's torso and together they lugged Zayde painstakingly up the stairs, stopping at the first landing to catch their breath.

Sara looked down at Jason's cast. "You okay?"

Jason nodded and looked over at Zayde, who looked quite drawn. His grandson lowered his body down so that Zayde could put his arm further across Jason's back. "That's it, Zayde. Hang on."

Zayde mumbled something.

"Sorry, what did you say, Zayde?"

"Dat's my boychick."

Jason smiled over at his mother.

"Okay, ready, dad?" asked Sara.

Zayde nodded.

"Up we go, then, dad."

The three struggled up the next two flights of steps. The whole time, Zayde, ashamed and depressed, looked away, anywhere but directly at them. When they'd reached the top of the stairs, Jason took a series of deep breaths and then headed back downstairs. On his next trip, he somehow hauled the wheelchair up the same flight of stairs and into the apartment.

But it didn't end there. Once they were upstairs, Jason watched his zayde clumsily try to navigate his way around the apartment, first banging into the coffee table with the feet supports, then backing up into the television with the back of the wheels. All the while, Bubbie feverishly moved the furniture out of his way.

Later that day, Zayde's frustration peaked when he had to use the bathroom. Jason initially heard him swearing as the wheels of his wheelchair scraped against the baseboards in the hallway but try as he might, he couldn't get his wheelchair to fit through the bathroom door. Not a moment later, his grandfather yelled, "Someone, help me."

Jason quickly rushed into the hallway realizing that it probably wasn't easy for his zayde to have to ask for help.

Jason studied his grandfather's face, his set jaw, beads of sweat pouring off his waxy-looking forehead. Zayde answered his gaze with a look of quiet exasperation. Not knowing what else to do, Jason lifted his grandfather out of the chair and lugged him into the bathroom. Not a word passed between them. Finally, as Jason was about to leave, his grandfather asked, "Can you pull down my underwear?" This was entirely new ground for Jason.

Afterward, Jason hobbled after Zayde as he once again wheeled into the living room.

Jason could tell that Bubbie found it especially hard. He realized that she suddenly had to shadow her husband around the apartment, anticipating and attending to his every need. Zayde now needed help getting dressed, being fed, and cleaning up after himself.

Later, Jason walked into the kitchen and watched his grandfather sitting helplessly in his wheelchair while his wife, standing on a step stool, reached high up to the top shelf trying to retrieve something her husband had asked for.

"No, not de Sugar Pops, gotdammit. De Frosted Flakes." Bubbie stared back down at her husband and dutifully obeyed.

"Bubbie, I can do that."

Bubbie shook her head. "I should do it."

Jason shook his head.

Still later, as he was leaving for work, Jason found his grandmother moving furniture in the bedroom. He walked over to her and asked, "Are you going to be alright alone with Zayde?"

Bubbie gave a shrug and nodded.

Jason choked and gave her a massive hug. She nodded and padded his shoulder.

Then, he turned to his grandfather and said, "Bye, Zayde. I'm off to the arcade."

Both he and Bubbie waited for Zayde to answer. But none came. Bubbie shrugged and motioned for him to go.

Jason gave her a peck on the cheek and left.

• • •

Later that night, Jason returned from the arcade feeling tired and spent. As hard as he tried, sleep eluded him. He lay on his lumpy couch bed for hours, staring up at the ceiling and replaying the events of the day. The quiet was only broken by the grunts and groans of his grandfather in the next room. He could hear every word clearly.

"My God damn foot."

"Vat?" Bubbie asked sleepily. "Vat's de mattah?"

"It hurts sumtink awful."

"So, rub it."

"How can I rub sumtink dat's not dere."

Jason shook his head and covered his head with the pillow. He felt sad that his zayde was suffering so. He had never known his grandfather to be so miserable. *What can I possibly do? What would make him happy?* No easy answers came to mind. But he eventually fell asleep.

With the air hot and humid, Jason woke earlier than usual. He heard music and wondered where it was coming from. He waddled sleepily into the kitchen where he found his zayde, in wrinkled shorts and a sweat-stained t-shirt, slouched in his wheelchair. He was listening to his favorite classical music radio station. The host of the show was rather formally introducing the next song.

"And now ladies and gentlemen, Enrico Caruso singing *'Una Furtiva Lagrima.'*"

With his announcement, his grandfather raised an eyebrow, and as the aria began, he closed his eyes and began humming the melody quietly to himself.

Jason would have been the first to admit that opera was not his cup of tea but that aria moved him in a way that surprised him. The poignancy and plaintiveness in the tenor's voice played on his emotions. After listening to only one verse, Jason got an idea.

That's it. I'll get him an opera record.

Turning to his grandfather, he said, "Zayde, I'll be right back." His grandfather simply nodded. Jason then turned to his little grandma and motioned, *I'm going out.* She gave him a mischievous little wink. Jason almost hopped over to the bathroom, changed quickly, and then hobbled down the hallway. He grabbed a light jacket and opened the door, coming back once to grab his crutches in the hallway.

He was on the way to the music store for Zayde.

• • •

Jason wasn't prepared for what happened next. After entering the store, he was momentarily dumbstruck by the sight. Stacked from the scuffed floors to the old copper ceiling were column upon column of vinyl albums and 78 rpm records, some old, some new, in no particular order. Jason had no idea where to look for an opera record. However, he was surprised to hear an unexpected, familiar voice.

"What are you doing here?"

Jason looked over, past the many bins of record albums, and spotted none other than Anna, standing at the far end of the aisle.

"Oh my gosh. I'm sorry I haven't called," Jason said. "There's been a lot going on with my zayde."

"Oh, that's okay," Anna said, thumbing through an assortment of albums. "I figured something was up. I tried to call but there was no answer."

Jason hobbled a little closer. "They had to amputate my zayde's leg."

Anna's hand flew to her mouth. "Oh, dear! I'm so sorry to hear that."

"He's home now."

"Well, that's good, right?" He could tell that she was worried about him.

"Yes. Except now, he's got nothing to do. He's miserable."

"Sorry to hear that." She reached out and put her hand on his arm.

He looked down at her hand and then leaned over to kiss her cheek. Then, he pulled back to look into her eyes. "Zayde was listening to opera this morning so I thought I'd buy him a record. Maybe it'll perk up his spirits."

Anna nodded and gave it some thought. "What kind of opera does he like?"

"You mean there's more than one kind?"

"Yes, silly. There's German, there's Italian. Some are funny, some are serious. My brother loves opera, too. I'll show you where they keep the classical music. You might find something you like."

Jason followed Anna past bins marked Chamber Music and Symphony. Many of the albums seemed misfiled and jutted out of the racks. Distracted by the lilting bounce of her ponytail, Jason got poked first by one album, then another. Occasionally, he stopped to rub his arm here and there.

Anna suddenly stopped and asked, "Who does he like?"

"Who?" Jason stopped and frowned, trying to remember what was playing that morning. "Well, a few minutes ago, he was listening to some guy. I think his name was Enrico. In fact, he was humming along with him."

Anna smiled.

"The title was something like, 'Una Lager'. Something like that. The announcer was speaking so quickly, I didn't catch the name."

Anna giggled. "Hmm. Could it have been 'Una Furtiva Lagrima?' Does that ring a bell?"

"That might've been it," Jason said, fiddling with his crutch.

"Good choice," Anna said. "It's a *romanza*."

"A what?"

"A *romanza*. A romantic aria," she said. Anna quickly thumbed through a bin and picked out an album. "Here it is," she said, handing it to Jason. "Looks like it's the last copy."

Jason eyed both sides of the album. "Thanks."

Anna looked at her watch and frowned. "Aw, shoot. I've gotta get back to my nonna's."

"That's too bad," Jason said, looking pleadingly at her. "I miss you."

"I miss you too," she said, smiling shyly.

"Can I call you?"

She nodded. "Sure."

Jason watched longingly as Anna left the shop and hurriedly crossed the street.

• • •

Nunzio was nursing his second coffee at the diner. He was waiting for Mario, one of his goons, to report back. Still suspicious about Anna's comings and goings, that morning he directed Mario to tail her. Nunzio looked up to see Mario approaching the coffee-stained table.

"So?"

"So, I followed her to a record store. Sure enough, ten minutes later, that heeb shows up." Nunzio nearly choked on his coffee.

"They left separately."

"That two-timing slut," Nunzio bellowed. "Who the hell does she think she is?" He slammed his coffee cup down on the counter and stormed out of the diner. Then, he jumped into his car and sped off in the direction of her grandmother's house.

• • •

Anxious to see Zayde's reaction to the record he'd purchased, Jason couldn't wait to get back to the apartment. However, today presented a special challenge. It was hot and humid that day and trying to climb the stairs while he gripped his crutches in one hand and held his prized record in the other, wasn't going to be easy. On top of that, the apartment was especially stifling.

When Jason entered their stuffy living room, Zayde sat slouched over in his wheelchair, dozing off and on in the living room. He looked frail and sweaty. Lil' Grandma was still sitting in the easy chair watching her favorite TV soap opera with the sound off.

"Zayde," Jason said proudly as he swept past him. "I got something for you." His zayde, half asleep, mumbled something unintelligible. Jason knew his grandparents stored their old Victrola on the top shelf of their closet. He carried the step stool into their bedroom and climbed up the steps to get it. Jason then lugged it into the living room and placed it on the dollied table by the window. He slipped the record out of its cover and placed it carefully on the turntable. Jason tried again.

"Hey, Zayde," he said.

"Vat?" Zayde grumbled dozily and lifted his head.

"I bought a record for you. Have a listen."

Great," Zayde said sarcastically.

Jason looked just in time to catch his zayde turning to Lil' Grandma. She looked back at him. Jason saw them sneer at each other. Then, Lil' Grandma lifted her chin and ignored Zayde, turning her attention back to the TV.

Jason shook his head and went back to carefully lowering the needle onto the record. He then turned his attention to his zayde. He couldn't help but see that his grandfather looked ten years older.

Zayde reached for his handkerchief to wipe his brow. When an oboe suddenly played the plaintive opening strains of the aria, he sat back in his chair. After a few moments, he dabbed at his eyes. Then, as the music began to wash over him, he relaxed and closed his eyes, mouthing the words to the music.

Jason smiled, taking heart in the fact that as weak as his grandfather was, the music had the power to move him.

• • •

Anna had a smile on her face as she walked back to her grandmother's house. Her chance meeting with Jason had brightened her spirits. As she continued deep in thought, at first she didn't hear a car racing up the street. When its tires suddenly squealed, Anna turned her head.

She saw the car and thought it looked like Nunzio's car. But that confused her. She wasn't expecting him. Not during the day like this.

The car screeched to a halt practically beside her and Nunzio jumped out. He raced over and stood directly in front of her blocking her path. Then, he grabbed her wrist and said, "Get in the car."

"Ow. Ow," she cried. She was shocked and tried to peel his hand off of hers. "You're hurting me."

"Get in the freakin' car," he repeated. Anna winced as he tightened his grip.

"I can't, Nunzio. My nonna's expecting me!"

"Don't be difficult. Just get in the car."

Anna didn't move. The last thing she wanted to do was to be with him today, or any day.

He shoved her. "You're nothin' but a puttana."

After regaining her balance, Anna stared at him coldly. Then, she turned and unexpectedly raced down the street.

"What the —?" Nunzio stood there shocked. He was momentarily stunned by her reaction. Then, not wanting to waste another second, he hopped in his car and took off in pursuit of her.

Anna frantically raced down the street without looking back. Her only thought was how she could get as far away from him as she could. Halfway down the street, she turned her head and spotted an alley. She quickly ducked into it. All the while, her mind raced, desperately trying to figure out what her next step might be.

Looking up, she saw a phone booth on the corner. Anna ran over and pulled out her small address book. She frantically rifled through it searching for Jason's name. Written beside it were two numbers, the first his parents' phone number and the second that of his grandparents. Anna pulled some coins from her pocket and plunked a dime into the slot. She dialed the second number. Anna anxiously shifted her weight from one foot to the other while the phone continued ringing.

"C'mon. Please, pick it up. Please," Anna prayed. While waiting for someone to pick up, she gazed down to look at her arm. The wrist that Nunzio had squeezed was now swollen and bright red. She began to cry.

• • •

When the phone rang in the kitchen, no one moved. Bubbie, who would've typically picked up, was out shopping. Lil' Grandma obviously wouldn't have been able to carry on a conversation in English, and Zayde had little interest in answering it. By default, the task fell to Jason. After it rang four times, Jason figured he'd better pick it up.

"Hello."

"Jason! I, um…" Anna's voice was trembling. Jason could tell she'd been crying.

"What's going on Anna?"

"I didn't know who else to call. I need to see you. Now." There was no mistaking the fact that Anna was panicked.

"What's wrong?" Jason had never heard Anna in such a state.

"Nunzio. He's after me."

"After you?" Jason's heart almost jumped out of his chest. He frantically looked around the living room. Lil' Grandma looked up, her eyebrows raised.

"Can you meet me downstairs? Now. I'm not far. I can be there in five minutes!"

"Yeah, sure."

"And Jason, meet me downstairs. I don't want to disturb your Zayde."

"Yeah, all right. I'll see you in a few minutes." Jason hung up the phone and grabbed the one crutch. Not knowing whether his zayde was awake or not, he yelled into the living room, "I'll be right back, Zayde." Then, he looked to his Lil' Grandma and gestured that he'd be back in *five minutes*. She nodded and she too closed her eyes. Jason hobbled across the kitchen and into the front hallway. He opened the door and hopped down the stairs.

Putting all of his weight on the crutch, Jason swung off the last step and looked up and down the hallway. Anna was just a few feet away.

Without saying a word, she brushed past him and went up a few stairs before turning back to face him as he joined her. Anna looked distraught and afraid. Her eyes were filled with tears.

"My God, where have you . . . ?" Jason asked.

Unable to talk, Anna reached for Jason. He grabbed her and squeezed her tightly. His heart leapt. He was at a loss for what to say or do as she continued weeping in his arms. All he could do was caress her hair, kiss her ear, whisper calming words. Finally, after giving her a minute to calm down, Jason took a step back and gazed into her eyes. "So, what happened?"

"Nunzio," she whimpered. "He, uh... He grabbed me and threatened me."

At that moment, Jason looked down and noticed the large red welt on her swollen wrist. The top button of her pink blouse was also missing.

"Let's go upstairs. You can clean up there."

She pulled at him. "No, no. I couldn't."

Jason reached for her hand. "Come with me. You'll be safer there." Slowly, he led her up the stairs to his grandparents' apartment.

• • •

Like a shark circling its prey, Nunzio sped up and down the streets of Coney Island, desperately trying to find Anna. Thinking that he'd caught a glimpse of her on 16th Street, he turned around and turned onto it. But it turned out to be someone else. Enraged, Nunzio then turned onto Mermaid Avenue and studied the crowd. Two blocks down, he spotted none other than Bubbie leaving the local bakery. He remembered having seen her one day at the arcade. There was something about her that reminded him of Jason, her grandson. He slammed his steering wheel. "Dat son of a bitch. I know where she is!"

• • •

After patiently leading Anna up the three flights of stairs, Jason needed a moment to catch his breath. As they walked through the hallway, he sensed something was different in the air. When they finally entered the kitchen, Jason turned to Anna. "Wanna wash up?"

"Maybe in a moment."

Jason suddenly heard a familiar sound, the repetitive rasping of a record skipping.

"Let me get this." He guided Anna into the living room and headed straight to the Victrola. Sure enough, the record was skipping. Without even turning to face him, he asked his zayde, "Want me to play it again?"

His grandfather didn't answer.

Jason looked over at Lil' Grandma. She was sleeping as well. Then, he turned to Anna and pointed at his little grandma and his grandfather. "Great audience, eh?"

She grinned. Jason tried again. "Want to hear it again?"

Zayde didn't answer a second time.

So, Jason turned to look at him. The sun's rays were pouring in through the window highlighting the many folds on his grandfather's face. Zayde was leaning to one side. His face was pale and his head was slumped on his chest. A string of drool hung from his gaping mouth and a tear rolled down his cheek. When Jason leaned in closer, his grandfather let out a long, deep sigh.

"You sure he's okay?" Anna asked.

"I don't know."

Anna came over and leaned toward his grandfather to study his face more closely. Then, she gently placed the back of her hand against his cheek and listened to his breathing. Jason looked on, hovering just behind her. Anna's eyes suddenly widened and she jumped back. "Oh, my God," she shuddered.

"What is it?"

"Call an ambulance!" she cried.

• • •

For three days, the air-conditioning in the hospital had been on the fritz. So, it wasn't surprising that when Jason and his bubbie arrived, the waiting room was hot and sticky. Their ears were bombarded with the sound of babies crying and the incessant chatter of loved ones. And it seemed like every ten minutes, they were being assaulted by the blare of an indecipherable public-address system.

Jason and Bubbie sat on the stiff rounded plastic chairs for over an hour, waiting for someone to give them an update on Zayde's condition. Jason already knew that it was only a question of time before the other relatives would arrive.

Bubbie suddenly got up and started pacing back and forth, wringing her hands and fretting. Jason was doing his best to distract her.

"Bubbie, can I get you some coffee?"

"No, tanks. Nuttink for me."

The hospital waiting room had become an all too familiar place for them. Bored and nervous, Jason tried everything to while away the time; thumbing through an old magazine, studying what snacks the vending machine had, and stopping for a sip at the water fountain. In fact, he'd made so many stops at the fountain that he'd already visited the bathroom three times.

Seeing his mother finally coming through the front doors was a welcome sight. Sara rushed over and gave each of them a warm hug.

"So, how's it going?" she asked, looking worried.

"Vee haven't hurd a ting," her mother said.

"Ma, they're just running some tests. He's strong as an ox."

Jason wished Anna was still with him. She initially had joined him and Bubba at the hospital. Then, she went to call her nonna to explain what had happened. Minutes later, she returned, crying.

Jason hobbled over to her and held her. "What happened?" he whispered, holding her by the shoulders.

"Nunzio showed up at nonna's looking for me and he was terrible. He really frightened her and she had to go after him with a broom to get him out of the house. I can't go back there tonight."

Jason held her to himself and looked around. He needed to protect her but he couldn't leave. He led her to a couple of chairs and sat her down. Then, he took her hands gently and looked lovingly into her face. "Listen, I'm going to call a taxi..."

Anna straightened up. "No, please. I don't want you to go to any trouble."

"Anna, I have to make sure you're safe, and you can't be any safer than being at your own place. I'm calling you a taxi and you're going home. You have to tell your father what happened to you today." He looked down at her swollen wrist and touched it tenderly. "Are you sure you don't want this looked at?"

She shook her head. Then, she wiped her eyes with the back of her hand and took hold of his hands. "Okay, I'll go home to my parents' place. I'm going to tell dad. He should know."

Jason felt relieved. "Yes, he should. Okay." He suddenly stood up, looked around and spotted the pay phone. "I'll be right back."

Just as Jason was dialing a taxi cab company, he looked over and saw his dad was coming through the front doors. His father walked over to him.

"Hi dad," he said.

Gary padded him on the back. "You okay?"

Jason nodded. "Mom's over there with Bubbie."

Gary looked over. "Okay, son."

Jason waited for someone to pick up the phone on the other end as he watched his father walking toward his mother and bubbie. He watched his father lean over and speak briefly to Anna. She, in turn, smiled up at him. Jason's heart melted. He suddenly realized that he wanted Anna in his life. He wanted Anna to be chatting to his mother and father. He wanted her around all the time.

Suddenly someone answered the phone and he was finally able to order a taxi for Anna. A moment later, he hung up just in time to see various aunts and uncles trickling in.

He walked over to join everyone over by the chairs and stood proudly by Anna. Soon, everyone was chatting. All at once. Every once in a while, he would introduce her to another one of his relatives.

"He'll pull out of this," said Jason's Uncle Al, scratching his ample belly.

"The man's built like a horse," his Uncle Julie said.

"Yeah. That's why Bubbie calls him a nag," Al joked.

Uncle Al, Julie, and the other uncles all got a good laugh out of that.

Suddenly, someone yelled out, "Has anyone called a taxi?"

Jason looked over and saw someone who looked like a taxi driver. He got up.

The man raised his hand. "Did you call a taxi?"

"Yeah, that's us!" Jason turned to Anna and helped her up.

"Where's she going?" Uncle Al asked. "We're just getting to know her!"

"I have to go home. It was so nice meeting you. I hope Zayde pulls through."

"Thank you," said Uncle Al.

Sara looked over from where she was sitting with her mother. She reached up to Anna. "You stay in touch, okay, Anna? You're always very welcome. And thank you for your support."

Anna blushed and mutely nodded. She sniffed and pushed her hair back over her ear. "Thank you."

Jason led her to the front doors and watched as the taxi driver opened the back door. Anna got in and Jason went around to the driver's side, waiting for the taxi driver to settle in. He leaned in the window and gave him two twenty-dollar bills. "My girlfriend will give you her address. She's in Queens. Keep the change."

The taxi driver nodded and then turned on the ignition. As he was about to pull away, Jason yelled, "Wait!"

The car stopped.

Jason hobbled over and opened the back door. Anna leaned toward him, looking up at him curiously. He suddenly leaned in and kissed her on the lips, holding her by the face with one hand. "See you soon, okay?"

She smiled softly and nodded.

Jason stood up and closed the door. He watched as the taxi drove away feeling so much older. And ten feet tall. As the taxi cab disappeared out of sight, he finally turned and hobbled back into the hospital. He was relieved to see that a doctor had finally appeared with the family. He quickened his pace.

Raising his voice above the din, the doctor shouted, "Are the Jacobowitz's here?"

Jason's uncles, Julie and Al both shouted back in unison, "That's us." All of the family members stopped what they were doing and formed a circle around the physician. Jason noticed that his bubbie was studying the doctor's eyes for some clue, some hint of what they'd found. The doctor nervously cleared his throat and began, "I'm very sorry."

The uncles turned to each other.

"Your husband arrived almost in a coma."

Jason heard his bubbie gulp.

"We did everything we could but I'm sorry to say that he passed away," the doctor, looking at his watch, continued, "Almost precisely ten minutes ago."

There was a stunned silence. "What?" Jason heard someone say. "That can't be."

Like a damn breaking, Bubbie suddenly burst into tears. Then, one by one, all of her daughters, Jason's aunts, followed.

"Oy, Herschel."

The uncles stared at each other in disbelief.

"I'm very sorry," the doctor said. "As I said, we did everything we could."

Sara instinctively reached for her mother and held her close. She whispered some words of consolation.

At the sight of this, Jason's eyes filled with tears. He felt his chest was about to explode. Now, he wished Anna was still there. To cling to.

His dad, sensing this, came over and gave him a hug. "Your zayde . . .," Gary began. The words, however, stuck in his throat. He too broke down, unable to finish his sentence.

Jason looked around the room. Everyone, including some relatives he'd never seen before were all crying openly. Jason was taken aback. He had never experienced anything like this before. His heart was in his throat. When he felt as though he couldn't take any more, he knelt down at his bubbie's feet and gently placed his hands lovingly on top of hers. "I'm so sorry, Bubbie," he whispered, stumbling over his words, "I loved Zayde very much."

Bubbie looked up from her handkerchief and looked Jason directly in the eyes. "He knew that," she said.

"I mean it, Bubbie." He choked. "With all my heart."

Bubbie's face was stained with tears. After a moment, she wiped her bloodshot eyes and added, "I never knew how sick he vas."

Suddenly, the atmosphere in the waiting room was almost too much to bear. Jason felt he was suffocating under the weight of the emotion. First, his fear for Zayde's health, then his fear for Anna's safety. Next, his zayde falling ill and his expanding love for Anna. And now this. An emotional roller coaster. Not knowing what else to do, he turned to his mother and said, "I've got to get out of here."

Sara simply nodded. He sensed that she clearly understood how he felt. With a gentle kiss on his mother's cheek, Jason slowly trudged out of the hospital like an old man. His heart was broken and his head was filled with questions. While he didn't exactly know where he was headed, he at least found the evening air a pleasant relief. All he knew was that he needed to be somewhere else. Exiting the hospital, Jason first looked to his left and then to his right. Then, he had an idea.

Jason headed in the direction of the subway station. He soon found the train's gentle rocking and swaying to be strangely comforting and felt increasingly better the closer he came to his destination. Letting his head lean against the cool glass of the subway car window, he allowed the tears to flow.

CHAPTER 20

*"Whoa, my love
My darling
I've hungered for your touch
A long lonely time."*

Unchained Melody
The Righteous Brothers

In later years, Jason wouldn't be able to recall how he got to the Conti's house. The little he remembered was that he stumbled through their front yard, the same yard in which years earlier he'd seen a younger Anna playing with her two sisters. Jason trudged right through into their backyard and then gazed up at Anna's windows on the second floor. At that hour, it wasn't surprising to see so few lights on and that the neighborhood was eerily quiet. Jason also noticed the rich ochre moon was three-quarters full.

"Anna," Jason whispered in the darkness.

There was no response. So, he tried again. "Anna. It's me."

Once again, there was no answer. For a brief moment, Jason didn't know what to do. Then, after looking around the yard, he spotted some pebbles at his feet. He reached down and grabbed one. Jason reared back and threw it at her window. But it missed. He picked up a second pebble and tossed this one at the window. That one missed as well. Unperturbed, Jason took another long look around the yard. As his eyes got accustomed to the dark, he spotted a tall trellis at the corner of the house. It supported the prized roses her father had so lovingly nurtured for the last twenty years.

Jason suddenly had an idea. If he were able to climb it, he could get up to the second floor and climb over to Anna's window. Then, he looked down at his cast. It wasn't going to be easy with his clunky cast and crutch. He hobbled over to the trellis and placed the weight of his foot on the first rung. He felt the trellis shake a bit. Then, he heard a tiny *ting* sound when he stepped onto the second rung. Anna must've also heard it because she instantly came to her window, opened it, and looked out with a shocked look on her face.

"Oh my gosh! Be careful, Jason," she whispered.

Jason nodded and placed his foot on the third rung. As he shifted his weight down and extended his leg, the entire trellis ripped away from the wall. Jason and the trellis teetered backward and fell hard to the ground.

"Oh, my God," Anna exclaimed as she looked down in horror and saw Jason sprawled in a messy clump of wood slats, nasty vine, and roses. Before he knew it, Anna was standing over him. He tried moving his leg. But it was stuck, entwined in a thicket of rose vines. Anna kneeled down and grabbed his leg. While trying to move his leg, she inadvertently pressed her knobby knee down on his cast. Jason stifled a scream in pain. Then, she tried lifting him by placing her slender arm under his shoulders. But he was clearly too heavy for her and together, they tumbled to the ground. "Ouch," she whispered as a thorn pricked her finger.

"Shhh," he whispered while clasping his hand over her mouth.

A light suddenly came on in her parents' bedroom. The two of them looked nervously at each other. Using all of her strength, Anna tried one more time to lift Jason. After some difficulty, she got him to his feet. They quickly wiped themselves off and found shelter behind the garden shed at the back of the yard.

Seconds later, her dad, gripping a Magnum 357, raced into the backyard. He took one look at his garden, a garden he had devoted his life to, and scowled. He was furious. Hearing something stir in the corner of his backyard, he raised his gun, aimed and fired. *Bam! Bam! Bam!*

"Take dat! You freakin' raccoon!"

Jason and Anna were hiding only fifteen feet away and the splinters of wood barely cleared them. Clinging tightly to each other, neither of them dared make a sound.

After what seemed like several long minutes, Sal finally went back inside, grumbling.

When Jason thought the coast was clear, he poked his head out from behind the shed. Then, he nudged Anna and together they walked to the front of the shed.

Jason carefully pushed the door open and guided Anna inside. The late August moon was shining in through the small corner window. In the barest of light, Jason took a quick look around and spotted a towel which he quickly spread on the cold concrete floor. Then, he motioned for Anna to come sit down. When he'd found a clean rag, he turned the make-shift faucet on, gave it a good rinsing, and wrung it out. Then, he joined her on the towel. Jason reached for her arm and began to gently swab at her bloody hand.

"Oh, Jason. You don't have to."

"Shhh," Jason whispered as he continued cleaning her wounds. He then brought her injured hand to his mouth and began sucking at the wound.

Anna pulled her hand away. "What are you doing, Jason? I'm bleeding!"

"My zayde used to —," Jason started to explain. But he stopped. He suddenly started crying.

"What's wrong? What happened to Zayde? Is he all right?" Anna got up on her knees and held him tightly to herself.

Jason took a breath. "He always said," mumbling through his tears, "that the best way to clean a wound is to suck the germs out." And with that, Jason began to weep uncontrollably. A floodgate of bottled up emotions he'd been holding back came pouring out.

Anna sat speechless, shocked by his sudden outpouring of grief. After a minute had passed, she asked, "What happened, Jason?"

"Zayde," he began, "He… he passed away almost exactly at the moment you got in the taxi."

Anna gasped. When she shifted her position, whatever little light there was suddenly illuminated her eyes.

Jason saw that they too were wet. Drawn into the deep brown pools of her eyes, he suddenly felt his heart stir anew.

Anna reached out and gave Jason a hug and cried. "Oh, Jason. I'm so, so sorry!"

While Jason tried to snuggle closer, he lifted his leg with the unwieldy cast and struck her knobby knee.

"Ouch," she cried.

"Shhh." He placed his hands around the nape of her neck. As he drew her face closer, his fingers got entangled in her long brown hair.

"Ouch," she shrieked again.

This time unperturbed, Jason pulled her closer and pressed his lips hotly on hers.

Anna instantly answered with a fervent kiss but bit his tongue by accident.

"Ow," he cried.

She pulled away, shocked. "Oh, sorry. I didn't mean to hurt you."

In the heat of passion, the two of them fell to the cold concrete floor. Jason planted sweet, moist kisses on her cheeks and ears, her lips and neck. They groped wildly at each other, tugging fervently at each other's clothing. Jason removed Anna's pajama bottoms while Anna pulled at his belt.

Outside the shed, the moon looked on, its rays shining upon the two young bodies safely hidden within.

Afterward, Anna and Jason lay together partially naked and breathless on the shed's cold concrete floor. Nestled in his arms, she lovingly stroked the few brown hairs on his chest. They both gazed up at the corner window. The sky was unusually clear that night and the moon shone an ochre glow. After a moment, Anna turned to him. "Lovely, isn't it?"

"Yup."

Jason and Anna savored the moment. The world seemed to slip away while they lay there in the soft afterglow. Jason visualized their future, that of living together, perhaps even studying together at the same school, marrying, and eventually raising children. Jason's mind drifted in and out of his reverie. That moment, however, didn't last long. A second later, two gunshots rang out. Anna and Jason sat straight up and looked at each other in fear.

House by house, the men in the neighborhood armed with various guns and rifles, were running out onto their front lawns firing round after round at what they thought were troublesome raccoons. Jason and Anna could hear someone in the distance yell, "I'll get you yet, you freakin' *procione!*"

Anna shook her head. Then, she nuzzled her head even deeper into Jason's chest and sighed. "I am just counting the days, Jason."

"Counting the days?"

She looked at him. "The days to when we can live our own lives."

CHAPTER 21

"A time to be born, a time to die
A time to plant, a time to reap
A time to kill, a time to heal
A time to laugh, a time to weep"

Turn, Turn, Turn
The Byrds

A light rain was tapping Anna's name against Jason's window when he woke up the next morning. He looked up at the window and he could almost feel her presence. He was now at his parents' place.

On any other day, Jason would've gone to work at the arcade. But today was different. Zayde's funeral was scheduled for 11:00 a.m. Out of respect, the family had decided to close the arcade for several days. And as is customary in the Jewish faith, Zayde's funeral and his burial were scheduled within days of his death.

The funeral was to take place at a small *shul* just three blocks from where Bubbie and Zayde lived. The dilapidated two-story brick building had once housed the offices of a local socialist labor association. The family had designed a simple ceremony and decided that only three people would speak at the service; two of Zayde's old friends and his only son Itzhak.

Jason stretched and yawned. There was a knock on his bedroom door.

"Jason? Are you awake?"

"Yeah, mom. I am. I'll get up."

"Good, we'll be leaving in about forty-five minutes. You got your suit ready?"

Jason looked over at his suit that hung on a wooden clothes hanger to keep from getting wrinkled. "Yeah, I do. Thanks, mom."

"See you in the kitchen. Your breakfast's ready."

Jason listened as he heard her footsteps going down the hall. He sighed and realized he was to face the day like a man. It was then, that he realized, he was no longer a boy.

He was indeed a man.

• • •

Saul, a large, gruff man, was the first to speak. Jason knew that after years of back pain, Saul was now resigned to use a walker. And everyone knew that he resented the fact that it now took him forever to get anywhere. The audience waited patiently while Saul made his way to the lectern.

Once Saul had steadied himself and looked out at the audience, he leaned his head back and shouted into the microphone, "Herschel had nuttink!"

People shifted in their seats.

"Ven he furst got here, vee had to feed him." At that point, Joseph, another one of Zayde's friends, wisecracked from the row behind Jason, "And vee had nuttink neither!"

Several attendees chuckled at his remark.

Unfazed by Joseph's comment, Saul continued, "But he loined quickly. On payday, ven his udder friends invited him out for a drink, Herschel refused. He vud go home, back to his tiny room and count his nickels and dimes. Den, he'd hide dem under his mattress." Saul gave a final nod of his head for emphasis and to indicate he'd finished.

With that, he turned away from the lectern. Saul took a full minute to finally be seated.

Then, following a long silence, the second of Zayde's friends, Jacob, stepped up to the microphone. Before he'd even opened this mouth, this small, unassuming man began fiddling with the microphone, adjusting it first upward, and then readjusting it back down.

"Vat are you? Georgie Jessel?" Oscar, another friend, shouted from the back pew, citing the well-known *borsch belt* comedian.

Once again, the audience snickered.

"Just speak, Yacob," Oscar reassured him. "Vee can hear you."

Jacob looked at the audience. Then, he took a moment to wipe away some tears. He finally whispered into the microphone. "Herschel vas devoted to his family. He didn't vant dat his children should go hungry. So, he vorked hard and he vorked long." Jacob turned away from the lectern and ambled back to his seat.

Finally, it was Zayde's son Itzhak's turn to speak. Jason knew that he was naturally shy and always chose his words carefully. Being Zayde's only son, Jason knew that he had worked many a summer at the arcade and had many stories to share. Jason expected to hear how stern his zayde — Itzhak's father — was, how hard he worked, the long hours he kept and how little Itzhak saw of his father in the earlier years.

Instead, Itzhak kept his remarks brief and to the point. "My father scrimped and saved," he shared. "He made a life for himself and for his family here in Brooklyn."

With that, Itzhak turned to go. However, just before he left the lectern, he took another look out into the audience and unexpectedly turned back and spoke into the microphone. "Would anyone care to say anything?"

The funeral attendees looked awkwardly from one to the other.

Something, however, stirred in Jason. On his walk to the *shul* that morning, he had debated whether he would say anything if given the chance. His heart was aching. Yet, he fretted about what he would say. *Would it be fitting? Would it be true?* Jason had so hoped that Anna could accompany him but her father had forbidden it. He could've used her support right now and it upset him that her father was so immovable.

At that moment, something prompted Jason to take a leap. He rose from his seat and carefully stepped up to the lectern. Before speaking, he took a deep breath and looked out at the faces of his family and Zayde's friends. He was actually surprised with the ease at which he spoke. "My zayde," he began, "was many things to many people. He was a grandfather, a father, a brother, and a husband. Many things. Zayde was most of all a warrior. He never gave up."

At that moment, Jason drew a blank. Somewhere deep down, he knew that something more needed to be said. He looked one more time out at the audience as if he were searching for that elusive thing. When he was unable to find it, he simply shrugged and turned to go. Jason had almost gotten back to his seat when he suddenly stopped, shook his head, and walked back to the lectern. Then, he cleared his throat.

"One more thing," Jason added. "My zayde," he gulped, "Was a man of mystery." And with that concluding remark, Jason went back to his seat. Many of the assembled stared blankly at each other with questions on their faces. When he took his seat, out of nervousness, Jason looked to his left. Zayde's old friend Saul was sitting next to him. He gave him a quick thumbs-up and a wink. When Jason looked to his right across the aisle, Zayde's old friend Joseph was staring at him. He gave Jason a knowing nod.

A simple reception followed the service. A long folding table covered with a white plastic tablecloth had been set up in the next room. Large platters were filled with an assortment of desserts and small paper cups were filled with drinks. Some in attendance stood quietly in the bare room munching on sponge cake. Others sipped sweet red Manischewitz wine or Slivovitz plum brandy. At the moment, Sara was putting another serving of bow tie cookies on the table. The atmosphere was reserved.

In the far corner, Jason's Lil' Grandma sat quietly on a folding metal chair. She watched as various uncles and friends chatted about Zayde, her son-in-law.

"He was a gruff man. Rough around the edges," Alvin, one of Jason's uncles, said.

Jason's Uncle Lenny chimed in, "He wasn't an easy guy to know."

"You could say that again," Uncle Julie said. They all nodded knowingly to each other.

At that moment, Lil' Grandma declared, "He vas a good man."

Suddenly the room went quiet.

Sara stopped what she was doing and looked up, surprised.

Whatever anyone had been doing in the room suddenly stopped. You could hear a pin drop as everyone turned to look at Lil' Grandma.

Finally, after what seemed like an hour, Sara spoke up. "But, Lil' Grandma. We… You… You speak English?"

Lil' Grandma smiled demurely and answered, "You never ast!"

Everyone laughed. In spite of their grief, Lil' Grandma's simple comment lifted their spirits.

It's funny what people remember about funerals. For Jason, this was his first funeral. To his final days, he would vividly recall three distinct moments of that day. The first occurred on their way home. As Jason sat beside his dad in their late model Catalina, he saw the never-ending stream of street lamps flashing past his passenger seat window. The second came as they were rounding a turn along the Belt Parkway in Brooklyn. Jason can remember seeing the Verrazano Bridge rise high against the overcast sky. And the third one was Lil' Grandma's unexpected comment.

• • •

Later that afternoon, Nonna was preparing supper. As Anna walked past the kitchen, her grandmother yelled, "Your mamma and poppa are coming over."

"Really?"

Anna had been relaxing, sitting in the living room reading the Virginia Woolf essay *A Room of Their Own*. The tempting aroma of garlic and onions filled the house.

"Your poppa said to make sure you're here."

Anna had no idea why her father would insist on her being there. She watched her nonna walk into the living room and rummage through her small liquor cabinet, searching for a bottle of liquor. Campari happened to be her son Sal's favorite aperitif. With Sal and his wife Maria coming over, Nonna wanted to be sure that she had a bottle or two around should he want some.

Suddenly, the phone rang. With her nonna busy in the kitchen, Anna took the call.

"Hello."

"Anna?"

"Oh, Jason! Hi!" Anna whispered shyly.

"Any possible way we can meet?"

While she listened to Jason's voice, Anna couldn't help noticing her nonna was talking to herself in the kitchen.

"Oh, *marone*. Where did I put it? I don't see any."

Reading the concern on her grandmother's face, Anna placed her hand over the receiver and said, "Everything okay, nonna?"

"Dere's a no Campari," Nonna said. "Your poppa he loves a dat."

Anna whispered into the receiver. "Just a minute, Jason, I think I know what to do." She cupped her hand over the receiver again and turned to her grandmother.

"Nonna, don't worry. I'll go out and get you some!"

"Dat would be great," her nonna smiled. "Pick upa two bottles, just in case."

"Okay, nonna," Anna said. "I won't be long."

Taking her hand off the receiver, she whispered, "Okay, Jason. I can meet you under the boardwalk. Give me twenty minutes." Then, she added, "I can't stay very long."

"Thanks, Anna. No problem. See you soon."

• • •

After speaking with Anna, Jason placed the phone back on the cradle and turned to his cousin.

"Mitch, I gotta head out for a little while."

"Let me guess. Anna?" Mitch wiggled his eyebrows.

"Not now, Mitch. Listen, I gotta talk to her. Can you handle this?"

"Yeah, yeah, yeah. Don't worry," Mitch assured him.

"Thanks," Jason said, getting off the stool.

As he neared the boardwalk, seagulls squawked overhead and the waves were gently lapping the shoreline. He immediately chose a quiet, shady spot as their rendezvous spot. As he trudged over to an old piece of driftwood, the sand cool and silky crept between his toes. With some difficulty, Jason lowered himself down and settled down to wait.

• • •

Nunzio took a long drag of his cigarette and peered through the windshield of his car. Luckily, he'd found a parking spot three doors down from Anna's grandmother's house. After waiting twenty minutes, there was still no sign of her. Nunzio had decided that today would be the day he'd have it out with her. He'd read her the riot act.

He slammed the dashboard. "Heck, I take her out. I spend money on her. I buy her stuff and what does she do? Take advantage of me. This has gotta stop!" he muttered, shaking his head. His heart was pounding and he wasn't used to not having full control. Anna's recent behavior really pissed him off. She was messing it all up.

Nunzio had plans. Big plans. He enjoyed working for her dad, earning good money, was building a career, and most importantly, he was getting the respect he felt he deserved from Sal. And here was Anna going out and two-timing on him. She was jeopardizing it all.

Nunzio had simple goals. He was going to marry Anna, have kids and, as his future son-in-law, he would eventually take over Sal's lucrative business.

Now, why is she going and messing it up?

As Nunzio was about to light another cigarette, he saw the front door suddenly open and Anna come out.

She stood on the stoop for a moment and looked up and down the street.

He ducked down and hoped she wouldn't be able to see his car hidden behind the car in front of him.

She finally went down the remainder of the steps and turned to walk in the opposite direction. She was hurrying. And then she broke out into a run.

Nunzio panicked quickly scrambling out of his car, giving his car door a good slam, and hurried to follow her. Not wanting to be seen, he kept a healthy distance behind her.

Anna had walked three blocks when she entered the corner liquor store. To avoid detection, Nunzio ducked behind a delivery truck parked across the street. Keeping his eyes peeled to the front door, he lit another cigarette and waited for his girlfriend to reappear.

A bell tinkled as Anna entered the shop.

"Ah, *buongiorno*," the cheerful owner, Mr. Esposito, said.

"*Buongiorno*, Mr. Esposito." Anna had known the shopkeeper since she was little. Nineteen years ago, Giovanni Esposito and her father had met at the local Italian Social Club and over the years her father had helped Mr. Esposito with some business matters.

"Ah, nice a to see you, Anna," Mr. Esposito said. "So, how's your fadder? He's a good?"

"*Bene, bene*," Anna said. "My parents are having dinner tonight at my nonna's. She sent me to pick up some Campari. Would you have some?"

"Of course."

"Can I get two bottles?"

"No problema for such a nice girl like you." Mr. Esposito turned to the shelves behind him. The Campari was conveniently stored on the third shelf. Giovanni grabbed two bottles and packed them in a crisp brown paper bag.

"Now, don'ta you worry," Mr. Esposito explained. "I put disa on de tab."

"Oh, thank you. I appreciate that."

"No problema."

Anna picked up the bag and headed for the door. Just before leaving, she turned her head and said, "*Ciao*, Mr. Esposito."

"*Ciao, bella*."

Spotting Anna exit the shop, Nunzio quickly snubbed out his cigarette and continued following her. He couldn't help noticing that Anna now walked with a distinct bounce in her step and she was smiling to herself. The closer she got to the boardwalk, the quicker she walked.

At some point, Nunzio had trouble keeping up with her. After following her for two blocks, he found himself panting for air. As someone who had always prided himself on being a smart dresser, Nunzio suddenly realized he looked a bit disheveled. His shirt flap was now out and when he looked down, he noticed little rivulets of sweat had formed on his new mint green Perma press shirt.

"Ah, shit," he said. "Dat girl. She's busting my balls."

Jason was pacing back and forth. He'd waited twenty minutes for Anna and there was still no sign of her. He looked at his watch for the third time. *What could be keeping her?*

Out of boredom, he hobbled over the sand and back to the street. His heart lifted when he spied her off in the distance. As she quickly approached, Jason could see her sleek black hair was tousled about, her smooth olive skin was now dewy, and her cheeks had a healthy glow.

"Hello, beautiful," Jason said, grinning. He was close to tears. *She's mine?*

"Aw, that's sweet," Anna said, throwing her arms around him. Then, she stepped back a little to catch her breath.

"I found just the perfect spot," he said, pointing to the large piece of driftwood he'd found under the boardwalk. "No one will be able to see us. Not even Nunzio." He looked at her concerned face. "Has he been bothering you and nonna? "Why didn't you stay at your parents?"

Anna shook her head. "Nonna was especially frightened after Nunzio did his thing with her and she didn't want to be alone."

"But you shouldn't be there. At least at home, you're safe under your father's protection against him."

Exasperated, Anna waved her free hand. "Dad says Nunzio wouldn't hurt a hair on my head because he knows what would happen. He thinks I'm exaggerating."

"And he thinks your nonna is exaggerating as well?"

Anna sighed. "What can I say? That's dad for you."

Jason looked around the street and then took Anna's arm with his free hand. "Let's go before Nunzio or one of his goons see us."

"Good idea."

Both of them tiptoed through the sand. Jason struggled to step closer and stroked her cheek.

"I love you, Anna."

Anna raised her head and didn't say a word. She smiled and blinked.

"All I know is you deserve better." He put his arm around her shoulders as they carefully made their way under the boardwalk. Carefully, Jason helped her lower herself down on the cool sand with his free hand. Then, he dropped his crutch onto the sand and eased himself down beside her. He took the paper bag of Campari and put it aside. The bottles in the bag tinkled.

"What's this?"

"Campari. For my dad. That was my excuse for leaving the house."

"Oh, got it." Jason smiled. He leaned toward her and was just about to kiss her on the lips when she pulled back. He leaned back in surprise.

"Jason. Please," Anna said. "Nunzio and my dad don't make it easy."

"Don't worry. We'll work it out. I'm not Nunzio or your dad."

Anna lowered her head. "I know, but …"

Jason leaned in again and planted a soft kiss on her forehead. Anna blushed. Jason brushed the hair away from her eyes and kissed her cheek. As he leaned even closer, wanting again to plant a kiss on the lips, Nunzio suddenly appeared from behind a wooden piling. He'd been spying on them the whole time.

"There you are," he shouted.

"Nunzio," Anna cried, jumping to her feet. "What are you . . . ?" The blood drained from her face.

"You filthy *puttana*," Nunzio spat out. "You're going to be in some trouble."

Jason awkwardly scrambled to his feet, lifting up the crutch to lean on. He looked from Anna to Nunzio with wide eyes.

"Wait," Anna said nervously. "Let me explain."

"You're nothing but a two-timing whore. Wait 'til your father hears about this."

"Don't," Anna said. "Please."

"Just wait and see."

Jason couldn't take anymore. He rushed up to Nunzio and pointed. "That's no way to treat her."

"Mind your own business, *Jew* boy."

"This *is* my business!" Jason said, lunging at him. He could hear the sound of fabric ripping as he grabbed Nunzio's jacket and pulled him to the ground.

"Son of a . . .," Nunzio cursed as he fell.

When he had scrambled back to his feet, he put Jason in a headlock and began pummeling his head. In their struggle, Jason tripped over a log and scraped his forearm on some shards of broken glass in the sand. While Jason was able to throw the occasional jab at Nunzio, he was unable to land a serious blow. The one thing, however, that he couldn't mistake was the anger in Nunzio's eyes.

Nunzio grabbed Jason's good leg and started kicking at his cast. Meanwhile, Anna stood by in horror. She winced and squealed with every kick that Nunzio made. Jason's screams were painful to hear.

Finally, not knowing what else to do, she reached down and grabbed a bottle of Campari from the bag. Then, she ran over to Nunzio and smashed it on his head. Glass and liquid flew in every direction.

Stunned, Nunzio stopped kicking and stood holding his head. When Nunzio looked down, he saw blood on his fingers. He then raised his bloody face and stared in disbelief at Anna. When he looked down at his expensive new pants and shirt, he realized they were now stained with blood and liquor.

Seething, Nunzio slapped Anna hard across the face. She reeled and twirled, falling down onto the sand. Scraping her right palm on a large, shard of glass, she yelped. Just for a moment, she nursed her hand before scrambling to her feet. With rage in her eyes, she slapped him back, her long nails digging into his face.

Nunzio eyed her contemptuously. "*Puttana*! Just you wait. You're in deep shit." Nunzio then turned to Jason who was still on all fours. "And I'm not done with you, *Jew* boy."

Jason didn't answer. He was still in pain and exhausted. It took Jason awhile to get back on his feet. As for Nunzio, he quickly realized there was no point in fighting. It wouldn't accomplish anything. He looked over to Anna, then back at Jason and spit blood out of his mouth. With his new clothes stained and torn and his head bleeding, he looked up to the heavens and shook his head in exasperation. Then, he took a deep breath and grunted as he gave Jason a final kick on his back. In exhaustion, Nunzio trudged off through the sand.

Anna shook violently. Suddenly bursting into tears, she bent down to Jason.

When Jason searched her eyes, he saw fear and embarrassment. "You okay?"

She nodded, not saying a word. Looking down at her cut hand, he quickly pulled out a handkerchief and wiped it. She let him put his mouth over the cut to soothe it, to stop the blood from flowing.

Helplessly watching Jason caring for her hand, it took Anna a full minute to gather herself together. She wiped the tears from her face and sniffled. Then, she peered at Jason questioningly and asked tearfully, "I wonder what he meant by trouble?"

"Aw, he doesn't know what he's talking about."

"Oh, you don't know Nunzio." Anna's eyes filled with tears once again. Overwhelmed by the emotion of the moment, she began to cry openly. Seeing this, Jason instinctively reached out and held her tightly. He forgot the terrible throb of pain in his leg and they remained so for several minutes. Just holding each other.

"Anna," he said trying to find the words. "I'm going to be out of touch for a while."

"You are? She lifted her head off his chest. "Why?"

"I have to sit *shiva* for my zayde this whole week."

"Sit what?" She sat back, looking at him questioningly.

Jason made an arc with his finger in the sand. "I'm going to be stuck at my grandparents for a week. Sitting *shiva* is how we Jews grieve. We spend the week sitting together, talking, eating, praying, and receiving guests. Would you be able to come? Perhaps I can ask my parents to take you in while this stuff is going on with Nunzio. I want to protect you."

Anna thought about that for a minute. "It'd be nice to join you," she said. She looked down at the arc in the sand that Jason drew. "But I know my dad would forbid me from coming. Also, there's no way I can stay over."

"Then at least go back to your parents' house. Tell nonna to go too, if she's afraid to be alone."

She sat and stared out into space for a moment. Then, she nodded. "Okay. I'll do that."

"We can meet when you're finished your *seeva*."

"*Shiva*," Jason smiled.

"*Shiva*," she repeated. "Then why don't we meet at Shepsy's next Sunday. Let's say at 11:00 am?"

"I'd like that." Exhausted and weary, Jason took a long moment to study Anna up and down. Her blouse and skirt were now dotted with red stains.

"Please, Anna. Whatever you do, please stay away from Nunzio, okay?"

"Oh, I will! Right now, I gotta get back to my nonna's."

"I understand. I'll see you next Sunday then."

Anna nodded wearily at Jason. Then, she got up to leave. He grunted to his feet, held her in his arms, and gave her a kiss on her lips.

Anna gently pushed away. As she disappeared around the wooden piling, Jason looked down at his own clothes and realized that his were also stained and in disarray. His left forearm also ached. It wasn't, however, until he began trudging his way back to the arcade that the full brunt of the fight hit him. He thought about recent events and realized that he'd been through a lot. *This growing up isn't easy.* On top of that, for the foreseeable future, he would have no one to talk with.

He would have to wait a week until he saw Anna again, the one person who understood him.

CHAPTER 22

"Unforgettable
In every way
And forever more
That's how you'll stay"

Unforgettable
Nat King Cole

Before opening the door to her nonna's house, Anna paused for a moment. She was out of breath and frazzled. She looked down at her stained and disheveled clothes. *How am I ever going to explain this?* She shook her head and opened the door. Looking down the hallway, she saw that her nonna was in the process of taking a casserole dish out of the oven. Nonna looked up. Seeing her granddaughter, she put the casserole dish down and made a quick sign of the cross. Then, she looked up to the ceiling and whispered, "*Mamma mia.*"

Anna fought back tears while she flipped her hair behind her ears. She watched Nonna as she shuffled closer with her arms out.

"Nunzio?" she whispered, her face wrinkled in shock.

Anna nodded.

"*Mamma mia,*" she said again.

Something didn't feel quite right to Anna. She hadn't taken three steps in before her father appeared in the hallway. Anna gasped and jumped back. She died many small deaths as he gave her the cold once-over.

"So, where's my Campari?" he asked sarcastically, knowing full well where the stains on her blouse and skirt came from.

"I'm sorry, Pop," Anna said, lowering her face in shame. "I, um, dropped them."

"That's one big fat lie," bellowed Nunzio, stepping in from the living room.

Anna jumped back again. "What are *you* doing here?!" She turned to her nonna. "Why did you let this brute in, Nonna?"

"I let him in!" Sal said.

Anna could tell her father was fuming angry.

Sal turned sternly to his future son-in-law. "And, *you. Basta,* Nunzio! Let me handle this with my daughter."

Nunzio ignored him. He was too upset. "I told 'ya, Sal," he said, relishing the moment. "Your daughter was just with that goddamn heeb. He's the problem."

"Nunzio," Sal shot back. "What'd I just tell 'ya? Stay outta dis."

Sal turned to his daughter, his furrowed brow darkening even more like storm clouds. Anna cowered knowing that look of his all too well.

"Nunzio was kicking him," she said tearfully, her chin quivering with emotion. "Hell, he was beating him. And he hit *me*!" She burst into tears and covered her face.

Nonna went to comfort Anna but Sal held her back. "That's enough," Sal yelled.

Everyone froze at Sal's dire warning. They could all hear the sporadic sputtering of the marinara sauce simmering on the stove.

Sal shook his head. He took a deep breath and pointed his well-manicured index finger at Nunzio. "I don't give a rat's ass about dat kid." Then, he turned to his daughter who was cowering under his glare. "Listen up and listen good," he said stepping closer to her. "I don't want you to see or have ANY contact with that boy. *Capisci?*"

Anna stood mute. After a moment, she slowly nodded her head. In her sixteen years, she had learned not to ignore her father's wishes and with every word he now spoke, Anna could feel all of her hopes, her dreams, and Jason dissolving into thin air.

• • •

The next morning, as hard as he tried, Jason found it impossible to sleep late. Even at 7:00 am, the apartment was already a beehive of activity. A generous neighbor had loaned Bubbie a large stainless-steel coffee urn and Jason could smell the slightly acrid aroma of coffee wafting through the apartment. Jason's mother and father had woken even earlier and picked up some freshly baked pastries at the local bakery.

Jason realized this day would mark the first *shiva* he had ever attended. He had never faced the death of a loved one before. Jason rose wearily from the couch, grabbed his clothes and stepped out of the living room into the kitchen where his mother and his bubbie were spreading a white tablecloth on the long table.

"Morning, morning, morning," he mumbled.

"Morning, Jason," his father, mother and his bubbie said in unison.

Bubbie then turned to Jason. "People vill be coming soon. So, you better get ready qvick!" She turned to her daughter. "Vee better open de door," she said. Sara nodded in agreement and went to unlock the front door. Bubbie was adhering to one of the many customs involved in sitting *shiva*; that is, by unlocking the front door, guests wishing to pay their respects could come and go as they pleased.

Jason would, in fact, discover many fascinating customs involved with sitting *shiva*. He had already noticed two unusual sights. The first was that the fabric of his bubbie's left sleeve was torn. Jason also noticed that a small black ribbon was now pinned to his father's shirt. Gary pointed to the ribbon.

"This symbolizes how grief can tragically tear at our hearts. You'll be wearing one, too. I'll put it on you. But first get dressed. It's going to be a busy day."

Jason nodded wordlessly and, as he was about to enter the bathroom, he noticed another custom. Someone had covered the mirror in the hallway with a black cloth. Somewhere in the dark recesses of his brain, Jason remembered that in the Jewish tradition, when someone is grieving, personal vanity is frowned upon.

Several minutes later, when Jason reemerged from the bathroom, he heard the distinct sound of water splashing out on the landing. His father had apparently placed a small table just outside the door. On it, he'd placed a basin, a pitcher of water and a small towel.

"What's that I hear, dad?"

Oh, that's also according to custom. It's a purification ritual. People ceremonially cleanse their hands when they come into the house during *shiva*."

Jason nodded. Suddenly, they both heard a knock on the door. As his father went to get the door, Jason scurried into the bathroom and raced to get dressed. He heard the door open and recognized Rabbi Feinstein's voice. He could see in his mind; the rabbi taking off his shoes and placing them neatly in the hallway. Jason knew that much at least. And he also understood that the rabbi probably wanted to pay his respects before the other visitors arrived.

Now that he was dressed, Jason hurried out of the bathroom just in time to see the rabbi bend over one of the platters of pastries on the kitchen table. He popped one in and said, "Good morning, Mrs. Jacobowitz."

Jason saw his bubbie jump and turn in surprise. He watched the exchange as he quickly folded his blankets and grabbed his pillow.

"Oh, good morning, Rabbi," Bubbie said. "Can I offer you sumtink?" She had been arranging some more pastries on a platter. She extended the platter filled with chocolate *babka* and smiled when she noticed that the rabbi's beard was already dotted with pastry crumbs.

"Sorry for your loss," the rabbi solemnly answered as he reached for another piece of pastry.

Suddenly, more people stumbled through the front door and into the kitchen and living room. As the growing throng filled the apartment, Jason quickly went to the bdroom closet and stuffed his bedding into the bottom crevice. Then, he quickly rearranged his hair before he walked back into the crowded living room. He returned just in time to hear the Rabbi speak.

"Please join me for the *kaddish*." Rabbi Feinstein motioned for everyone to come closer.

When everyone had gathered, he began, "*Yisgaddal veyisqaddash shmeh rabba …*"

As the rabbi and those assembled prayed, Jason thought about how his grandfather had never really been that observant a Jew as long as he knew him. While he knew that Zayde respected his wife's faith, Zayde himself rarely attended services at the *shul*. Bubbie, on the other hand, went to the synagogue regularly with her mother and together, they observed the many customs, ceremonies, and rituals of the Jewish faith.

When Jason's eldest aunt and husband arrived next, she was carrying a large white box of *mandelbrot* (biscotti). Once Esther had set it down on the table, she gave her mother a hug. Then, she began arranging pieces of the dessert on a nearby plate. Whenever Jason spotted *mandelbrot*, his first thought was invariably that there is no middle ground with *mandelbrot*. It's either moist and tasty. Or, it tastes like dry cardboard. Guaranteed to break a tooth.

As the morning wore on, the kitchen table became chock-full of delicious pastries; macaroons, apple cake, chocolate *babka*, honey cake, various cookies as well as dishes of dried fruits and nuts. Throughout the day, people came and went, typically sitting in the rickety folding chairs around the coffee table in the living room. One long candle had been lit and photo albums of Zayde and the family were spread open on the coffee table. Through the day, family members and his friends took turns telling stories about Zayde; many of them humorous and some of them sad.

Around noon, the sun began pouring in through the windows and the air in the apartment quickly became stifling. While nibbling his umpteenth piece of *babka*, Jason looked over toward the windows and noticed that many tiny specks of dust were suspended in the air. At that point, as if she were telepathic, Bubbie pointed to the windows and said, "Jason, be a good boy."

"Sure, Bubbie. What is it?"

"Close de curtains."

"Sure, grandma."

Jason hobbled over to the windows. From his vantage point, he had a clear view of the street. A woman who appeared to be in her 40's was pacing back and forth on the far side of the street. She raised her right hand to her eyes as if she were blocking out the late summer sunlight. *Oh, my God.* Jason suddenly realized that she was, in fact, the woman who had been with Zayde on the subway platform several weeks earlier.

Jason closed the curtains in every window and then turned and motioned to his bubbie. "I'll be right back." He quickly meandered between the visitors in the living room and hobbled down the three flights of stairs as fast as his legs and his crutch would carry him. Then, he opened the front door.

Turning around and being surprised to see someone crossing the street toward her, the woman turned away in embarrassment and began retreating in the opposite direction. Jason tried his best to catch up to her.

"Excuse me!"

Hearing him calling, the woman quickened her pace. Jason struggled to keep up with her.

"Excuse me," he repeated. "Please, don't make me run."

The woman then reluctantly stopped and turned to face him. Then, she looked down shyly at the pavement. For several seconds, they both stood silently in the bright, warm sunshine.

"I think I know you," Jason said.

It took her a moment to look into his eyes.

"You're the woman who called the ambulance, aren't you?"

She hesitated. Then, she nodded demurely. A look of relief slowly came over her face. Jason noticed that tears were forming in the corner of her eyes.

He took a step closer. "You loved my zayde, didn't you?"

The woman nodded her head again and sniffled. Holding a small box of pastry in her right hand, she used her free hand to search for a tissue. Jason handed her his handkerchief.

"Thank you," she said while she dabbed at her nose.

"By the way, what's your name?"

"My name? It's Gail," she answered, averting her eyes.

"Well, Gail, on behalf of my family, I want to thank you."

"Oh, well, I..."

"Please come upstairs."

"Oh, no. I couldn't!"

"Please. Please join us. My zayde would've liked that."

Gail gazed nervously down at the sidewalk as she considered his invitation. Then, she quickly nodded and followed him across the street and up to the apartment. When they had eventually climbed the three flights of stairs, Jason opened the apartment door and motioned for her to enter. Gail hesitated again.

"Don't be shy. Please, come in."

Gail followed Jason down the hallway. The kitchen was a beehive of activity, people conversing here and there, preparing and serving food. Jason saw Gail's eyes widen when she saw the sheer number of platters of cakes and cookies as well as casseroles which adorned the kitchen table. Jason helped her find a space on the table and she placed her small box of pastry down.

Jason then reached for her arm. "Don't be nervous," he whispered. "I'll introduce you as the woman who called the ambulance."

Gail looked at him and simply nodded. Then, she followed him into the living room. A heated discussion was ensuing between Bubbie and her youngest daughter.

"I never saw him," Aunt Leah said. She was referring to her deceased father.

"He vas busy, Leah," Bubbie said. "Alvays vorking."

"Yeah, but he was never around."

Bubbie took her daughter's hand and gazed into her eyes. "He loved you," she said, patting her daughter's hand.

Jason took that opportunity to clear his throat. Several people looked up from their conversation and eyed the woman who was accompanying Jason with some curiosity.

"Excuse me, Bubbie?"

His grandmother turned her head and looked up at her grandson.

"I'd like to introduce someone."

"Oh, okay," his bubbie said, readjusting her posture on the couch.

"Bubbie, this is Gail."

"Uh huh," his bubbie said, with some weariness.

"She's the woman who called the ambulance."

You could suddenly hear a pin drop.

"You? We didn't…," Bubbie was groping for words. "Where were you when…?" Many questions raced through her head.

As if anticipating the question that she really wanted to ask, Gail said, "My father is Harry's friend Joseph. That's how we met."

Bubbie nodded and chewed that over. At the same time, Jason flashed back to having met Gail's father earlier that summer on the boardwalk. After a long gap, Bubbie finally said, "Tank you. Tank you for vat you did."

"Oh, it was my…" Gail nodded demurely and stopped talking. She smiled shyly.

"Please join me." Bubbie patted the one spot still available on the couch beside her.

"Oh, no. I couldn't."

"Please." Bubbie implored her.

"I simply wanted to express my sympathy."

"Please. Come. Sit," Bubbie suggested.

Gail reluctantly sat down beside her. Taking that as his cue, Jason politely excused himself and disappeared into the kitchen. After studying the long table laden with sweets and pastries, he indiscriminately picked up two platters, intending to offer them to the guests in the next room. When Jason returned to the living room, he stood in the doorway and took his time studying all of the people gathered, his grandmother, his great grandmother, his aunts, their friends, and Gail. He felt his heart soften.

When will I ever see all of the women in my zayde's life all assembled in the same room at the same time again?

• • •

Getting through that first day of *shiva* was no problem. However, confined to his grandparents' apartment, Jason found the next six days to be insufferable. The constant flow of people in and out of the apartment, having to dress nicely every day and having to be on his best behavior was a pain. At many moments, he just wanted to get up and run, to be anywhere but at his grandparents'.

With Anna constantly on his mind, he frequently wondered how she was doing and how she was coping with her father about Nunzio.

By Thursday, Jason had had his fill. Late that afternoon, he impulsively rose from the couch, walked into the kitchen and picked up the phone.

• • •

Anna's mother was stirring some *marinara* sauce in the kitchen when the phone rang.

"Hullo."

"Hi, Mrs. Conti," she could hear Jason saying excitedly. "I'm Anna's friend Jason. Is she there please?"

Maria's eyes darted over to the couch where her daughter was reading. Anna looked up. "Uh, sorry. Can I take a message? She's out."

Her daughter ran frantically into the kitchen. Maria quickly placed her hand over the receiver as Anna stood in front of her mother and whispered beseechingly, "Please, mom. please. Is that Jason?" Her mother shook her head.

"Yes," Jason said. "Just tell her I called and that I'd like to see her."

"Yes, Jason. I will tell her."

"Please, Mrs. Conti. Please make sure you tell her I called."

"I will, Jason. *Ciao.*"

Click.

Anna covered her face and ran to her bedroom upstairs.

Maria continued stirring the *marinara* sauce.

• • •

By the time Sunday rolled around, Jason was beside himself. Not only excited that he'd finally get to see Anna, but that he'd also get to reconnect with the world at large, a world he left seven long days ago. After dressing quickly, he bounded down the stairs and headed to Shepsy's Restaurant as fast as his legs would carry him, thankful that he no longer had to rely on crutches.

Even though it was drizzling, Jason waited patiently for Anna in front of the restaurant. He was growing more and more impatient by the minute. Having waited twenty minutes, she had still not shown up. *Something must be keeping her.* Just to be sure, Jason decided to wait another ten minutes. When there was still no sign of her, Jason sighed. He took one last look at his watch and went into the restaurant.

Jason walked straight over to the woman behind the till. A cigarette hung from her lips. "Do you have a phone here?" he asked.

She pointed nonchalantly to the payphone at the back of the restaurant.

Jason walked past several booths that had yet to be cleaned. He stuck his hand into his pocket and came up with a dime. After plunking it into the slot, he dialed the Conti's number and waited to hear it ring. The only thing he got was a low hum. Jason shook his head. He retrieved his dime and popped it in one more time. Once again, Jason waited and all he heard was a low hum. A balding waiter shuffled past him. "It's broken," was all he said.

"Thanks." Jason wasn't quite sure what to do next. Then, He remembered he could use the phone at the arcade. To counter the morning drizzle, he fastened the top button on his shirt. Jason's heart was aflame and he longed for her. Badly. He was so deep into his thoughts that he was surprised to find himself standing in front of the arcade before he knew it. He unlocked the gates and quickly ducked inside, locking the gates behind him. Not wanting anyone to know there was someone inside, he only flicked on one of the lights. Then, he walked over to the counter and reached for the phone. He dialed the Conti's number. This time, he got a busy signal.

Shit. Jason tried dialing it again. Once again, he was met with a busy signal. *What is it with these phones?*

Out of frustration, Jason looked around the arcade. Something prompted him to reach for his guitar which he'd stored under the counter. He took a seat on the stool and studied it for a minute. Then, he cradled it in his lap and caressed its neck. It felt like weeks since he had played it. After a quick tune up, he strummed a chord. He liked what he heard. Jason tried a second chord. Then, he combined the two. Slowly, he added a third and a fourth chord. Jason then put the four chords together, C, A minor, F, G. He played that combination again. And again. Out of the blue, a simple melody came to him. He tried singing it with the chords. Then, he adjusted it a bit. Over time, a more elaborate melody emerged. He sang it again, this time picking up the tempo a bit. After thinking about it a bit more, Jason put his guitar down.

Jason pulled his small notebook from his back pocket and turned to the page that he'd scribbled lines of verse for Anna. In the dim light, he looked them over. He reached for his guitar once again, and tried weaving the humble lyrics with his simple melody. As an experiment, he tried a full chorus of the song. This time, he added a tasty little frill here, a turn of phrase there. By honing the song again and again, Jason slowly but surely crafted a beautiful and humble love song to Anna.

As if arising from a dream, Jason looked up. For a moment, he had forgotten where he was. When he surveyed the arcade, one machine, in particular, intrigued him. *That's it.* Jason realized that he could actually record the song. As if possessed, he grabbed his guitar and his notebook and walked over to the recording booth. After stepping into the booth, he put his things down and searched his pockets for coins. The machine required four quarters, but Jason could only come up with three. Then, he had an idea. *There's always petty cash.* Jason raced over to the counter and, sticking his hand underneath, found the frayed straw basket of coins. He looked up to the heavens. *Sorry, Zayde.* Jason grabbed a quarter from the basket and rushed back to the booth.

He stepped inside and opened his notebook. Before plopping the quarters in, he took a huge breath and thought about Anna, her beauty and her intelligence. Her heart and her humor. *This is for you, Anna.* One by one, Jason plunked the four quarters into the slot. Then, he reached for his guitar.

A moment later, when the green flashed on, Jason said, "I wrote this for you, Anna," into the microphone. With that, he opened his heart and sang. He sang simple and he sang true. When he'd finished, he carefully propped his guitar against the door and closed his notebook. In the quiet of the booth, an unusual weariness, a sense of fatigue, came over him — not unlike how he'd felt after his romantic interlude with Anna.

Jason carried his guitar and notebook back to the counter. By the time he returned to the recording booth, his newly made recording was ready. Holding it by his fingertips, he carried it carefully back to the counter. Jason found a paper sleeve underneath the counter and slipped the record in. He studied the record one more time, turning it over and over in his hands. A feeling of pride swept over him. In the process, he also realized that the labels on both sides were blank. Jason mulled over a title for the record. Then, he grabbed a pen and, at the risk of sounding cheesy, he carefully wrote the words, 'To Anna, With All My Heart'.

Jason thought about Anna. Especially now that he was armed with the recording, he longed to see her. So, he thought he'd try to reach her again. Jason reached for the phone and once again dialed the Conti's phone.

"Hullo," he heard Maria say.

Jason was relieved that someone finally answered. He desperately wanted to let Anna know that he had something for her.

"Mrs. Conti. Hi, it's me again. Jason."

"Oh, hi, Jason. She hasn't called you?"

"No, she hasn't."

"Well, I did give her your message."

Jason sighed. "Can you please let her know that I called? I have something for her."

"Oh, that's nice. I will. *Ciao*, Jason."

"*Ciao*, Mrs. Conti."

Sadly, he hung up the phone, feeling deflated.

Something didn't feel right.

• • •

Several days later and there was still no word from Anna. Jason sat staring at the record. He was quite aware that, in his cousin's eyes, he may have seemed distracted all morning. Mitch walked over to the counter, pointed at the record and asked, "What have you got there?"

"Oh," Jason said, rousing himself from his trance, "It's just a recording I made."

"Really?"

"Yeah," Jason blushed. "For Anna."

"Cool." Mitch studied his cousin's face. "So, what's going on, Jason?"

Jason just stared blankly at Mitch, not answering his question. He was clearly preoccupied. After a moment, he finally said, "I haven't heard from her since before the *shiva*."

"That does seem strange."

"Exactly."

Jason wasn't sleeping well. He was clearly frustrated, haunted by a whole host of questions. *Why hasn't she returned my calls? Did I do something wrong? Does she still like me?* Jason bit his lip and looked down at his record again. "This song captures every feeling I have for her." Jason picked up the record and looked at his cousin. "I have to give this to her."

Mitch nodded. "Jason, do what you gotta do."

Taking his cousin's advice literally, Jason suddenly stood up. "Can you hold down the fort?" he asked.

"Sure. What do you have in mind?"

Jason's mind was made up. He was going to take matters into his own hands. "If she won't see me, I'm going to see her."

"Wow." Mitch was impressed. "Go for it."

Jason tucked the record under his arms and trekked up to the Stillwater subway station. Ten minutes later, he was sitting on the train on his way to the Conti house. As his subway car rocked and swayed, Jason held the precious vinyl record delicately between his fingertips as if he was holding a baby.

• • •

Anna's youngest sister Bella answered the door holding a cherry lollipop in her sticky hand. Jason spotted several suitcases in the hallway behind her.

"Hi. Is Anna here?"

Bella nervously turned her head and looked up the stairs. "Uh, sorry," she said. "She's not here at the moment."

"Oh, okay. Can you just tell her that I came by?"

"Sure. No problem," Bella replied, looking down at her bunny slippers.

Bella shut the front door. For a moment, Jason just stood on the concrete stoop. He initially felt befuddled, not sure what his next step should be. After a moment, he shrugged forlornly to himself and turned to go. As he walked away, Jason turned and looked back at the Conti house several times.

• • •

Jason had still not heard from Anna when September arrived a week later. At this point, he was at wit's end. His heart felt empty. He was lonely and confused. It was also the start of Jason's last year in high school. A few days later, on the first day of school, Jason made a point of asking Anna's friends if, in fact, they had heard from her.

Each of them responded that they hadn't.

When Friday rolled around and he'd still not heard from her, he thought it best that he speak with Anna's favorite English teacher. Mr. Ellison was a decent guy and Anna loved his classes. Jason caught up with him late that afternoon as he was packing up for the day.

"Now that you mention it," he said, "I haven't seen her either."

"I'm concerned about her."

"Have you tried speaking to her boyfriend?"

Jason rolled his eyes. "Well, thanks, Mr. Ellison." Jason shuffled out of his classroom and down the hall.

With the suspense now killing him, Jason walked into the principal's office and stepped up to the front counter. The secretary seemed to be photocopying some forms.

"Mrs. Bender, would you have any information about Anna Conti?"

She looked at Jason curiously. "I'm sorry, Jason. I don't. Apparently, she hasn't returned to school."

"I know."

"Have you tried speaking with her friends?"

"Yup. None of them have heard from her."

"Well. Sorry I can't be of more help."

"That's okay." Jason shrugged and pessimistically left the office.

Unable to contain his anxiety any longer, Jason decided to return one more time to the Conti house. Even from a distance, Jason could sense that something was different. Anna's father's Black Cadillac Seville wasn't parked in the driveway and Jason noticed that the flowers in the front garden were wilting. There wasn't even a bicycle or toy-strewn on the front lawn.

Jason once again stepped onto the porch and rang the doorbell. He swatted at a bee that buzzed noisily around his head. After waiting a minute, no one answered the door. Jason rang the doorbell one more time. Once again, there was no answer. While he waited, his attention was drawn to the sound of water spraying in the next yard. The Conti's neighbor, a portly, balding man in his early 60's, was watering the flowers. Jason approached him.

"Excuse me," he said.

The man turned to Jason and pointed his hose to the ground.

"Any idea where the Conti's might be?"

The neighbor answered immediately, "Nope." Then, he returned to his watering.

Jason was at a loss. He didn't know where to turn or what to do. As he was about to leave, the neighbor's wife, a platinum blond with a big blond bouffant hairdo, came strolling down the street carrying a Toy Poodle and a bulky purse.

Seeing Jason in the yard, she shouted, "Looking for the Conti's?"

"Matter of fact, I am. I'm a friend of Anna's."

"Oh," she replied, joining him on the Conti's front lawn. "They went to Italy."

"What?" Jason was stunned.

"Yeah. From what I heard, she's getting married."

"What?" Jason stood back as if he had been punched in the diaphragm. His mind spun and it took him a moment to recover his equilibrium. After a moment, he was finally able to speak. "Well, thank you," he said sadly.

Jason was just about to walk away when the neighbor added, "Do you need to reach her?"

Jason was momentarily shocked. "Yeah. I'd love to."

"They did leave a forwarding address. You want it?"

"Sure," Jason answered, his spirits lifting.

The neighbor raised her index finger indicating that he should wait. Then, she put her Toy Poodle back on the grass, took hold of the leash and guided her dog back into the house. While he waited for her to return, Jason studied the two statues in the Conti's front garden. Each of them was peeing into a stone basin. Two tiny birds were bathing in one of them. A minute later, the woman reappeared holding a small slip of paper.

"Apparently, they're staying in Palermo," she said handing Jason the slip of paper.

"Thanks." Jason quickly looked it over.

Once again, the neighbor raised her index finger to her lips. "Now, don't tell nobody you got this from me."

Jason smiled and nodded eagerly. "I won't. I promise."

The woman gave him a quick wink. "Remember. Don't tell nobody."

"I promise. Thanks again."

"*Ciao.*" She smiled.

"*Ciao.*"

As soon as Jason was back in his grandparents' apartment, he grabbed a pad of paper and a pen and walked into his unofficial office, the tiny tiled bathroom. Jason sat on the toilet and feverishly began writing the first of what would be many letters that he'd send to Anna. While writing, he realized that it had been ages since he had written a letter to anyone, never mind someone who was the love of his life. His future.

Dear Anna:

I think about you night and day. I sincerely hope you're well. As you can imagine, I was quite surprised to learn that you and your family are now in Italy.

I was especially surprised by the news that you are going to marry Nunzio. I don't believe it. It must be a rumor because I know you can see clearly who he really is.

I think you can do better. You deserve every opportunity to pursue your plans and dreams. And I want to be part of those dreams.

Please let me know how you are . . . and if there's anything I can do to help. And I mean ANYTHING! Let me know! I would even come to Italy and find you.

All my love,
Jason

Over the following weeks, Jason wrote many similar letters to Anna. And after mailing each one, he'd wait patiently for a response. But none ever came. It crossed his mind that perhaps her father made it his business to intercept and burn his letters. That thought made him feel helpless. He could only hope that one would reach her.

Whether it was his youthful enthusiasm, his ignorance, his tenacity or that his love was truly real, the fire continued burning brightly in his heart. Jason refused to give up. Somehow, he persevered through this difficult and lonely time and continued to hope for an eventual reply.

CHAPTER 23

*"Bells will ring, the sun will shine, whoa-oh-oh
I'll be his and he'll be mine
We'll love until the end of time
And we'll never be lonely anymore"*

Chapel of Love
The Dixie Cups

The weather in Italy had been perfect since the day the Conti's arrived in Palermo. The temperature continually hovered in the pleasant mid-sixties and the family couldn't have been happier. All that is except Anna.

She was miserably depressed. She was being railroaded into marrying Nunzio by her father.

She could tell that her father, in particular, was overjoyed to be back in the old country. As they drove in from the airport, along its dusty country roads, past row upon row of citrus trees, her father had eyed the scrubby mountains in the distance and smiled non-stop. Anna, on the other hand, had remained quiet since they left their house in Queens.

Vincenzo, Sal's younger brother, insisted that Sal and the family stay with him at his villa which was nestled in the ancient hills of Palermo. No sooner had they entered the villa than Anna peered into the sunroom to the right of the marble foyer. She quickly spotted a dozen wedding gifts lying in the corner and a healthy stack of envelopes, many of which were tied with delicate white, pink or purple ribbons, all on the long glass table along the far wall. Each of them was invariably stuffed with a wad of American dollar bills.

"Word isa quickly spreading about your wedding," said Vincenzo, turning to Anna.

She immediately felt a knot form in her stomach. "My wedding?"

"*Si*, Anna. Your wedding."

She looked at him askance. She felt ill. "You mean, you've already arranged it? These are all for me? To Nunzio!?"

Sal grabbed her arm and pointed at his daughter. "Anna, you are getting married to Nunzio and that's that. As your father, I say how it's going to go!"

Anna tore her arm away from her father's grip. Her eyes darted in all directions. She felt trapped and confused. She was frightened of losing her mind. She covered her face and wept.

• • •

With the Mediterranean sun peeking in through the windows that September morning, Sal awoke feeling refreshed and excited. Later, over breakfast, he suggested that everyone head into town and stroll through its bustling cobblestoned streets. Sal longed to visit La Vucciria, one of the city's many open-air markets.

His wife, Maria, was more than happy to join him. Sal knew it had been more than twenty years since she and he had lived in Palermo and that she would be only too happy to be back.

Anna, however, begged to stay behind. She claimed she wasn't feeling well.

Sal only read it as her usual way of fighting back. He knew he was going to ensure that she not leave the house while they were gone. One of the servants would have to keep an eye on her.

Sal and Maria smiled at each other as they strolled along the streets of the open-air market. Maria couldn't recall the last time they had held hands. She took particular delight in gazing at the many stalls of ripe local tomatoes, billowy cauliflowers, plump zucchinis, and succulent oranges. As they neared one of the local fish stalls, she heard someone calling Sal's name. A man roughly Sal's age was standing out front, his apron stained with the blood and guts of seafood.

"Salvatore? Is data who I tink it is?"

Maria saw a smile come across Sal's face as he stepped up to him.

"*Come va?*" Mario asked.

"*Bene, bene.* Is data really you, Mario?" said Sal, warmly shaking his old friend's hand.

"*Si.* So, what a brings you here?"

"My daughter. She's a getting married."

"Ah, *bene, bene.* Datsa wonderful." Mario looked down at Maria and extended his hand.

She shook his hand and smiled.

"We're just making some of de final arrangements," Sal said.

"Oh, you don't have to tell me. I know what datsa like."

All three of them laughed.

Sal suddenly felt a rare feeling of hospitality. "Say, why don't you bring your wife? Maria, wouldn't dat be wonderful?"

Maria nodded. At first, she had misgivings with Sal's forceful way of ensuring that Anna marry Nunzio. But now that they were in Italy, she knew that family unity was the most important aspect of any Italian marriage. And with Nunzio working with Sal, it would now be a given. She thought Anna would come around. Surely. And now, finding more old friends made her excited about the upcoming wedding.

"Please, do come, Mario. We would love you anda your wife to come."

"Ah, *grazie*, Maria. *Grazie*, Salvatore."

"It'sa soon. De first of October."

"Ah, *bene*!" grinned Maria.

Mario then eyed some sardines in a bin that a local fisherman had just delivered. Grabbing some manila paper, he quickly wrapped several handfuls of them. With a healthy grin, he handed them to Maria, then he turned to Sal.

"*Ciao*, Sal."

Maria graciously accepted his gift.

"*Ciao*, Mario," Sal said.

• • •

With the wedding scheduled to take place in only two weeks, Maria faced a mountain of details to deal with. She still had to select the cake, the wedding dress and more. When they returned from the market that afternoon, Maria had arranged to meet with a chef as well as a bridal gown dressmaker. Maria insisted that her daughter attend these meetings.

While Anna did, she seemed to choose to sit silently in the villa's sumptuous living room. Judging by her bowed head, she still hadn't come around to the arrangement. But there was nothing Maria could do. She also noticed that Anna hadn't been feeling well since they arrived. She realized it was a difficult position for her daughter.

After a lengthy discussion with the chef about the menu, Maria concluded, "Now remember, we only have two weeks."

"Dat'sa not much time," the chef said.

"You don't have to tell me."

When that meeting ended, the dressmaker from the bridal store, who'd been waiting patiently in the next room, took the chef's place. Rushing into the living room, she quickly spread the proposed wedding dress out on the couch.

Seeing how beautiful it was, Maria clutched her heart and sighed. "Oh, my God. Datsa beautiful."

"*Grazie*," the dressmaker said.

"Anna, what do you think?" Maria asked, looking over to her daughter.

Anna just sat there and didn't say a word.

"Anna? What do you . . . ?"

Without warning, Anna suddenly clutched her stomach and cried out in pain.

Maria rushed to her side and grabbed her daughter's hand. "What's wrong?" she asked searching her daughter's eyes.

In great distress, Anna looked up at her mother. "My stomach. It hurts."

"Could be she's a nervous?" the local seamstress said.

Disregarding her comment, Maria raced out into the hallway. Her husband and her brother-in-law were in the middle of a conversation.

"Sal, call da doctor. Now."

Anna staggered out of the living room and leaned against her mother. "I need to lie down." Without waiting for a response, she moaned clutching at her belly and turned to go to her bedroom.

"Sal, quick." Maria then turned to her brother-in-law. "Vincenzo, please call your doctor!"

Vincenzo hurried to the phone in the front marble hallway.

Doctor Gallo arrived later that afternoon. Sal and Maria stood by helplessly as Dr. Gallo visited Anna in her bedroom. After introducing himself, he politely asked Anna to disrobe. He didn't have much to say during his examination, electing instead to poke, prod and palpate her stomach. After ten minutes, he simply turned to her and said, "Please get dressed."

Anna obeyed.

"Anna needs to come to de hospital," Dr. Gallo explained.

"De hospital?" her father asked.

"Si. She needs to take a test or two."

"A test? For what?"

"To see what de problem is," he said, lifting his shoulders.

"When?" asked Maria, concerned and worried.

"Today. Immediately."

Maria and Sal gathered their light coats together and escorted Anna outside to their car. Together, they followed the doctor back to the hospital.

As much as they wanted to stay by her side, the nurse insisted that Anna go on her own into the laboratory. The nurse told them that X-rays would be taken and blood would be drawn for some tests. "De results will be ready disa Friday."

"Friday?"

"Si. De specialist will a see Anna den."

• • •

Jason continued having a difficult time. Constantly racking his brain, trying to make sense of things, he couldn't for the life of him imagine why Anna would've been willing to go ahead and marry Nunzio. On many occasions, Anna had shared her hopes and dreams with him. He knew that she had big plans, completing her last year of high school and then attending university. Anna took great pride knowing that she'd be the first in her family to go beyond high school. Jason also knew that she loved literature since she was very young and she dreamt of the day that she'd get to share that love with others.

Anna often described the life her mother led, how she waited on her husband hand and foot. And countless times Anna had asserted that she had no intention of pursuing that same life. Jason could not imagine why Anna would now suddenly jeopardize all of her plans.

As September unfolded, Jason felt as though he was straddling two opposing worlds. Like any other seventeen-year-old boy who was starting the 12th grade, his head was filled with sports, music, and friends. However, in every other respect, his life was now different. He now felt acutely alone, unexpectedly thrown into a world of adults, now forced to tackle adult emotions and considerations.

Not only had his summer in Coney Island introduced him to the heady realm of love. But it also introduced to the pain which accompanies it. There seemed to be some cruel irony in the fact that Jason's very first taste of love occurred at the very same time he lost his grandfather.

It was no surprise that Jason's grades suffered and he had trouble concentrating. While he was physically there, he became increasingly distracted. Frequently he'd start a project for school with the best of intentions. However, within minutes he'd lose interest, often obsessing about Anna. Jason's friends quickly noticed how distant and preoccupied he became.

One cool autumn afternoon, his friend Paul invited him to play catch at the local ball field.

Before leaving the apartment, Jason thought he'd put on his favorite Mickey Mantle baseball jersey. When he got to the ball field, Paul was standing along the first base line, stretching and warming up. Jason walked up to him.

"Hey. How's it going?" he said.

"Great. Why don't you run out there and I'll throw you some balls?"

Jason sauntered out to second base and stood there pounding the pocket of his well-worn glove with his fist. Just to make sure, before Paul threw the first pitch, he called to his friend, "Okay, Jason. You ready?"

"Yup. Let her rip," Jason called.

Paul reared back and, just as he was about to release one of his feared curveballs, a flock of rock pigeons flew across the sky.

Jason looked up and quickly became lost in thought. He raised his glove up to his face trying to shield his eyes from the glaring sun.

Realizing there was a potential accident in the making, Paul yelled, "Jason. Watch out."

"What?" Jason turned absentmindedly.

Paul's blazing pitch struck him on the shoulder.

"Ow!" Jason winced.

Paul raced over to him. "You okay?"

"Yeah. No problem," said Jason, rubbing his sore shoulder. This only added to his misery.

• • •

When Friday finally arrived, Anna's parents, as well as Nunzio and his parents, accompanied her back to the clinic. For over an hour, everyone waited anxiously before Anna's name was called. Sal and Maria wanted to accompany their daughter into the specialist's office. But, as they followed their daughter into the room, the nurse quickly stopped them. "Sorry. Please wait here."

Anna was led into the office of Doctor Scarpone, a stout, balding man in his early '70's. She sat quietly while he took a long look over the results of her tests. Then, he guided her over to the examining table and proceeded to inspect her belly, poking and prodding at this spot and that. He repeated the words, 'Does disa hurt?' so many times during his examination that Anna might've thought that those were the only three words he knew.

When he'd finished his exam and she'd gotten dressed, Doctor Scarpone bluntly said, "You have an ectopic pregnancy."

Anna was shocked and speechless.

"The right tinga to do," he explained, "Isa discuss dis with your famiglia." The doctor then accompanied Anna, who was at a loss for words, out into the waiting room where her family was waiting anxiously.

Dr. Scarpone cleared his throat. "De blood tests and my examination confirm dat Anna isa pregnant."

Anna's face turned white and she felt queasy.

Her father looked at his wife incredulously, then back at the doctor. Sal joyfully said, "Pregnant? Datsa a wonderful!" Sal gave Nunzio, his future son-in-law, a hearty slap on the back. "You did a goot, Nunzio."

"*Pero…,*" the doctor interjected.

Only Anna looked at him with concern. She saw that even though he hadn't finished giving his diagnosis, the group was ignoring the doctor and, overjoyed by the news, was beginning to celebrate. At the same time, she saw that Nunzio sat frozen in his chair completely dumbfounded.

Her father pointed to Nunzio's father Frank with a broad smile on his face. "You gonna be a grand poppa," he said.

Frank was also beaming and so full of joy that Anna watched him bound over to his son and hug him tightly. "Nunzio, you did it. You make a me proud."

Nunzio meanwhile sat there with a confused look on his face.

"*Pero,*" the doctor once again tried to get a word in. But the group, in their joyous state, still continued to ignore him. In their excitement, both fathers were now slapping Nunzio repeatedly on his back, hugging and kissing him.

Anna, tears welling up inside her, saw that Nunzio remained perplexed. They had never ever gone so far as to have any such intimacy and Anna saw Nunzio look over at her. She was suddenly consumed with fear.

Suddenly, she heard her father speak to Nunzio. "Don'ta you worry, Nunzio. I felt de same way. You got a family now. We all a gonna help you."

"*Pero, per favore!*" the doctor repeated.

Nunzio leaned forward in his chair toward Anna. She watched as he searched her eyes for any clue, any sign of acknowledgment. While Anna recognized that this was an opportunity to let everyone believe what they wanted, she deliberately remained quiet.

"Oh, I can see it now," Sal said. "Playing wita my little bambino out in de garden. Wit a little truck and a gun."

"Datsa my boy," Nunzio's father said.

Finally, unable to contain his frustration any longer, Nunzio blurted out, "But, it's not mine."

Everyone stopped.

Anna died inside.

"It's not my kid," he repeated.

"What are you talking about?" Sal asked, taking a step toward him.

"It's not mine."

"*Basta!*" Anna suddenly yelled. "Poppa. Enough."

"What?" Sal said, turning to look at his daughter.

"Poppa," Anna exclaimed. "He's right. It's not his child."

"Not his baby?"

Anna lowered her head in shame as the light slowly came on in her father's head. Sal looked warily at his daughter. He looked at Nunzio and then back again at Anna. She could tell that her father was growing angrier and angrier as the light continued to dawn. Making a fist with his right hand, he started pounding it repeatedly in his left hand.

"Sal, I am willing to marry her," Nunzio said, in a rare moment of gallantry. "To respect your family name."

Anna looked over at Nunzio in shock. "You still don't get it, do you?" Anna yelled at Nunzio. "I don't love you. I don't want to marry you," she said, slapping him across the face.

The whole time, Dr. Scarpone had been trying to get everyone's attention. Finally, out of exasperation, he climbed up awkwardly on one of the plastic chairs and loudly cleared his throat. At the top of his lungs, he shouted, "*Signore e signori, scusami*. Dere's a one more ting."

Once again, everyone stopped.

"One more ting?" Sal asked angrily. "What's dat?"

"Right now, it'sa dangerous," the doctor explained, "for de baby and for Anna."

"What?" everyone responded in unison.

Suddenly Anna felt a massive sharp pain in her abdomen. She grabbed her stomach.

"An operation is necessary."

Anna burst into silent tears from the pain.

"An operation?" Sal asked incredulously. "Dat can't be right." He looked at his daughter who was now hunched over in pain and crying.

"And de operation isa scheduled for dis afternoon."

"Dis afternoon?" Sal said. "You gotta be kidding," pounding his fist more intensely.

"No, I'm not."

Nunzio exploded. "She's damaged goods. Now, there's no way I'm going to marry her." Nunzio's comment infuriated his future father-in-law.

Sal stepped right up to the specialist and scowled at him. "Dis isa too much," he shouted, forming a fist with his right hand. "You don'ta know what you're talking about. You're nothing but a quack." In his fury, he hauled off and punched the specialist in the jaw. Then, just as quickly, he turned to his daughter and pointed his finger accusingly at her. "You have embarrassed me! And the whole family."

And with that, Anna watched through tears as her father stomped out of the hospital.

• • •

Anna underwent surgery later that afternoon. While her mother was relieved that it went well, she was also concerned that her daughter looked weak and frail. Using a wet compress, Maria dabbed at Anna's forehead. Then, she looked into her daughter's eyes and smiled. She was happy to have her daughter back. "Can I get you anything?"

Anna shook her head. "No, Momma. But, please, I want to be alone. I don't want to see anyone just yet."

"Everyone will leave you alone."

"But poppa . . ."

"Anna, he's still very upset. He doesn't want to see you anyway."

Anna suddenly burst into tears.

Maria opened her purse and took out a small package of food that she'd prepared. "Have some."

Anna, sniffing, dutifully opened her mouth. Spoonful by spoonful, Maria fed her daughter the homemade soup and tasty clumps of sesame seed bread that she'd brought along. After, she gently stroked her daughter's hair. Anna started to cry anew.

"Momma. I'm sorry," she said.

"Oh, don't be."

"I feel so ashamed."

"You have no need to be. It'sa gonna be alright," her mother reassured her. Maria reached over to give her daughter a hug. She wanted to give some relief to her daughter's overwhelming guilt and shame she must surely feel.

• • •

The next day, Anna returned to the villa where she was consumed by a deep sense of dread. The only person willing to be with her was her mother. Anna felt unwelcome and unloved. Her fiancé and her father both refused to speak with her and she felt most ashamed that so many relatives and friends had flown so far and would now be upset that the wedding was canceled.

Feeling miserable and beset by lingering pain, Anna didn't sleep well, spending much of her first long, endless night tossing and turning. Sometime after midnight, while lying awake in bed, she overheard her parents through the thin walls arguing in the next room. Being the good wife, her mother never argued in public.

"Why, Sal? Why are you so hard on her?" Anna could hear.

"She's a tramp."

"But, she's our daughter," her mother yelled. Anna could hear her start to cry.

"What kind of woman did you raise?"

"She's a good girl, Sal," her mother answered tearfully.

Sal tutted. "I *thought* she was a good girl."

"Sal, she made a mistake. We all make mistakes."

"A mistake, eh? Some mistake. From disa day forward, she's nuttink to me."

Anna gasped. She took a handful of her nightgown and squeezed it. She couldn't believe her father would say that.

"But Sal, she's a good girl," her mother cried again.

Anna wiped the tears from her eyes. She had already had a disturbingly restless night. But now hearing her parents argue made it that much more painful. While she lay there feeling particularly vulnerable, Anna let the other recent painful moments replay in her mind; her family's surreal episode at the hospital, how she had allowed herself to get pregnant and more. For hours, she lay there, restless and troubled. In that hellish state, Anna also knew enough that she needed to figure out what she'd do next.

It would no longer be what her father wanted.

Anna dragged herself out of bed and sorted through her belongings. In the process, she came across the address of her friend, Stacy, who she knew was currently in France. With shaking hands, she wearily placed the scrap of paper in her purse. Then, she went about packing her bags and got dressed, making sure that her passport was packed securely in her purse. Then, as quietly as she could, she picked up her bags and tiptoed out into the darkened hallway.

Placing her bags beside the door of the sunroom, she quietly opened the door. At first, she had trouble seeing anything. But slowly, as her eyes adjusted to the little light there was, she walked over to the side table and studied the wedding envelopes stacked there. It only took a moment of consideration before she grabbed a healthy handful of them. She stuffed them quickly into her leather backpack.

When she walked out into the hallway, to her surprise, her mother was standing in her nightgown directly in front of her. Anna felt an immediate pang in her stomach. Her mother had been crying, her eyes puffy, her face lined with tears.

Maria sniffled and stepped toward her daughter. She took a long look at Anna and when she looked behind her, she saw the luggage sitting in the hallway. Without saying a word, Maria reached for her daughter and gave her a long hug. Then, she took a deep breath and placed a gentle kiss on her daughter's cheek. The two of them, both in tears, held each other tightly for several minutes.

Afterward, she pulled away and whispered into her daughter's ear, "Anna *mi*a."

Anna found that almost too much to bear. "Yes, mamma," she said tearfully.

"Do what you feel isa right."

Anna tried to maintain her composure. She took a deep breath and whispered, "I will, momma, I will." Her face collapsed in miserly and pain before she managed to control her emotions enough to be able to function. Finally, without saying another word, Anna silently picked up her bags and carried them to the door.

Maria quietly watched her oldest daughter open the heavy wooden door and slip out into the night. With a broken heart, Maria stood at the door and watched as she walked out into the night. With tears in her eyes, Maria then looked up to the heavens and, making the sign of the cross, turned and shuffled back into the kitchen.

CHAPTER 24

*"With her went my future, my life is filled with gloom
So, day after day I stay locked up in my room
I know to you, it might sound strange
But I wish it would rain, oh yeah, yeah, yeah, yeah"*

I Wish It Would Rain
The Temptations

"Mom, I don't know what else to do," Sara said. She was exasperated. Jason had been in a foul mood for weeks. He was obviously down in the dumps. Sara was at a loss as to how to deal with him. Being at her wit's end, she thought her mom might offer some advice. "He's moping around the apartment. He won't clean his room and he's got no appetite. What am I supposed to do?"

Bubbie thought it over for a moment and said, "Vy don't you all come for Tanksgivink?" Then again, her answer to just about anything was food. Sara knew that in her mother's eyes, a home-cooked meal was a surefire, time-tested remedy for just about anything that ails anyone, in this case, a way to cure her grandson's heartache and pain. Before hanging up, she added, "But I could use your help dis time."

"Sure, Mom, what do you need?"

"Can you make de toikey?"

"Sure, Mom." Sara recognized that her mother didn't have the energy this year.

"And I'll make de stuffing."

"Sounds good."

On Thanksgiving Day, Jason, Sara, and Gary piled into their Catalina and drove out to Coney Island. While their meal was scrumptious and it was lovely to get together as a family, Bubbie was evidently struggling.

As they were finishing the main course, without any warning, Sara turned to her mother and said, "Mom, we think you should sell the arcade."

Everyone stopped and Bubbie looked up in surprise, shocked as she was by her daughter's suggestion. "Who's we?" she asked.

"Your daughters and your son," said Sara, wiping her mouth. She recognized that this wasn't an easy topic. But she also felt that the issue needed to be addressed sooner rather than later.

"You vant I should sell it?"

Sara placed her napkin down and readjusted her posture. "Mom, there's no one else who can take care of it."

Bubbie was taken aback by her daughter's comment. "Vat about Itzak? He could do it."

"He's too busy, Mom. With work of his own. And there's no one else."

Bubbie did not have a response.

Sara rose from her seat and carried the dirty dishes over to the sink leaving her mother to consider her argument. Sara then looked over at Jason who was staring idly at his plate, playing with what left of his potatoes. "Jason, can you help us clean up?"

She watched him rise listlessly from his seat, then gather a few dirty dishes and bring them over to the sink. Then, he took his seat again at the table. In the meanwhile, Bubbie had gotten up and went into the kitchen to put on some coffee. Within minutes, the rich aroma of freshly brewed coffee filled the kitchen. Sara watched as Bubbie reached for a plate of pastry and shuffled back to the table.

Sara came back for more dirty dishes and watched Bubbie place the dessert smack dab in front of Jason.

"Vant a piece of cherry danish?"

Jason eyed the dessert halfheartedly. "No thanks, Bubbie. Maybe later."

Sara could sense that Jason probably would be upset at her suggestion that the arcade be sold. It would probably raise many questions in his head.

Suddenly, Jason quickly excused himself and left the living room.

Jason snuck into his grandparent's bedroom. As quietly as possible, he slid the top drawer of the dresser open and pulled out a set of keys. Jason stuffed them into his front pocket and returned to the living room looking for his mother. She wasn't there so he went in the kitchen again. She was at the sink. She looked up, concerned.

"I think I'm going to get some fresh air."

Sara nodded and wiped her hands on a towel. Before she had a chance to question him, Jason left the kitchen and living room, slipped on his jacket, and made his way down the stairs and out onto the street.

Jason had only one thought in mind as he walked along Coney Island's overcast November streets. That is, to make one final visit to the arcade where he'd spent so much of his summer. As he unlocked the rusty front gates, he could hear a distinct pitter patter coming from within. With the power now turned off, however, it was difficult for him to see anything inside. Barely two months ago, the arcade had been alive: a brightly lit, noisy and festive place. Jason now found it dead, silent, and dormant.

Something inexplicable drew him over to the skeeball machines. He smiled thinking of the many joyful moments he had playing them. After looking at their long ramps and their large round concentric holes, an odd thought occurred to him. He had never seen what was behind them. So, he thought he'd take a look.

Jason stepped over to the dusty wall and peered down. He discovered a snake pit of coiled electrical cords, tumbleweeds of dust, and a healthy sprinkling of mouse droppings.

Vat's keeping you? Clean it up already, gotdammit!

Jason laughed. He could clearly hear his zayde.

With the echo of Zayde's voice in his head, he walked back to the counter. A sudden wave of memories flooded over him. He recalled the many times that Anna and Nunzio had shown up, the many moments he'd shared with Zayde and Mitch, and the highs as well as lows of working there. When Jason turned his head, he spotted the public bathrooms and fondly remembered his first day of work and how disgusted he'd felt first seeing them. Jason smiled recalling how insistent his grandfather had been about cleaning them up.

As if it were only yesterday, Jason also remembered his zayde steering him over to his private bathroom.

Letting curiosity get the best of him, Jason walked over and unlocked the door. Then, he took a long look around. The same blue suit, dark red tie, and starched shirt were still hanging there on the wall. And the postcard which had so intrigued him months ago was still pinned to the wall. Out of curiosity, Jason removed it and studied the photo on the cover again. This time, Jason looked even more closely. *Yup, it's her.* Just as he suspected, the photo was of Gail.

His mind suddenly flashed back to that fateful evening he saw Zayde and Gail on the subway platform. Jason turned the postcard over and reread the message. *What a sweet message.* After thinking that over for a while, he nodded to himself. There was no reason for Bubbie to see the card. Jason stuck it in his shirt pocket, took one last look at the bathroom and shut the door.

As Jason walked back to the counter, his mind was suddenly awash with many poignant memories of his summer; how often his zayde had reminded him to return promptly from lunch, the time his grandfather yelled at him for changing the radio station, and how forcefully Zayde always dealt with Nunzio and his cohorts. Jason felt a lump in his throat. At that moment, he felt tremendous love and affection for his zayde.

Looking out onto the street, he realized that daylight was quickly fading. Jason took one last look around and bid the penny arcade a fond farewell. He then strolled over to the light panel and studied the many light switches. Jason smiled recalling the grand symphony his zayde had treated him to months ago.

When Jason had finally locked the rusty gates, he raised his gaze and looked across the street. To his great surprise, he saw his old nemesis Nunzio standing in front of the Steeplechase Amusement Park. An attractive blonde girl was draped on his arm. Feeling all of his emotions rise to the surface, Jason bolted across the street.

"Where is she? he asked. "Where's Anna?"

"How should I know!?" Nunzio was just as shocked to see Jason and he took a moment to look around. Then he sneered at Jason. "And I don't care. She's nothing but a tramp!"

"How dare you call her a tramp." Jason was so enraged that he lunged at him.

The two of them grabbed, shoved and jabbed at each other while Nunzio's girlfriend looked on in horror. Jason grabbed

Nunzio's shirt collar and hauled him to the ground, scraping his neck against the gravel.

"You sonofabitch!" Nunzio said clutching his neck and scrambling to his feet. When he drew his hand away, he spotted blood. Then, each of them took a hard, hateful look at the other.

"Did you marry her?" Jason demanded.

"No way. Once I realized you were the father, I wanted nothing to do with her."

Jason suddenly shot up straight. "What are you talking about?" Jason said, staring at him incredulously.

"You have no idea, do 'ya? She got pregnant 'cause of you."

"What?" Jason said, having difficulty processing what he just heard. He slowly took his hands off of Nunzio's shirt and took several steps back. Then, he stared off into space for a long while. Finally, he said, "Admit it. You never loved her."

"You're probably right," Nunzio said.

The two of them stared intently at each other.

"I would've married her to protect her family's reputation but that bitch refused."

"That's no way to talk about her." Jason was furious.

Nunzio looked down at his clothes, splattered with blood. "*Che palle*. Is there anything you won't ruin in my life?" With nothing more to say, Nunzio simply spat on the ground and shook his head in frustration. Then, he reached for his new girlfriend's hand, his signal for her to follow, and walked off in a huff.

Jason was equally speechless. For several minutes, he stood motionless watching as Nunzio and his girlfriend walked away, wrestling with what Nunzio had just revealed. Then, slowly, he turned and absentmindly started walking back to his bubbie's place. He walked blindly past Coney Island's retail shops and its fruit stalls. Jason thought about Anna. It was as though she'd fallen off the face of the earth or into some black hole.

Jason realized he now had to decide what his next step would be. Should he continue waiting for her? Or had she disappeared totally out of his life?

• • •

By the time Jason returned to the apartment, he was emotionally spent. He trudged up the stairs with every last ounce of effort, When he lumbered into the kitchen, Bubbie looked him up and down and said, "Mein got. Vat in God's name happened to you?"

Jason was so lost in thought that he had frankly forgotten what he looked like. His shirt was in tatters and splattered with blood. There were several buttons missing and his face was scratched.

"Come. Sit down," his mother said, while she rinsed out a cloth. At the same time, his bubbie began wiping the blood and dirt from his face and hands.

"So nu? Vat happened?" she said.

Jason hesitated before answering. "I got into a fight."

"What did it concern?" Sara asked.

Jason took a long, deep breath. For a moment, he debated whether he should reveal the full story.

"Well, it's about Anna."

"De Italian vun?" Bubbie asked.

Jason nodded shyly.

"We started seeing each other and we fell in love."

"Oy, gevalt."

"But she had a boyfriend who didn't love her or treat her right."

"Yeah. But, dat doesn't explain dis," said Bubbie, pointing to the cuts on his face.

"Then, she suddenly disappeared."

"Disappeared?"

"Yeah. She and her family went to Italy. Supposedly to marry this guy."

"Yeah," Bubbie said, trying to coax him on.

"Well, I just ran into him."

"Oy."

"We had a fight and I just learned they didn't get married."

"And?" said his bubbie, continuing to prod him.

"Well," he paused, not knowing if he should tell them. He took a deep breath and looked at his mother in embarrassment. "He claimed I got her pregnant."

There was a heavy silence. He knew that neither his mother nor his grandmother quite knew what to say next.

At that moment, Jason's little grandma, who'd been sitting quietly by herself in the corner of the kitchen, unexpectedly pitched in, "Got is closest to dose mit a broken heart."

Jason gave her a surprised look while his mother and grandmother looked quizzically at each other.

"Lil' Grandma, your heart's been broken?"

His great grandmother lowered her head. Then, she looked directly into Jason's eyes and nodded slowly. "De secret vill die vit me," she said, giving him a mischievous wink.

Bubbie stared at her mother incredulously.

Everyone took their time considering what Lil' Grandma had just revealed. After a lengthy silence, his bubbie finally asked, "So, haf you hurd from her?"

"Nothing. Not a word."

Bubbie then pulled her chair closer and looked into her grandson's eyes. "Don't vorry. Somevun vill come alonk," she whispered.

Jason leaned forward in his chair. "But I don't want someone else."

With that simple declaration, Jason set his future course. From that day forward, he would forever search for Anna, his first love, in bars, in his travels and through his network of friends and family.

CHAPTER 25

"All these places have their moments
With lovers and friends, I still can recall
Some are dead and some are living
In my life, I've loved them all."

In My Life
The Beatles

Sunday, August 8, 1999

Standing at the kitchen counter, Jason felt a strange comfort as the boiling water slowly turned a light shade of brown and wisps of steam rose from the glass mug on the kitchen counter. As Jason methodically bobbed his tea bag up and down, the sweet, woody aroma of peppermint filled his nostrils and he found the steady rhythm and repetition hypnotizing and soothing.

Jason hadn't been himself in the days following his divorce. With the ground shifting beneath his feet and his life suddenly thrown into limbo, he'd been tense and irritable. He desperately needed some order, some routine, and predictability in his life. So, he naturally sought out the simplest of tasks, the ordinary, tired and true rituals that he'd always taken for granted.

Like making a cup of tea.

Jason pulled the tea bag from his cup and, pressing it against his spoon, he squeezed every last drop out of it. Then, he turned to toss it into the garbage. When he turned back, his dear cousin was standing right beside him, staring at him eye-to-eye.

"Geez, don't scare me like that."

"Oh, sorry," Mitch said. "So, you coming this Saturday?"

"This Saturday?" Jason drew a blank.

"Hello? Remember?" Mitch said. "This Saturday is Zayde's *yahrzeit*. His memorial. I placed an announcement for it in The Jewish Week newspaper."

"Oh, yeah. Sure. You can count me in."

"Great."

Jason reached for his steaming cup of tea and just before leaving the kitchen, he turned to his cousin and said, "Listen. I really appreciate you letting me stay here."

"Oh, sure. No problem."

Jason ambled down the hall. While it wasn't exactly home, Jason found that staying in his cousin's guest room was a welcome relief, a temporary refuge for him to touch down, clear his head, and get back on his feet.

Once Jason settled into the easy chair, he took a comforting sip of his tea. Then, he took a deep breath and unexpectedly felt his shoulders drop. He grinned when he realized that that was the first deep breath he'd taken in weeks.

Jason was frankly happy to be alone. Letting his eyes wander around the room, he got a strange feeling of satisfaction in seeing his weathered suitcase by the bed, his trusty guitar propped up against the wall and the old cardboard box of mementos that he'd placed near the door.

Jason took another sip of his tea. When he looked over at the cardboard box, a hodgepodge of old papers, photo albums, and documents, there was something about it that intrigued him. He instinctively rose out of his chair and dragged the box closer to the chair. Tucked between two binders was an old 45 record. Jason reached over and pulled it out. The first thing he noticed was that there was a blank label on one side.

Jason turned the record over. Seeing the words, *To Anna, With All My Heart,* in his own sloppy handwriting on the other side, suddenly transported him back in time. Jason vividly recalled the very afternoon he made it. That summer, he'd worked at his grandfather's penny arcade, when he'd fallen in love with an Italian girl named Anna. He remembered slipping into the cramped recording booth and recording a simple song for her. Jason took heart in the fact that he had forever captured his heartfelt feelings for Anna on vinyl.

Oh, man. This is too much.

When he took another look across the room, he spotted his old guitar. It was the guitar he used to record the song. Jason fell to his knees in stunned silence. He felt a lump in his throat and his eyes filled with tears. It took him a moment to settle down. He looked again at the cardboard box and this time, he spotted two photo albums. One was marked '1970's', the other '1960's'. Jason leaned over and picked up the second album. Placing it on his lap, Jason began leafing through its many pages. He was intrigued by all of the faded black and white photos, many of them of himself. As he looked closer, he was struck by how innocent he looked.

Several pages in, he spotted a photo of himself arm-in-arm with one of his former girlfriends, Olivia, taken in their high school hallway. Jason chuckled at the sight of his Afro hairstyle. Despite her attire, her faded jeans, a plaid work shirt and boots, she exhibited an unmistakable sense of grace. However, what attracted him most about her, Jason recalled, was her skin, her clear Mediterranean coloring not unlike that of Anna's.

Turning several more pages, he spotted a photograph of a woman he didn't recognize at first. When he studied it more carefully, he realized that it was a photo of a one-time neighbor when he lived in Queens. Brenda, a divorcée, was sitting cross-legged wearing bell-bottomed jeans and a blouse. Three of the buttons of her blouse were open revealing her cleavage. Even from that dated photo, Jason felt her ineffable animal magnetism. He recognized that one quality which had always attracted him to women was their gusto, their lust for life. She, like Anna, possessed a fire, a simmering life force.

Turning to the next page, Jason discovered a long, empty rectangular space that was surrounded by three photos and yet it was lighter in color than its cardboard backing. After pondering that for a while, something possessed Jason to take his wallet out and open it. Tucked away behind the dollar bills, he found an old strip of two black and white photos. It was half of the strip that he and Anna had taken one afternoon at the arcade's photo booth. He grinned at the memory of giving Anna the other two.

When Jason studied the photos more closely, he was immediately struck by the light emanating from Anna's eyes. Her innocence and lust for life were unmistakable. He had trouble recognizing himself however. Out of curiosity, Jason walked over to the full-length mirror hanging behind the door and, leaning in closer, took a moment to really examine his face. He took another look at the photos and then again at himself in the mirror. Jason was shocked by how little light there was in his eyes.

Taking one step back, he began to cry as he reflected on his many one-night stands and how often his heart had been broken over the years. At that moment, he understood, perhaps for the first time, how important his relationship with Anna had been. Their brief summer romance had taught him about love, its fundamentals; mutual respect and communication. And while he appreciated that his relationship with Anna was the first of many pearls on a long string of love, he also realized that his deep feelings for her still lingered.

Even now.

Thirty years later.

• • •

Saturday, September 14, 1999

A cool drizzle was falling while Jason drove to get his daughter for his zayde's memorial later that morning. He issued a deep sigh and marveled at the fact that his zayde had now been dead more than thirty years.

When Jason finally pulled the car into the driveway, he was surprised to see his daughter Tess waving at him from the living room window. He smiled and waved back. She quickly disappeared and before he knew it, Tess was sitting excitedly beside him in his car. While they drove out to the cemetery in Staten Island, she sat contently in the passenger seat holding his hand. For most of the ride, they sat silently together. She occasionally, however, looked up at him and smiled.

At some point, Jason cleared his throat and asked, "Tess, do you know where we're going?"

"Sure do. We're gonna see your grandpa."

"Yeah. I guess we are." He chuckled.

A few minutes later, when Jason looked over at his daughter, she was studying the back of his right hand. Jason once again cleared his throat. "He died a long time ago. We're going to where he's buried."

"Yup. I know." Tess once again took her dad's hand.

Letting her cradle his large hand in hers, he felt content and he bathed in the blissful feelings that were pouring through him. She was very healing for him.

Then, before he knew it, they were passing through the cemetery gates and Jason noted that, even at this time of the year, the lawns were still quite green. As they approached the gravesite, he was surprised by the number of cars parked on either side of the gravel road.

Jason made a point of parking his car fifty yards away. Even from that distance, Jason recognized his uncle Itzhak, his aunt Phyllis and some of his grandfather's friends from the old country who were already gathered around the old monument.

Jason turned the ignition off. Even before he had a chance to run around the back of the car and open the rear door, his daughter came flying out. Jason gazed lovingly down at her and patted the top of her head as she looked around at the people.

"Can I walk through the monuments?" she asked, squinting up through the light drizzle.

"Yes, but stick around."

"Don't worry, Daddy. I will," she said giving him a penetrating look.

Tess followed her father up to the gravesite. As they approached, Jason removed his baseball cap. "*Shalom, shalom,* everyone," he said, nodding respectfully to his aunts, his uncles, and to Zayde's friends. Then, he took his daughter's hand and found places to stand near the monument next to Mitch and his family.

Noticing that the area surrounding the monument was overrun with weeds, Jason bent down and started pulling at a few stubborn weeds clump by clump. Then, he rose to his feet and tossed them into the woods.

Suddenly, his uncle took his place next to the monument. That seemed to be the cue to start the ceremony. Opening his prayer book, his uncle Itzhak began to recite the *kaddish*, the sacred prayer in honor of the dead.

"*Yit-ga-dal v'yit-ka-dash sh'mei ra-ba ...*"

One after another, the others joined in. While he recited the prayer, Jason happened to spot some pebbles to the right of the monument.

"*B'al-ma di-v'ra chi-ru-tei ... ba-a-ga-la u-viz-man ka-riv, v'im'ru: A-mein.*"

Once everyone had finished reciting the *kaddish*, Jason bent down and picked up one of the pebbles. Then, he placed it on the top of the monument. Others soon followed his lead. For several minutes, everyone stood with their heads bowed.

Suddenly, their silence was interrupted by the sound of a car's tires spinning on gravel. An older model Toyota Camry had pulled up behind Jason's car. Even before the engine quit, the right rear door of the car swung open and a young girl hopped out.

Jason noticed Tess looking over and her eyes lighting up.

"Hey. There's Katie!"

Jason watched as his daughter ran excitedly over to greet the young girl. From that distance, Jason watched the two girls give each other a hug.

"What are you doing here?" he could hear Tess ask.

"My mom said we should come."

"Why?"

"She said she knew the man."

Jason thought nothing of their conversation and briefly wondered who the mother was. A friend of the family, certainly. Then he saw the two girls darting in and out of the rows of the stone monuments. Hearing a car door slam, Jason instinctively looked back at the car that was parked behind his. A black-haired woman got out and looked nervously up to the gravesite. He could tell that she was hesitating to approach the monument.

Mitch, who'd been watching all of this unfold, turned to his cousin and whispered, "Hey, Jason. She looks familiar. You know her?"

Jason squinted but couldn't quite place her. However, there was something about her that intrigued him. It may have been her long black hair or how she was dressed.

Wearing heels and with the grass damp, it took her several minutes to walk up to the gravesite and when she'd gotten ten feet away, Jason gasped. Then, he broke out into a grin.

It was Anna.

"*Bonjour*," Jason chuckled.

"Ah, *bonjour*. Is that you, Jason?" Anna asked, holding out her hand.

"Yup, it's me." Jason took several steps toward her and grabbed her, giving her a big hug. Then, they stood back and took their time taking each other in.

"Gosh, it's been awhile," he whispered, drinking her in.

"You could say that again." She smiled.

Jason felt a lump in his throat. "Thanks for coming."

"I wouldn't have missed this for the world."

Jason's eyes welled up. He took her hand and guided her up to the grave.

YIDDISH GLOSSARY

Balaboosta	A perfect housewife: Someone who tirelessly cooks for, cleans, and serves anyone in their household
Bissel	A little bit
Boychick	Affectionate term for a young boy
Bubbala	Affectionate term for a girl, a darling
Bubbie	Grandma, grandmother
Bupkes	Worthless
Challah	Braided egg bread
Chazerei	Junk or garbage
Chutzpah	Nerve, gall
Dreck	Shit
Ess/Essen	Eat
Fershtay?	Do you understand?
Fress	To eat like an animal
Gay shlufen	Go to sleep
Gonif	Theft, swindler
Gotteniu	My God (with an anguished cry)
Kvell	To beam with pride
Kvetch	To complain
Mazel tov	Good luck
Mensch	Person of character

Meshugga/Meshuggina	Crazy
Noodge	To bother
Nosh	Snack
Oy	To express sorrow
Plotz	To explode, to burst
Shayner Maidela	A pretty, attractive girl
Shmatta	A rag
Shmeer	To spread
Shteibel	Talmudic reading room
Shul	Temple or synagogue
Veizmear	Woe is me

ACKNOWLEDGMENTS

Only as a result of completing the arduous journey of writing and publishing this book did I realize I'd been leading an incomplete, unresolved life. The writing, editing, publishing, and marketing of this novel has proven to be a true odyssey for me. Through this process, my life has become richer and more complete. Many people helped and guided me along the way.

I would especially like to acknowledge the love and dedication of my partner Liesje, a fellow author. Without her continual encouragement and her steadfast resolve, this novel would never have been written. I would have given up many times had it not been for her patient and critical ear, her bountiful patience, her guidance, insight, and her humor.

I would like to also acknowledge and thank my beloved children, Joshua, Tessa and Jared for their patience, their love and wisdom.

I would particularly like to acknowledge those at Author Academy Elite; especially Kary Oberbrunner. His continual encouragement, his knowledge, and inspiration have been humbling and awe-inspiring. I have continually valued his wisdom.

The journey of writing and editing is often long, circuitous and frustrating. I found that the input and the commitment of my fellow authors, as well as the helpful staff at the Igniting

Souls program was often inspiring. In particular, I have greatly appreciated the insight and creative ideas which the editor Nanette O'Neal and graphic designer Geno Valloni shared with me.

I would also like to acknowledge the writers who have so eloquently described and evoked memories of 1950-1960's Coney Island in me:

Reed Farrel Coleman
Joseph Heller
Alice Hoffman

In the early stages, I listened to Stanley Fox describe his memories of the glory days of Coney Island. As one of the original 'Coinsmen,' Mr. Fox operated a penny arcade.

• • •

Finally, I would like to acknowledge the love and support of my family far and wide. My dear parents, now departed, Gerald (Gerry) and Charlotte (Sara Jacobowitz) Smith, created a safe and colorful world, a cradle of loving-kindness, for my sister and I. Hopefully, we have imparted a good dose of that to our children.

I would also like to make a special mention of my sister Elyse, her husband Reuven as well as their children and numerous grandchildren. They have served as a continual inspiration.

• • •

One of the people I wrote this book for and hoped that she'd get the opportunity to read it, was my youngest aunt, Lillian Countess (Jacobowitz). I was fortunate enough to spend time with her during one of our winter stays down south. Fortunately, during that visit, I got to consult with her, ask her specific questions concerning her parents, my maternal grandparents. More importantly, I had the pleasure of listening to her describe what it was like growing up with her family, their rich lives and the Coney Island neighborhood they lived in.

Sadly, my Aunt Lillian, a dear, wise and critically minded woman (right up until the end), passed away before this book was published. May the memory of her long rich life serve as a blessing to all.

> *"We are family*
> *I got all my sisters with me*
> *We are family*
> *Get up everybody and sing*
> *We are family."*

Manufactured by Amazon.ca
Bolton, ON